PRAISE FOR

THE
CHRONICLES OF NEVER
AFTER SERIES

"Satisf[ies] the fractured fairy tale itch."

—*School Library Journal*

"Fans of fantasy and fairy tales of all kinds will delight in catching all the references to classics."

—*Booklist*

"A fast-paced fantasy that Land of Stories fans will enjoy."

—*Publishers Weekly*

"Equal parts whimsical and adventure-packed, Filomena's journey will entrance readers and have them rooting for the young, witty heroine . . . A refreshing twist on well-known fairy tales."

—*Kirkus Reviews*

ALSO BY MELISSA DE LA CRUZ

THE CHRONICLES OF NEVER AFTER

The Thirteenth Fairy

The Stolen Slippers

THE DESCENDANTS SERIES

The Isle of the Lost

Return to the Isle of the Lost

Rise of the Isle of the Lost

Escape from the Isle of the Lost

Because I Was a Girl: True Stories for Girls of All Ages
(Edited by Melissa de la Cruz)

NEVER AFTER

THE BROKEN MIRROR

MELISSA DE LA CRUZ

ROARING BROOK PRESS
New York

Published by Roaring Brook Press
Roaring Brook Press is a division of Holtzbrinck Publishing Holdings Limited Partnership

120 Broadway, New York, NY 10271 • mackids.com

Our books may be purchased in bulk for promotional, educational, or business use.
Please contact your local bookseller or the Macmillan Corporate and Premium
Sales Department at (800) 221-7945 ext. 5442 or by email at
MacmillanSpecialMarkets@macmillan.com.

Library of Congress Cataloging-in-Publication Data is available.
First edition, 2022
Series design by Aurora Parlagreco

Printed in the United States of America by Lakeside Book Company,
Harrisonburg, Virginia
ISBN 978-1-250-82725-8 (hardcover)
1   3   5   7   9   10   8   6   4   2

For Mike and Mattie, always

CONTENTS

OF THIEVES AND PRINCESSES

Magic mirror on the wall,
Who runs Never After after all?
If our heroes set out to rescue a friend,
What happens if trouble appears before the end?
And if trouble comes disguised as a thief,
Where should our heroes turn?
Can they turn a new leaf?
Magic mirror on the wall,

A princess and a thief can be friends through it all.
But if the princess has a jealous sister,
Will she betray?
And who will run Never After
at the end of the day?

PART ONE

Wherein . . .

Filomena Jefferson-Cho and her
three best friends get fleeced by
a mysterious charmer.

A princess welcomes weary travelers
into her castle in exchange for
their help.

And our heroes get a little too
attached to the royal treatment.

CHAPTER ONE

FOUR HEROES ARE BETTER THAN ONE

"So how cold are we talking, exactly, when we talk about Snow Country?" Alistair asks between huffs and puffs. Filomena, Jack, Alistair, and Gretel have been walking for a few hours now. But Filomena doesn't mind one bit. When in the company of her gang of friends, the hours tend to go by like the swoosh of a swoop hole.

How wonderful it is, Filomena thinks, to have people who like hanging out with her. And not only that—she can count on them to have her back both when she needs emotional support and also in *battle*. Back in middle school, she was dumped by her closest friend and bullied by a group of literal trolls. But now she knows where she belongs: right here, alongside her friends, trudging on a dirt trail with nothing but their wits and their courage to keep them safe on this long and perilous journey. It's much better than being stuck in Algebra One Honors, even if *anything* is better than Algebra One Honors.

"Is it hot-chocolate-with-vanilla-marshmallows-for-every-drink cold or sledding-as-a-main-form-of-transportation cold?" Alistair continues.

"I'm not sure what scale you're using here, but I'm going to guess it's haute-winter-couture cold," says Gretel with a gleam in her eye. "I can't wait to put together some winter *lewks*. I *never* get to wear cold-weather fashion! Turtlenecks, knit sweaters, earmuffs, oh my!"

Like Filomena, Gretel is biportal, spending part of her time in the mortal city of Los Angeles and part of her time in . . . well, whatever part of Never After needs her most. Filomena can't help getting caught up in the cold-weather excitement, too. Though she knows their quest to Snow Country will likely involve risking their lives, that fact seems to pale in comparison (at least for the moment) to the excitement of traveling to a new Never After kingdom. And one with snow, no less!

"You know, guys, I've never actually seen snow," Filomena tells them.

Jack, Gretel, and Alistair turn to her as if she's just told them she's actually a friendly goblin and not Filomena Jefferson-Cho of safe, sleepy, suburban North Pasadena, California.

"What do you mean, you've never seen snow?" Jack says. "Isn't there snow in the mortal world? I didn't know snow was magical."

"It's not magical in the mortal world, but it is magical to me! I'm from California, remember? There's no snow there—I mean, unless you drive up to the mountains, but my parents are terrified that I'd get into a skiing accident, or any accident, as you know. All my mom does is read about people crashing into trees on ski runs. And where I live, it's pretty much always sunny and warm, no matter the time of year."

"And you thought Never After was weird!" Alistair shakes his head. "You come from somewhere that doesn't even have *seasons!*"

Gretel, Alistair, and Filomena all laugh and settle into fantasies about quaint snow-covered villages, ice-skating on frozen lakes, and resting their stocking feet by a roaring fire.

But Jack isn't looking so dreamy. Filomena's vision vanishes upon seeing his face. Once again, Jack the Giant Stalker is carrying the weight of the worlds on his shoulders. And it's been only a fortnight since Filomena learned she and Jack have a lot more in common than she thought.

It's still hard to believe that only a short time ago she'd been reading the Never After books in the mortal world (which, at the time, she'd thought was the *only* world). She loved poring over Jack's heroic adventures and laughing along with his sidekick, Alistair, from the comfort of her home in North Pasadena, safe and sound. The series always felt real to her, but she never knew just *how* real it would become. And she never would have guessed that the real writer of the Never After series was her aunt Carabosse, the thirteenth fairy of Never After. Carabosse had come to the mortal world to write books that would address the fairy tales the mortal world *thought* it knew and set the record straight. But she died before she finished writing the thirteenth book, and now it's up to Filomena to do the job—because she's living it!

Oh, and don't forget: Filomena just found out that Jack the Giant Stalker (now her friend and not just the hero from her favorite book) is also the Winter Knight, the prince of Vineland, and a gift from the fairies to Never After, intended protector of the kingdoms. Seriously, the guy is certainly dashing, but how many titles can one boy have?

Filomena tries not to look at Jack while thinking about this, lest her face give away her inner thoughts. They're on a mission here; this is no time for blushing!

But Jack's not the only one with titles. Filomena only recently found out that *she* is Princess Eliana of Westphalia and a gift from the fairies, too. Just like Aladdin's Lamp and the Stolen Slippers. The Prophecy about the fate of Never After says there were thirteen blessings from the fairies that the ogres crave, and apparently Filomena and Jack are two parts of that thirteen. That's why the ogres won't stop chasing them through the kingdoms. The Prophecy states that once the fairies' gifts fall into their hands, Never After is theirs for the taking. So far, though, Filomena and company have been successful in undermining the ogres' plans. It seems that Filomena and Jack are tied by more than their friendship and ability to fight ogres together; Filomena's beginning to feel like their destinies might be tied together, too.

The four are so deep in their respective thoughts, plodding along the path to Snow Country, that they don't notice a shadowy group emerge from the surrounding trees and creep up behind them.

"Hey, what the—" Alistair starts as the weight of the heavy pack he's carrying lifts off his shoulders.

"Wait a second, excuse me—" Gretel says as she senses something swipe her leg.

Filomena feels something tugging at her, but when she turns around, no one is there. She keeps turning, certain that someone's behind her. The others are doing the same. The four companions form a circle, facing outward with their backs together.

Suddenly a group of boys surround them, appearing as if out of thin air. One boy with jet-black hair and a terrifying mischievous glint in his eyes must be the leader of the pack; Filomena can tell by the way he's grinning and pacing around them. In his all-black outfit, he looks a bit like a wraith.

"Sorry to bother you," the boy says. "We were hoping

we'd be able to lighten your load without causing you any trouble. But it seems you've caught on, so now we'll have to do this the old-fashioned way."

The boy lunges at Jack, who's unsheathed his Dragon's Tooth sword. Jack swings at him, but the boy shifts out of Jack's range, quick as a river.

"Would you take a look at that beautiful sword!" the black-haired boy says. "Now you're just tempting me."

The rest of the thieves start taunting Filomena, Gretel, and Alistair, circling them with quick steps and jeering.

"Oh, come on now, kids," the leader boy says. "Don't be scared. We only want to see what you have in those bags! Didn't your mothers teach you to share?"

Jack leans toward Gretel, Filomena, and Alistair, who all still have their backs together in defense. "Whatever you do," he instructs, "don't take your eyes off them, not even for a second."

"Oooh, lookee here, this one thinks he's some kind of hero," jeers the leader. "Is that what you are? A hero?"

Jack reddens and slashes with his sword, but the boy ducks away easily, cackling loudly as he goes.

Filomena reaches for her Dragon's Tooth sword, but when she pats her hip, nothing's there.

One of the boys brandishes it. He laughs wildly. "Looking for this?"

"Hey, that's no fair!" Alistair yells. He looks around to

check for his own weapon, and as soon as he takes his eyes off the boys, they charge.

Without her sword to defend herself, Filomena has little to rely on. She tries to swing her bagful of Never After books at the thieves (they are heavy tomes, after all, and could do serious damage), but she loses her balance and, in doing so, gives the thieves an opening to relieve her of her belongings.

Gretel gives a bloodcurdling scream as she tries to hold on to her pack, pulling it away from the thieves. But there are two of them and only one of Gretel, and with a mighty tug, they rip it out of her hands.

"Who's the hero now?" the leader of the pack sneers.

"Will you shut up about that?!" seethes Jack. In Jack's haste to secure his sword before flicking his vines, the thief is able to swipe the blade from its sheath as quick as a blink.

"What the—" Jack curses, but it's too late.

The muggers run off with the four friends' weapons and packs, and the group is left standing in the clearing empty-handed.

"Did that just happen?" asks Gretel, who's still in shock.

"Unfortunately, yes," groans Alistair.

They're still trying to come to grips with the situation when a now all-too-familiar voice calls from a distance: "It was so nice to see you all again! I do hope we keep running into each other. And thanks for the gifts!"

A chorus of laughter fades into the woods as the four friends are left looking dumbfounded at one another.

"Tell me that didn't just happen," Gretel repeats. "We were like sitting ducks!"

"Only cowards attack from behind!" Jack fumes. If Jack was grim before, he's absolutely livid now. He's pacing frantically back and forth while Alistair and Gretel pat their pockets and assess their losses.

"My scissors! They even took my scissors! How will I make my Snow Country collection now?!" Gretel yells in despair. She shakes out her empty pockets. "And my entire makeup kit! All my mascara wands! I'm going to look like I have no eyelashes until we get them back!"

Alistair is even more upset. "All my cooking gear is gone! And I was just starting to get good at it! How am I supposed to learn to make tulip cakes without my supplies?"

Filomena freezes as she just realizes what *she's* lost. "You guys, you guys, my Never After books are gone! I need those! How am I going to help us if I don't have them for reference? I read about Snow Country a long time ago; I was relying on those to refresh my memory!" Now she is really panicking.

Jack turns around, his eyes blazing. "We'll get everything back—every single pot, every single book, every single mascara wand! I swear!" Then he hangs his head. "Our dragon-hide armor is gone, too, and we'll need that when we get to Snow Country. I'm so stupid; I should have had us all wearing it. This is all my fault. I should've defended you all."

Filomena can't stand to see him this way. "Jack, come on," she says, putting a hand on his shoulder. She feels her stomach flip a little as he looks at her with wounded eyes. She goes on, "You're not single-handedly responsible for fighting off every danger for us. You may be a hero, but you're not the only hero here." Filomena smiles at Alistair and Gretel. "We're all in this together. We can all be one another's heroes."

Filomena looks at her three friends. Standing in this clearing empty-handed, discouraged, and totally robbed of their armor, weapons, and treasure: This isn't exactly how she pictured their next quest starting. But then again, when have things in Never After ever happened in the way she thought they would?

"You know what we need right now? A group hug!" Filomena declares.

And so Jack the Giant Stalker, Alistair Bartholomew Barnaby (aka Ali Baba), and Gretel the Cobbler's daughter all surround Filomena in a tight hug. Turns out that even getting robbed isn't so bad when you've got friends like these.

CHAPTER TWO

THE FORBIDDEN FOREST

"Well, you know what I'll say about hanging out with you three?" Gretel says as they break apart from their embrace. "There's certainly never a dull moment."

"I love group hugs!" Alistair says, considerably cheered. "What kind of magic are hugs? Fairy magic?"

Filomena smiles, thinking of her parents and their group hugs. She wonders how they're doing. Back in North Pasadena, her parents have their house rigged with an elaborate security system to keep them all safe. Filomena always thought they were being paranoid, but if they knew she'd just gotten robbed on a quest, they'd be freaking out too much to even say *I told you so!* A thread of homesickness worms its way into her chest and lodges there. Her parents always did everything within their power to keep her safe. She could really use one of her mother's takeout dinners right now, or maybe a big bowl of plain pasta with butter and cheese, which is the one dish her mom knows how to cook.

"Just the magic of friendship and love, Alistair," she says, trying to bring herself back to the present and the task at hand.

Jack is squinting into the distance. "I think they went that way," he says, motioning to the valley below.

Filomena is relieved to see his spirits returning. *Jack really does come alive in a crisis. Underdog extraordinaire. And, oh gosh, he does look so cute when he's making a plan . . .*

Ah! Focus, Filomena! Why did she keep going back to thinking about how cute Jack was when being heroic? (Although she thinks he looks cute all the time.)

Wait! She thinks Jack is cute? She's always thought he was cute, of course, but . . . Oh dear. This feels deeper than a book crush for sure. Filomena hopes no one's noticed how crimson she's turned.

"All right," says Jack. "No time like the present to pick up the pace. Let's go!" And with that, he's off and running in the direction of the thieves.

"You know," Gretel says, "the one thing that's actually good about getting robbed is that we have a lot less to carry."

The four of them are jogging at a quick clip now, with Jack in the lead.

"So," Gretel continues, "one way to look at this: The thieves are actually, like, our helpers, you know—like packhorses? Carrying the heavy stuff for us until we get to our destination!"

"Right," Filomena responds, "except we wouldn't be running right now if we weren't robbed in the first place."

"I can't believe I haven't learned by now not to wear my designer boots on these trips," Gretel says. "Man, I really need to invest in some athleisure."

"'Athleisure'?" Alistair questions. "Is that some kind of potion? What witch are you working with, Gretel?"

Filomena giggles. It never gets old, listening to Alistair and Gretel. Ever since spending so much time together at the Queen of Hearts' castle in Wonderland, they'd been bonded like squabbling siblings.

As they banter, Jack peers through his Seeing Eye to look just ahead. Luckily the tiny gold telescope hung from a chain wrapped around his neck, and the thieves hadn't gotten close enough to grab it.

"How's it going, Jack?" Filomena asks.

"We're on their tails; I can see them ahead. It looks like we're getting close to Northphalia. Not exactly the part we were planning to cut through, though."

Another *North* is on Filomena's mind again. It was only yesterday that Filomena thought she'd be going home to North Pasadena. She'd even packed her bags. She was excited to see her parents, give them a huge hug, and tell them everything that had happened since the last time she was home. And a LOT had happened. She'd tell them all about meeting the supposedly wicked stepsisters, Beatrice and Hortense; barely escaping death in a gingerbread house; spending the night in a beast's castle; and, of course, going undercover at the Queen of Hearts' palace! (Doesn't sound familiar? Better check out book two of this series. The adventures just keep coming!)

When Filomena got back from her first visit to Never After (remember when she was denied her genie wish but still managed to banish the ogre Olga with help from a wolf pack?), she thought they'd never believe that this other world existed. But when she came clean about it, it turned out they'd already known—or at least had suspected. Filomena had always known she was adopted, but what she hadn't known until that moment was that she was adopted by her parents after Carabosse, the thirteenth fairy (her aunt, remember?), rescued her from the evil ogre Queen Olga on her christening day, after her birth mother, the fairy Rosanna, died. Carabosse brought Filomena to the mortal world to keep her safe. There Filomena's mortal parents found her and raised her as their own, protecting her from evil—and, sure, sometimes they were a little *too* protective. Yesterday she had been so excited to see them and to explain how she'd helped defeat the ogre queen (for now), bring the real Queen of Hearts back to Wonderland, and free Byron Bessley from his beastly curse.

But just as Filomena was about to return to her other life, a page from the Queen of Hearts' castle had come bearing news that the fairy Scheherazade (also known as Filomena's aunt Zera) was in Snow Country, and that she had found Colette, one of the thirteen fairies who'd gone missing after the Last Battle. And Zera needs help, desperately.

So going home would have to wait for now. Thank fairies, time works differently in Never After; when Filomena eventually did get back to her parents, it would be as if only a few hours, or a day, had passed.

"You know," Alistair squeaks out between huge breaths, "if I'd known how big a part cardio was going to play in saving the worlds, I don't know that I would've signed up for this."

The four laugh between gasps of air.

"Oh, you signed up for this? That's nice. I didn't realize it was optional!" Gretel huffs.

"We really should be training in our downtime, shouldn't we?" responds Alistair.

"Downtime?" Gretel laughs. "Since when do we ever have downtime?"

The path they'd been running along through the woods suddenly breaks into a clearing on a hill that overlooks a tiny town at the bottom of a valley. At the edge of the village is a forest that looks much different from the one they've been running through. It's darker and denser, with trees that seem almost sinister; they have bare black branches, and the lines of bark on their trunks look like scowling faces.

And from their vantage point on the hill, they can just barely spy the band of thieves with bags, glinting swords, and other assorted goods beelining toward that sinister forest. Soon the thieves have disappeared into it.

Jack lowers his Seeing Eye. "It won't penetrate through those trees," he says dejectedly. "The forest is covered in defensive magic."

"What is that place?" Filomena asks while Alistair and Gretel take deep breaths, hands on knees, beside them.

"Sherwood Forest," says Jack grimly.

Gretel's and Alistair's heads snap up.

"Are you sure?" Alistair says.

"I'm certain," Jack responds.

"I thought no one ever goes into Sherwood Forest?" says Gretel.

"Why? What is it?" Filomena asks. "I don't think it's covered in any of the Never After books I've read so far. But it sounds familiar."

"It's enchanted. No one knows much about it, but Gretel's right that no one ever goes there. At least, that's what they say. But it seems our little gang of thieves begs to differ." Jack kicks some pebbles on the path.

There's a chill in the twilit evening air; stars are just starting to glint above them. It's growing late, and Filomena can't tell if the cold is because they're getting close to Snow Country or because of this mysterious forest and its creepy energy.

Jack looks out over the vast landscape ahead of them. To the left is Sherwood Forest; to the right a small village. Beyond is Snow Country and all that comes with it. "It looks like we'll finally have some of that downtime Alistair was talking about. Let's follow the path to the village for now."

And with that they scramble down the hill, hoping to reach the village before the sun fully sets. An unspoken agreement lies among them: They aren't sticking around to see whatever might come crawling out of Sherwood Forest.

CHAPTER THREE

THE PRINCESS AND THE PLEA

The village is so pretty, it should be on a postcard or a billboard advertising trips to Never After. (COME FOR THE MAGIC! STAY FOR THE GREEN VISTAS!) Filomena can't believe her eyes as they walk around; it's like a town right out of a medieval British folktale! (She *does* read books outside the Never After series, you know.)

Gretel feels the same and claps her hands with glee as

they walk the charming village streets. "Oh, this town is so darling! Don't you think, Filomena?"

"It's very cute. It reminds me of a story, though I can't think which one."

"When you read so many, it must be hard to keep them all straight," Jack teases.

"Don't worry, the Never After books are still my favorites. Turns out the characters in them are pretty fun to hang out with," Filomena says, bumping Alistair's arm. Her eyes catch Jack's. He smiles back, and she feels that delicious tingly feeling once more.

The buildings in the town are lovely low houses and storefronts on cobblestone roads. From the windows, golden candles cast a warm glow onto the streets.

"Yeah, sure, it's cute all right, but you know what would be *really* cute? A huge plate of steaming hot food and a big comfy bed with a hundred pillows," says Alistair.

It's true that they haven't eaten in a long time now, and if they've learned anything from their travels together, it's that finding yourself on the road and without shelter at night is a recipe for a sticky situation. (We're looking at you, Rory Hexson, witch's son!)

"It looks like there's a pub right up there. Do you think we can get in?" Filomena says.

"Why wouldn't we be able to go in?" Jack responds.

"Aren't pubs like bars? Don't they ID at the door?"

"What is this *eye dee* you speak of?" Alistair asks. "They check our eyes for something?"

"Oh right. Sometimes I forget that the rules of the mortal world don't apply here," Filomena says, slapping her palm to her forehead. "I guess being underage doesn't really matter when you're immortal."

"I suppose that's true," says Jack. "It'll be a useful place to rest, anyhow, and there are probably rooms for rent upstairs. Good idea, Filomena."

The four friends take seats at a long wooden table inside the Merry Greenwood Tavern. Jack sits next to Filomena, and Gretel and Alistair sit across from them. The tavern is spilling with life: Rowdy locals are laughing and toasting with bubbling jugs of drink, and a band plays a fiddle and a lute in the corner. A group of well-dressed foxes and bears dance to the beat, and a bunch of pretty maidens with flowing jewel-tone dresses sit together at a table, chatting.

"I need to ask where those girls got such fabulous frocks," Gretel says, looking over at the maidens. "Maybe we can stop tomorrow for some shopping?"

She looks hopefully at Jack, but a white rabbit wearing a waistcoat and a timepiece and holding a pen and paper hops up onto their table before Jack can respond. Filomena stifles a gasp. She supposes a rabbit waiter is not the strangest thing she's seen since stepping foot in Never After—not by far. Foxes and bears are dancing over by the band, after all. But isn't this *the* famous White Rabbit of Wonderland?

"Welcome, weary travelers!" the White Rabbit says in a thick Cockney accent. "What nosh can I get for you this evening?"

"No chance you have cheeseburgers and fries, is there?" Alistair asks hopefully.

"Can't say I know what that is, son, but I do have bangers and mash. Maybe that'll tickle yer fancy?"

Alistair nods, resigned.

"Lasses? Lad?" the White Rabbit asks, turning to the rest. "Same?"

"Sure . . . ," says Filomena. "But aren't you late for something?"

"Late?" The White Rabbit blinks and checks his timepiece.

"Don't you work for the Queen of Hearts?" she persists.

The White Rabbit chuckles. "Oh yes, yes. A long time ago, lass. But when my cookbook *The White Rabbit Entertains!* went to the top of the bestseller lists, I was able to open my dream pub." The White Rabbit proudly looks around at his establishment. "How is the Queen of Hearts these days?"

"Restored" is all Filomena says with a smile.

"Tip-top," says the White Rabbit, who hops away to put in their order.

"Does anyone know what bangers and mash is?" Gretel asks with her nose wrinkled. "The White Rabbit might be a celebrity chef now, but he could at least give us a menu! If bangers and mash is anything like kidney pie or liver with onions, I'm *so* out."

Jack is shaking his head, food the furthest thing from his mind.

"You're still thinking about the robbery?" Filomena leans in to ask. Gretel and Alistair continue debating the topic of dishes they are least likely to eat.

Jack nods. "I just don't get what happened. Normally I can take on twenty highway thieves! I've done it before, even *without* a Dragon's Tooth sword. I don't understand how they got everything from us so easily."

"We weren't prepared for them. Don't be so hard on yourself, Jack."

"It's not that I'm being hard on myself. I'm always able to fend people off. If I can't protect us against a bunch of kids, something else is afoot. They must be more than they appear. And who was that guy? He almost seems familiar." Jack frowns, thinking.

Filomena considers this. At first she thinks Jack is still just being too hard on himself, but it did seem odd that Jack the Giant Stalker, the prince who slayed the ogre king, could be so easily hoodwinked by a bunch of teenage ruffians.

"He said something when he left," she says. "Remember?

He said it was nice to see us again. What was that about? We've never met him before, have we?"

Just then the White Rabbit comes back carrying a tray of frothy hot drinks. "Courtesy of the young lady at the next table," the White Rabbit says, motioning to the group of pretty maidens.

"Hot cocoa! No way!" Alistair takes a mug gleefully. "Do you guys think the girls over there have a crush on me?"

Filomena looks over at the girls, puzzled. She turns back to her friends and wrinkles her nose. "Well, I don't know why they wouldn't, Alistair, but maybe we should be careful before drinking these. You remember what happened the last time we took something sweet from a stranger?"

Gretel shivers, remembering the days they spent in sugar-fueled fugue states. "Can we please stop bringing up the gingerbread house? I'm really trying not to relive that in my dreams."

One of the maidens walks over to their table. She's a beautiful Black girl with a crown of curly dark hair. She looks to be about sixteen years old and wears a red velvet dress with golden lace cuffs and collar.

"Do you not care for hot cocoa?" she asks the table. "I thought that was a safe choice; I thought everyone likes hot cocoa. I can get you some mulled wine if you prefer."

"Oh no, we love hot cocoa! We were just wondering why it was sent over is all, and we hadn't gotten to drinking it yet," Filomena responds.

"Of course! How rude of me to proceed without introductions!" The maiden giggles. "I'm Princess Jeanne. It's a pleasure to make your acquaintances."

The princess holds a hand in front of Jack for him to kiss, which makes him redden profusely. He looks to Filomena as if to say *help*, and she just shrugs. But the princess isn't discouraged and waits for Jack to take her hand. He kisses it sheepishly.

"Pleased to meet you, Princess Jeanne," he says.

Filomena ignores the pinprick of jealousy that blooms in her stomach. He's just being polite, after all.

"May I join you?" the princess asks, still looking at Jack.

"Yeah, sit down!" Gretel cuts in. "I was actually dying to ask about your dress . . ."

"Oh, this old thing? It's so out of style now, I know, please don't think any less of me! The locals can just get quite rowdy around the tavern, spilling and such, so I don't like to wear my good gowns here. You know how it is."

Gretel looks dejected, so Filomena gives her hand a squeeze under the table and mouths *I think it's very cute.*

Alistair's looking a little dejected, too, come to think of it. Princess Jeanne didn't ask *him* to kiss her hand. Wearing a hot-cocoa mustache, he asks a reasonable question: "If you're really a princess, where's your crown?"

"Well, Alistair, that's actually very pertinent to why I wanted to speak with you all."

The four trade glances. Filomena gets that feeling again: The plot is about to thicken.

"Wait," Alistair says, frowning, "how do you know my name?"

Princess Jeanne laughs, and it's a sweet melodious sound. Despite her suspicions, Filomena starts to warm to the girl. Besides, it's obvious Jeanne's way too old for Jack, who's only thirteen.

"Why, I know all your names! Dashing Jack the Giant Stalker, fashionista extraordinaire Miss Gretel, and of course the brilliant Filomena, or should I say Eliana? What name do you go by these days?"

"Filomena's fine," Filomena says, slightly confused now.

"Wait, wait, wait," Alistair butts in. "Don't I get a descriptor?"

"Of course, Alistair the Adorable," Princess Jeanne says, tapping Alistair on the nose with her pointer finger. "You four have been splashed all over the pages of my favorite magazines. Every time I go to get my nails glittered by the sprites, I always read the *Palace Inquirer* and the *Daily Crown*."

Gretel perks up. "Hold on, are we famous?"

"Well, it takes more than one feature in the *Palace Inquirer* to be *truly* famous—and I should know—but you certainly got a lot of coverage during Hortense's and Beatrice's weddings. A gorgeous ceremony, by the way! So lovely, I can almost forgive the fact that I wasn't invited," she says, pouting coyly. "But anyway, that's not what I'm here to talk about. I need help. And after reading about you, I think you lot are the ones I need."

The four friends look at one another. More people to help? This is the last thing they need right now. Don't they themselves need help? And aren't they on the way to help Zera?

"Plus I just overheard your little conversation about getting robbed? I think I know exactly who was behind it," Jeanne says.

Okay, now they're interested.

"Go on," Jack says.

"Okay. First let me back up a little. Does the name King Richard mean anything to you?" Princess Jeanne asks.

Filomena's drawing a blank, once again cursing the fact that she doesn't have her Never After books on hand. Gretel shrugs. But Jack and Alistair look at each other with an air of dread.

"Yes, it does," Jack responds.

Princess Jeanne can see that Filomena and Gretel are lost here, so she explains. "King Richard is my uncle," she tells them.

Jack's face has gone stony, cold, closed up. Filomena can sense that any interest he had toward getting to know Princess Jeanne and whatever she wants has vanished. That name clearly means something to him, and it's not good.

He coughs. "We know of King Richard. At least, Alistair and I do."

Princess Jeanne nods. "Then you know he's caused a lot of harm in Never After, especially here, up north. He's notorious for forcibly wiping out villages, sending all the creatures who live there away from their homes and their communities, so they're left with nowhere to go. All just so he can clear the land and build his own properties there."

"He targets some of the most beautiful villages in Never After," Alistair explains to Filomena and Gretel. "Especially ones near the sea or on lakeshores. He conquers them for his own greed. The oldest and loveliest villages in the kingdoms, those that used to thrive under the protection of the fairies. But since the fairies are gone, there's no one to stand up to him and his army. He just builds castles for himself and his friends, castles that sit empty most of the time."

Filomena is shocked. How awful! Running people out of their homes? Just to build empty showpalaces? "How can he do that? That's horrible! Hasn't anyone stopped him?"

"We've tried," Jack says, still stone-faced. "But since the Last Battle, all of Never After is either controlled by ogres or falling to despots like him."

"Right. I'm relieved you know how truly horrible he is. Some in the North have rallied to his cause. But here's the thing: King Richard isn't even technically a king. He just took the title and makes everyone call him that. *I'm* the rightful heir to the throne."

"So you're not aligned with your uncle?" Jack asks, skeptical.

"Not at all! I don't stand for anything he's done. He's reprehensible. Not to mention he's sabotaging me!" Jeanne's getting quite agitated and takes a deep breath before continu- ing. "That's what I need to talk to you about. Our kingdom does not recognize its true ruler until that person is crowned with the ancient crown of the North. You asked where my crown is. Uncle Richard stole it. He knows I can't be the true queen without it. But while I'm alive, he can't declare him- self king, either."

Alistair's eyes widen at this.

"It's only a matter of time before he tries to get rid of me. Right now he's content styling himself as King Richard the Lionhearted even though his heart is smaller than a kitten's. More like Richard the Mouse King. But one day he *will* place that crown on his head."

"So what are you going to do about it?" asks Gretel.

"Steal it back, of course," Princess Jeanne replies. "Here's where you all come in. For better or worse, I know my uncle, and I know he doesn't do his own dirty work. I have reason to believe that the person who stole the crown from my castle is the same sneaky black-haired boy who stole from you today. None other than Robin Hood."

"Robin Hood?" Filomena's ears perk up in recognition. Could it be the same Robin Hood she read about in the mor- tal world?

Princess Jeanne clucks her tongue. "Horrible chap! He's been terrorizing our kingdom and the surrounding villages for years. He's unbelievably tricky, stealing from the poor and making himself rich."

Filomena frowns. "But wait—in the stories I know, Robin Hood steals from the rich and gives to the poor." In the traditional fairy tales, that is. "He's a hero."

"Filomena," Gretel says, "remember how the mortal world's story of Cinderella has no mention of Cinderella being a spoiled ogre? It seems like this might be another case of the wrong story spreading across the portal border."

"He's no hero! He is nothing but a thief!" Princess Jeanne says hotly. "He's stealing from the poor to make himself rich, just like he stole from you."

"Hey, who you callin' poor?" Alistair says, crossing his arms.

"Well, no offense, darling, but have you looked at your outfit recently?" Princess Jeanne says, giving Alistair a sympathetic smile. "Gretel's got it going on, though."

Gretel smiles, tossing her hair over her shoulder. "I do know how to do beauty on a budget!"

Still, Filomena isn't totally convinced by Princess Jeanne yet, and the princess can clearly sense it.

"I know we just met, but trust me, I'm on your side. I'm in trouble, and so is my kingdom, but most pressingly, so is my friend. He went to steal the crown back for me, but he hasn't been seen since he left. I'm really worried about him. That's mainly why I'm coming to you for help." Princess Jeanne looks so forlorn that the four friends immediately feel sorry for her. She takes a huge breath and regains her composure. She drums her fingers on the table. "That guy who stole from you—black hair, annoyingly handsome, and so slippery that you couldn't seem to get a hold of him, right?"

"*So* handsome," Filomena agrees. Wait, did she just agree that Robin Hood was handsome? In front of Jack? Did he notice? Is that why he's looking at her and frowning? "I mean, um, if bad boys are your type, which, um, they're not mine!" she quickly adds.

"Like I was saying, the thief who stole your belongings is the same thief who stole my crown and who's possibly holding my friend hostage: Robin Hood!" Princess Jeanne declares. "It's him. I know it. We have history. Uncle Richard is behind all this, but Robin Hood is his henchman. And I need you to help rescue my dear friend, Sharif of Nottingham, from his clutches."

"You mean *the* sheriff of Nottingham?" asks Filomena, who is a stickler for grammar. She's read about him, too. He's the mean old sheriff who rips off the townspeople, isn't he? Seems like a strange fit for a friend of Princess Jeanne's, but stranger things have happened in Never After.

But now it's Jeanne who looks confused. "The sheriff of Nottingham? I don't understand. Although his name is Sharif and he is from Nottingham. Lord Sharif of Nottingham, to be precise."

"Oh," says Filomena. She notices Jack's brows furrow

at the mention of that name. Does Jack know everyone in Never After? The guy does get around.

"Did you say Sharif?" Jack asks. "Goes by Riff?"

"Exactly!" Princess Jeanne says brightly. "Do you know him?"

Alistair guffaws with surprise. "We do! We fought with him in the Last Battle!" he cries happily.

Jack's face softens. "Riff was one of our best soldiers. He served in our battalion with Byron Bessley."

"Splendid! Well, what do you say, then? Will you help me rescue him?" Princess Jeanne asks. "I know he went into Sherwood Forest to help get my crown back, and I couldn't stand it if he's come to any harm because of me!"

The group confers silently, exchanging glances, but of course there's only one answer. Filomena didn't need to read all twelve Never After books to know that heroes like Jack and Alistair don't disappoint innocent strangers who ask for their help. And since she and Gretel are part of the team, too, she knows how they'll respond.

"Of course we'll help," says Alistair. "Right, Jack?"

"There's Zera to consider," Jack replies thoughtfully. "We were on our way to Snow Country."

"Zera's a powerful fairy. She can hold her own for a while yet," says Alistair, and at once Filomena sees the brave sergeant at arms that Alistair used to be and not just her goofy, cheeseburger-obsessed friend. "Riff and Princess Jeanne need us now."

"And we can't go to Snow Country without getting our stuff back," reminds Gretel. "We need our Dragon's Tooth swords and our armor."

"She's got a point," Filomena murmurs, even as her heart starts to beat rapidly at the thought of the rescue mission.

"So you'll do it?" asks Princess Jeanne.

"Yes," says Filomena.

"Definitely," says Alistair.

"I don't see how we can say no," adds Gretel.

"We'll go at once," says Jack.

"Oh, thank goodness!" says Princess Jeanne, clapping her hands in relief. "Thank you, thank you!"

"But first we've got to eat," says Alistair just as the White Rabbit returns to the table and sets down four plates of bangers and mash.

"No, no, this simply won't do," Princess Jeanne says, shaking her head at the sight of their supper. "You need better sustenance than this. Dearest White Rabbit, can we please have a large shepherd's pie, three beef Wellingtons to share, and a full Sunday roast with extra gravy? With all the vegetables from the garden? I know it isn't Sunday, but for me?" She bats her lashes. "Put it on my tab."

The four friends are practically drooling at the sound of the order. They haven't eaten like that since the royal wedding feast.

Alistair laughs. "It's sure helpful to have a princess's budget when you have a princess's palate!"

"As far as princesses go, you're far better than Cinderella in my books," Gretel agrees.

"Not all princesses are alike, you know!" Princess Jeanne says, dipping her finger into the whipped cream on Jack's hot chocolate. "Don't judge a girl by her crown! Or, in my case, by the lack thereof."

CHAPTER FOUR

ENEMY OF MY ENEMY

The next day, after a good night's rest at the inn, Gretel, Alistair, Jack, Filomena, and the most recent addition to their group, Princess Jeanne, are on their way for an early morning rescue.

Princess Jeanne isn't just a pretty face; she's been tracking Robin Hood for a week, ever since she figured out that he must have captured her friend Riff. Filomena is impressed. She didn't expect the princess to be such a sleuth. Princess Jeanne tells them she's got Robin Hood's schedule down pat.

He likes to strike during lunchtime, when people have their guard down and are trying to rest.

"Disrupting the sacred hour of luncheon! The guy truly *is* despicable," Alistair says.

As such, Princess Jeanne tells them that their best bet to rescue Riff and look for her crown will be when Robin Hood and his gang are out prowling at midday, leaving only two dopey guards at their hideout.

Today Princess Jeanne is wearing an outfit much more appropriate for a break-in than her red velvet dress. "It's the kingdom's latest in battle-ready-wear," she tells Gretel as the Cobbler's daughter admires the thin gold chain mail outfit with envy and while Alistair plods along beside.

Jack and Filomena are hanging a few paces behind the group. Filomena can tell that Jack wants to talk to her alone. She's his primary confidant. She smiles to herself.

"So what do you think, Fil?" he asks.

"About what?"

"Can we trust Princess Jeanne? We've been burned before. We know Queen Olga has spies everywhere."

Filomena considers this. She's starting to get a pretty good read on whom to trust, but with each passing day in Never After, the stakes get higher. Although, she was once quite suspicious of the wickedly fun stepsisters Hori and Bea, and now they're some of her closest friends.

"You know, there's a saying in the mortal world: *The enemy of my enemy is my friend.* That's what I thought when

I first met you and Alistair, when you helped me escape the Fettucine Alfredos. Robin Hood certainly seems like our enemy, and he's definitely Princess Jeanne's enemy. By that equation, she might have a good shot at becoming our friend."

Jack nods. "You're right. You always know how to think your way out of a trap, Filomena. I admire that about you," he says with his customary shy grin.

She smiles back at him, and a realization hits her hard. There's no denying it: She likes Jack. She really likes Jack. It's awful. It's terrifying. It's electrifying.

"What are you two smiling about, huh?" Alistair says over his shoulder, snapping both Filomena and Jack out of their doe-eyed trance. "I'm not feeling so smiley right about now. I think I had too much of that full English breakfast."

A loud belch escapes him as they exit the village and start into Sherwood Forest.

"If I get killed because of one of your burps, Alistair, then I swear to all thirteen fairies, I will haunt you forever!" Gretel whisper-yells.

Princess Jeanne shushes them both, and that's when Filomena realizes they've come upon their destination. The gang gathers in a dense cluster of trees. "Robin's lair is through there," Princess Jeanne says, beyond their makeshift hideout to an old, decrepit-looking castle with a pair of guards in front. Filomena tries to pull her thoughts away from Jack and back to the mission at hand.

"It used to be one of the finest castles around," Princess Jeanne says sadly. "Now look at it. Gone to ruin. Just like everything in this cursed forest."

It's one of the spookiest sights Filomena's seen in Never After. Tall Gothic arches and spikes that have chunks missing. Gargoyles growling and displaying sharp teeth, or what's left of them. The castle even seems to have its own weather; a storm cloud is hanging above it.

"It looks like bats will fly out at any second," Gretel says. "Major ick!"

The five huddle close and speak in hushed voices.

"The important thing to remember about Robin Hood is that he's mostly all bark and no bite," Princess Jeanne says. "He's not violent, but he is quick."

"Yeah, we got a taste of that," Jack answers, remembering how their belongings were stolen without them even realizing.

"With that in mind, we need to approach this the way Robin would," Princess Jeanne offers.

Filomena can't help but wonder about Princess Jeanne's past with Robin Hood. It seems they've known each other a long time. But she feels she doesn't know Princess Jeanne well enough to ask yet.

"Hmm, not sure how we would do that," Gretel inserts, "because we have absolutely no weapons."

"I'm sure that wouldn't be a problem for the likes of you all," Princess Jeanne says. "So here you are. I've led you to

Sherwood Forest, I've given you background info, and now I think it's time for my hired heroes to take over."

"'Hired'? You mean we're getting paid for this?" Alistair retorts.

Princess Jeanne ignores him. "Well, go on, then—rescue Riff, and see if you can snag my crown while you're at it!"

Jack is staring at the castle doors, a plan formulating in his mind. "Those guards seem pretty bored, which means they can probably be easily distracted," he considers.

"My teachers always told me I was a great distraction to the class. I could give it a shot!" Gretel volunteers.

"I guess I could help, too. I'll go with you, Gretel," Princess Jeanne says, threading her arm through Gretel's. "We'll pretend we're lost and looking for directions."

"Perfect," Jack says. "Try to lure them away from the doors and keep their backs facing the castle. Filomena, Alistair, and I will sneak in and find Riff."

"Then what?" Alistair asks.

"Then we run."

Filomena watches Gretel and Princess Jeanne talk to the guards and make them laugh. Filomena wonders why, when it comes to adventures, tasks like these seem to get split between girls and boys, with girls doing the distracting and boys the rescuing. But Filomena's with the boys. Is she "one of the boys"? Is she "not like other girls"? Ugh, she hates that phrase. Just because she can't match shoes to a handbag doesn't mean she's not a girl like Gretel. Or just because she can run faster than Alistair doesn't mean she's just like Jack. (Also, there are probably a lot of people who can run faster than Alistair.)

Anyway, this is too much to think about while on a quest! She makes a mental note to bring this up when conversation runs dry during their next five-hour hike to a faraway kingdom.

Gretel gives Filomena, Alistair, and Jack the all clear with a brush of her left shoulder and a touch to her nose. The three friends beeline into the castle.

The inside is even creepier than the outside. Dim and damp. No carpets or tapestries, no warm fire, nothing. Just spiderwebs in corners and silence. Filomena was once trapped in the Beast's dungeon, but this is even worse. Jack heads into the darkness, leaving them behind.

"Is Robin Hood goth?" Filomena jokes. "He does wear a lot of black."

"Goth? Well, according to my studies, this architecture *is* rather Gothic," Alistair offers.

"Your studies?" she asks.

"Oh, my dear Filomena, I've lived many lives. There's so much you've yet to learn about me." Alistair winks.

Jack comes back from wherever he'd been checking out. "No sign of Riff," he reports. "There are way too many rooms in this place. We don't have time to check each one and risk Robin Hood returning while we're still here."

Filomena thinks. If Robin Hood is all about wits, she can work with that. She tries to think like a trickster. It is difficult; Filomena is so honest, truth serum would barely make her act differently . . . unless she was asked a *really* personal question after taking some. Like who she was crushing on. She has a crush! And he's standing right there!

Her focus is wavering. Filomena starts pacing to keep her mind on track.

If she were to capture Lord Sharif of Nottingham—not that she, in any world, would ever capture anyone!—where would she put him? Somewhere far from reach, yes, but Robin Hood would do worse. Robin Hood seems to have a mean streak. If Robin captured Riff just to mess with Princess Jeanne, then where would he think would be a funny place to hold Riff hostage?

It hits her like an Ogre's Wrath attack.

"The tower! He put Riff in the tower, I bet you," Filomena shouts.

"What?" Jack questions.

"Just trust me, let's check it out."

The two boys have learned by now that when Filomena has a hunch, it's worth inspecting. So they run up the stone stairs to the eastern part of the castle, where a large tower is located. At the top of the stairs is a heavy stone door.

Filomena tries to open it, but it's locked. Robin Hood wasn't taking any chances there. Jack twists his vines around the handle and pulls, but it doesn't budge an inch.

"Let me try," says Alistair, stepping forward. "Have you forgotten who you're with, old chap? Your brave companion, your sidekick, your chief lieutenant?"

Jack whips his vines back around his wrists and regards Alistair with an amused smile. "If I remember correctly, Byron was my lieutenant."

Alistair makes a dismissive gesture and motions for them to give him some space, then puts his hand out and booms, "OPEN SESAME!"

The door remains closed.

Alistair scratches his chin. "OPEN SESAME NOODLES!"

Nothing.

He rocks back and forth on his heels. "OPEN SESAME CHICKEN!"

Nada.

Filomena whispers in Alistair's ear.

"Huh? I've never heard of that one," he says.

"Trust me, it's big in the mortal world," Filomena assures him.

Alistair clears his throat and gestures toward the door again. "Right, right. How about . . . SHOW ME THE WAY TO SESAME—"

"STREET!" Filomena and Alistair chorus.

There is a deep silence.

Then, slowly, oh so slowly—so slowly at first that they're sure nothing is happening—the heavy stone of the door crumbles and becomes a pile of sand, leaving an open doorway.

Filomena gasps. "It worked!"

Jack slaps Alistair on the back. "Nice one, Ali Baba!"

Alistair grins. "Sand is made out of rocks, and you know the desert is my home turf," he adds modestly.

"Pardon me, but . . . who are you?" a voice asks.

In the doorway stands a tall boy of about seventeen years with a brown buzz cut and bronzed muscles like Michelangelo's *Statue of David*. (Filomena saw that statue on a trip with her parents once. She feels a pang for them—her art-loving, pasta-eating parents.)

But she snaps back to reality when she realizes, *Oh no, I was wrong!* They've accidentally rescued some Greek god, not Sharif of Nottingham. How many people does Robin Hood have locked up in this castle, anyway?

"Apologies! We are supposed to be rescuing Lord Sharif of Nottingham, but it appears we open sesame'd the wrong door," Filomena tells him.

"Oh, but that is me! I am Sharif! But please, call me Riff," the handsome boy says with a blinding smile. He turns to the others and his face lights up even more. "Now, this can't be Jack the Giant Stalker, Winter Knight, General of the Thirteen Armies, can it?"

"One and the same. Good to see you, man," says Jack with a wide grin on his face.

Filomena watches as the two engage in what the mortal world calls a bro hug. When they pull back, they look so delighted that they hug again, this time normally, with both arms, slapping each other on the back.

"I can't believe this, mate! And, Alistair, I forgot you could crumble doors like that." Riff grins, giving Alistair a hug. "How long has it been since I saw the likes of you two?"

"Since the Last Battle, it must've been," Jack responds. They all look somber for a moment. But then Jack perks back up, throwing an arm around Filomena. "Riff, you have to meet our best friend, Filomena," he says.

Filomena's shoulders tingle a bit at Jack's touch. He hasn't been this happy since the success of their last rescue. Filomena could've stayed like this for a long time, but the logical part of her remembers that they have a mission at hand, not to mention a cunning antagonist who might be on his way here.

"It's so nice to meet you, Riff, but I think we better get out of here while we're alone," she ventures. "Let's catch up once we're out of enemy territory?"

"Wait! Aren't we supposed to try and find Princess Jeanne's crown while we're here?" Jack exclaims.

"I looked everywhere before I was captured. It's not here," says Riff.

There's no time to look for it anyway. Luncheon is over; they heard the clock chime. Robin Hood could return at any moment.

The four dash back down the stairs and out of the castle.

Outside, Gretel and Princess Jeanne are still distracting the guards. Gretel is showing them how to play a game on her phone. "So you see, you populate your little island."

Filomena signals to Gretel to get out of there, and then she and the three boys hide in the forest until Princess Jeanne and Gretel are able to sneak away.

When Princess Jeanne catches sight of Riff, she runs straight into his arms.

"Jeannie!" he cries, catching her and swooping her around in a circle.

"I was so worried!" she tells him. "Are you okay? I hope they didn't do anything too terrible."

"I'm fine. Nothing I couldn't handle. But I'm so sorry, Jeanne—I don't have it," he tells her.

Princess Jeanne shakes her head. "It's okay. It's just a crown." She shrugs.

"We'll get it back. I promise you," Riff tells her, giving her another squeeze.

"That's Riff?" Gretel whispers to Alistair.

"I know, right?" Alistair whispers back to Gretel, leaning in.

"Wow. The mortal fairy tales really did a number on him," she says incredulously.

"Why? What's he like in the fairy tales?" Alistair asks.

"Let's just say he doesn't look like that! Hubba, hubba!" Gretel says, fanning herself.

Filomena laughs, overhearing the two gossip like a couple of hens.

"Thank fairies you got Riff out of there when you did," Princess Jeanne says to her hired heroes.

Riff nudges Jeanne with a smug grin. "Missed me, did you?"

But Princess Jeanne isn't having any of that right now. "I suppose. But also, once the henchmen gave us directions to the nearest village, they noticed my new gold chain mail and got really chatty. Like they haven't spoken to anyone new in centuries. Then they started mansplaining my own battle gear to me! The nerve! I was getting so annoyed, I'd have blown our cover any minute."

VERY MERRY

At Princess Jeanne's castle, a feast is in session.

"Now this is the kind of royal treatment I could get used to," Alistair says.

Alistair, Jack, Gretel, and Filomena are seated around a long dining table resplendent with large roasted fowlkens, roasted zucchonions, mashed sunsquashes, and razzleberry pies for as far as the eye can see.

After rescuing Riff, Princess Jeanne said it was about time they saw the much more welcoming castle of Northphalia, which—*cough*—just happened to be her own. *Smaller than*

Robin Hood's creepy hideout, sure, she'd said. *But much better decorated. And insulated.*

It's true. Filomena had been swept away by the beauty of the castle the instant they entered. It's even grander than Hortense's and Beatrice's home, Rosewood Manor, which Filomena had thought was the height of luxury. But Princess Jeanne's castle is on another level. It's like the grand royal palaces Filomena's read about in history or seen on television: marble floors, gold and silver everywhere, brocaded walls, and furniture upholstered with the richest velvets and silks.

"Welcome to the Court of the North!" Princess Jeanne announces when they enter the dining room, where dozens of guests are gathered. "These are the Merry Men and Women, and this is my dear baby sister, Little Jeanne!"

"I may be your baby sister, but I'm not a baby," Little Jeanne says, walking up to the newcomers with her arms crossed and a pout on her face. She's just as pretty as her older sister—and as it appears, much more spoiled. She looks a few years younger than Princess Jeanne—so about the same age as Filomena—but she's definitely acting like a toddler having a tantrum. "I can't believe you went on an adventure without me again!" Little Jeanne says, practically stomping her feet.

"Now, Little Jeanne, I told you, Sherwood Forest is too dangerous for you!" says Princess Jeanne, trying to placate her sister.

"*Little* Jeanne?" whispers Gretel. "She doesn't even get her own name?"

After Little Jeanne stomps off, Princess Jeanne turns to the group and sighs. "Her real name is Veronique, but when she was little—I mean *younger*—she looked so like me that the court nicknamed her Little Jeanne, and it stuck. Believe me, neither of us is happy about it. It causes way too much confusion. But what can you do?" Princess Jeanne rolls her eyes. "Anyway, sorry about that. Please, come sit for dinner," she says, and leads them through the warm and inviting royal dining room.

They follow her to the center of the enormously long head table. Members of the court are dressed in luxe outfits similar to those Filomena and her friends are now wearing. Northphalia's castle is the complete opposite of the damp, silent hideout they just fled. So much chatter and laughter! Filomena smiles. Merry men and women indeed!

When they arrived, Princess Jeanne had insisted that Filomena and her friends all change out of their "filthy travelers' clothes" and into fresh outfits. Filomena and Gretel wear hand-me-down gowns, and Alistair and Jack are dressed in royal regalia. Only Gretel seems to feel at home in such garb; she's admiring her reflection in the tall mirrors on the dining room walls. Filomena would much rather wear her regular hoodie and jeans, but at least she still has on her purple combat boots. They match the purple color of her gown quite perfectly.

"How wonderful you all look!" Princess Jeanne says.

"Now you really look like the prince that you are," says Little Jeanne when she comes back and takes a seat across from Jack, coyly batting her eyelashes.

Jack smiles politely but doesn't respond. Filomena knows he's never been one to enjoy throwing around titles. Among all the guests, Filomena sits between Jack and Riff; Princess Jeanne and Little Jeanne across from her, next to Gretel and Alistair.

At Princess Jeanne's nod, footmen around the table begin to serve the meal, heaping food onto their plates. Filomena's mouth waters at the sight of the mashed sunsquashes and the crispy roasted fowlken.

Little Jeanne gestures to a jug of sparkly pink liquid. "Peony fizz," she says, as a footman pours some for Jack. "A Northphalian specialty."

"So, Filomena," Riff says, "what part of Never After are you from? We haven't met before, have we?"

"We haven't. I'm kind of new around these parts." Filomena laughs.

"We found Filomena in the mortal world," Alistair interjects between bites of fowlken. "It was the most amazing accidental meeting ever."

"Well, I don't know how accidental it was. Jack the Giant Stalker here totally stalked me," Filomena adds. She catches Jack's eye, and they share a laugh, remembering their first meeting. Wasn't it just yesterday that she'd run from an Ogre's Wrath with him? Time flies when you're trying not to be an ogre's dinner.

"So hold on—you're a mortal?" Riff asks, scratching his head.

"Well, not exactly . . . ," Filomena responds.

"Oh, Riff, don't you read the *Never After Daily* at all?" Princess Jeanne squeals. "She's Princess Eliana, the fairy Carabosse's niece and Queen Rosanna's daughter! She just grew up in the mortal world."

"We're both biportal," Gretel adds. "My dad is the Cobbler."

"But she's not just the missing princess; she's Filomena Jefferson-Cho of North Pasadena," Jack says. "She's excellent at casting spells and fighting ogres."

Filomena tries not to look too pleased by this description.

"Hey," Gretel says, putting down the peony fizz she's been sipping and turning to Riff. "How did you come to be captured by Robin Hood, anyway?"

Sharif shakes his head in annoyance, remembering. "I went out in search of Jeanne's crown, and that abandoned castle was one of the first places I decided to look—it's well known as one of Robin's hideouts. I searched pretty much the whole place but came up with nothing. I was about to leave when I heard a girl's voice crying out for aid from the tower." He shrugs his broad shoulders. "I figured it must be a damsel in distress, so of course I ran up to rescue her. But when I got to the highest tower, where the voice was coming from, only Robin Hood was there."

Jack nods in sympathy with Riff.

"Before I could even realize what was happening, he'd slipped out the door behind me and locked it! Then he mocked me through the door for trying to be a hero." Riff glowers at the memory.

"Of course you wanted to help!" says Princess Jeanne, taking his hand across the table and squeezing it.

Riff smiles and looks around at Filomena and her friends. "I haven't thanked you enough for saving me, by the way. I thought my only escape might have to follow Rapunzel's approach. But growing out my hair to the length of hers would've taken years!" he jokes.

Princess Jeanne starts telling Alistair and Gretel all about the redecorating she's done in the castle over the last year, and Filomena looks around the dining room. The Merry Men and Women are all gossiping, chatting, eating, drinking, and living up to their moniker.

Hold on. The Merry Men? As in *Robin Hood and his Merry Men*? Aren't they on *his* side? She leans over to Jack. "Correct me if I'm wrong, but if Robin Hood is a bad guy who steals for his own good in this world, then wouldn't his Merry Men also be in cahoots *with him*?"

Before Jack can comment, Riff chimes in from Filomena's other side. "Oh no, these Merry Men are excellent blokes! They fought in my battalion during the war. Jack, you remember, right?"

Jack nods, leaving Filomena perplexed—not for the first time.

Filomena would be first to admit that Robin's group of scrawny teenagers were far from jovial. His men being merry is not the only lie perpetuated in the mortal world, however. As noted by Princess Jeanne when she introduced them, these are her Merry Men *and Women*.

"Trust me," Riff says, noticing Filomena's hesitance, "I'd never fraternize with anyone who works with Robin Hood. He's stolen far too much from this neck of the woods. And now he wants to put that pretender, 'King' Richard, on the throne! That would be a disaster for this kingdom. Everyone knows the rightful heir is Princess Jeanne."

While Riff is speaking, Filomena notices Little Jeanne's expression shift, as if something's not quite right. Then it shifts back into a neutral smile. *She's been very quiet this evening,* Filomena notes.

Having heard her name across the table, Princess Jeanne merges her redecorating conversation with Riff's. "You know what ballroom I would *love* to see? The Queen of Hearts' in Wonderland! I can't believe I didn't get invited to Prince Charlie's and Cinderella's ball," she pouts. "I mean, I know it ended up being ruined by ogres, but still."

There's been so much going on that Filomena has hardly thought back to that occasion, when Cinderella was revealed to be an ogre . . . Something clicks in the back of her mind. There were so many people in attendance from across all the kingdoms, so many fairy-tale characters she'd only ever read about. She remembers being starstruck by Lord Peter and Lady Wendy of Neverland and who else . . . ?

"Robin Hood!" she exclaims suddenly. Everyone jumps, thinking she's just spotted him. "No, no, not here—he was at Cinderella's ball! He was a guest!"

"You don't think . . . It can't mean . . . ," Gretel says.

Filomena finishes the thought on everyone's mind: "He must be working with the ogres."

Chapter Six
The Three Dancing Princesses

Everyone's quiet for a moment, even the Merry Men and Women. A realization washes over them: If Robin Hood is working with the ogres, then this just became way more serious than getting back Alistair's cooking supplies and Gretel's scissors. It means the ogres want King Richard on the throne and are aiming to keep Princess Jeanne's crown far, far away from her head. Filomena sighs. It always comes down to the ogres, doesn't it?

Princess Jeanne breaks the silence. "No!" she despairs. "It can't be true! I mean, I suspected as much, but I can't believe it. Robin's a thief, but he's not . . . he's not *evil*."

Riff tries to comfort her. "He's not the boy you knew anymore," he tells her. "I'm sorry."

"How do you know?" Little Jeanne asks scornfully. "You don't even know him! He's not really like that!"

Filomena raises her eyebrow at Little Jeanne's passionate defense of Robin Hood.

"We grew up with him," her sister explains. "He was one of us. The three of us were something of a gang."

It doesn't matter that Robin Hood was a childhood friend. If he's working with the ogres, then they know what they have to do. Gretel, Alistair, Jack, and Filomena look at one another, communicating silently. Their journey to Snow Country will have to be delayed for now, with the hope that Zera can hold out just a while longer.

"We really can't leave until we help Princess Jeanne get her crown back," says Filomena, looking at her friends.

"I'll send a messenger to Snow Country," Jack agrees.

"Yeah, looks like we'll have to deal with that slimeball," says Alistair.

"Gladly." Gretel nods. "I really need my cleansing cream back. When I use regular soap, I always break out!"

"Oh, grand!" Princess Jeanne claps. "My own private brigade!"

"We're not exactly working *for* you," Alistair jokes, "but we are working in your interest."

Princess Jeanne ignores this comment. "Okay, okay, enough of this dour mood! Nothing else we can do about all this tonight. Let's enjoy the evening, shall we?"

As Princess Jeanne says this, empty plates and bowls start levitating and float toward the kitchen door.

Filomena watches in awe. "How on earth?"

"Our head of staff here at the castle came up with a great spell for cleaning dishes that allows the staff a break," Princess Jeanne says in answer. "She's distantly related to the fairies. I can get her to teach it to you sometime if you want. Since, according to Jack, you're so talented at spellwork."

"I would love that," Filomena says, shyly accepting the compliment. How handy! She never considered that spells could be used for anything other than preventing mortal danger.

As the dishes fly away, musical instruments in the corner of the room start to play: A cello's bow zigzags across its strings, violins float in midair, a harp plucks itself, and a piano's keys press themselves down.

"Nothing takes the edge off like dancing!" Princess Jeanne says to the group.

Soon the dance floor is full of Merry Men and Women swaying, cheering, laughing, and dancing. Filomena's feeling a bit shy. She's never been to a dance. School was always so horrible thanks to her bullies, the Alfredos, that she never even considered participating in after-school activities. But this isn't home; it's Never After. Where instruments magically play themselves!

"Come on, then!" Gretel grabs Filomena's hand and brings her to the dance floor.

Gretel and Filomena dance together, and soon Alistair joins in. The three friends do the twist.

The song ends, and when the next one begins, Gretel whispers to Filomena, "Go ask Jack to dance."

"Me?"

"Yeah, you! He's just sitting there. Go on . . . Ask him!" urges Gretel.

Filomena is paralyzed. "Shouldn't he ask *me* to dance?"

"What is this, the eleventh century? Actually, it *is* the eleventh century in Never After. But *we're* from the twenty-first!" says Gretel, rolling her eyes.

"What about you? Shouldn't you ask Riff?"

"Just because I think he's attractive doesn't mean I like him. It's just an observation, like saying the sky is blue," says Gretel. "Besides, look—he's taken." They watch as Princess Jeanne and Riff dance in each other's arms. The two appear as though they were made for each other.

"Who *do* you like, Gretel?" asks Filomena. She is curious.

Gretel shrugs. "I don't know. I like myself. I like making things. I like my friends. I haven't really felt that way about anyone yet. Maybe I never will. Who knows?"

Filomena nods. That sounds reasonable. Not everyone needs a someone, and Gretel is certainly enough on her own.

As the night goes on, Princess Jeanne and Riff are graceful and fluid on the dance floor. Alistair and Gretel, on the other hand, seem to be involved in a dance battle; they're trying to outdo each other's moves. Alistair is pretending to be a watering can while Gretel is doing the robot.

Jack, however, sits alone at the head table. Filomena wants to ask him to dance or to pull him up off his feet, to join them. But she's paralyzed. What if he says no? Does that mean something, if he says no? If he doesn't want to dance with her, does that mean he doesn't like her in the way she likes him? And if he doesn't like her in the way she likes him, will she just melt into a humiliated puddle?

She feels ill and suddenly thirsty, and notices the jug of peony fizz on the head table is empty. Ready for a break from dancing, she grabs the jug and makes her way to the kitchen to refill it. Surely there's no shortage of peony fizz in the castle.

She walks across the dining room and through the kitchen door. A person wearing a pink silk dress is leaning out the window. Little Jeanne? Filomena gets a pinprick of fear, though she doesn't know why. *What's she doing with her head out the window?* Filomena thinks she can hear Little Jeanne speak but can barely make out what she's saying.

Filomena thinks she hears Little Jeanne whisper, "Don't worry! I've got it covered," but when she steps closer, trying to hear more clearly, Little Jeanne seems to sense her presence and whips around. Her face is a mask of surprise and anger, but it quickly smooths into a laugh.

"You scared me!" Little Jeanne says forcefully. "Sneaking up on me, are you?"

"I was just refilling the peony fizz," Filomena says. The same feeling of suspicion from earlier is washing over her once more.

Little Jeanne smiles. "Oh, that's what I was doing, too!"

"But you don't have a jug."

"There are more jugs here in the kitchen. I was just getting a breath of fresh air when you walked in. The dining room can get stuffy with so many people." Little Jeanne continues to smile so sweetly, it's giving Filomena a toothache.

"All right, well, I'll leave you to it!" Little Jeanne says, sauntering out of the kitchen and leaving Filomena with an empty jug and a pounding heart.

When Filomena comes back to the dining room with a full jug of peony fizz, a dreaded slow song starts. Oh, the horror! Filomena panics. Why is there slow dancing in Never After? That terror should be exclusively mortal. Gretel and Alistair are slow dancing together, chatting and smiling like the friends they are. At least some people are enjoying this.

"Jack, care to dance?"

What?! Filomena's head whips around. Well, since she hasn't, it seems someone else is asking Jack to dance.

It's none other than Little Jeanne. She looks so pretty in her light pink gown and with her hair in a myriad of plaits down her back. Filomena flushes. Jack won't say yes, she's sure of it. He can't.

"Oh, um." Jack looks around the room. He makes eye contact with Filomena. She quickly looks away, but she hears him say, "Sure, why not." He leads Little Jeanne to the dance floor, bows, and takes her into his arms.

Filomena wants to kick something. *Jack is just being polite, isn't he? He doesn't actually like Little Jeanne . . . Or does he?*

With her arms around Jack's neck, Little Jeanne grins right at Filomena before laying her head on Jack's shoulder.

This can't be happening. Is this really happening? Why does this feel like an attack? This is worse than being almost eaten by ogres.

Filomena feels a sudden need to exit stage left. She feigns a massive yawn. "I'm beat!" she says to Gretel and Alistair, who are now both sitting at a table on the edge of the dance floor. "I think I'll head to bed."

Filomena runs upstairs to the bedroom that Princess Jeanne showed her earlier, which she's sharing with Gretel. Alistair's and Jack's shared room is right across the hall. In a huff she changes out of her gown and into pajamas Princess Jeanne lent her, then crawls into bed.

That was so weird, that moment with Little Jeanne in the kitchen. And then right afterward Filomena walked in on something, though she's not sure what. Little Jeanne dancing with Jack . . . Could it be a coincidence? It almost seemed like Little Jeanne was trying to say, *Don't mess with me.* But if that's true . . . Oh no. She must suspect that Filomena *cares* if she dances with Jack. Which means she could see that Filomena *likes* Jack. Filomena just admitted this to herself today! Is it that obvious? Does everybody know? Does *Jack* know?

Even worse: Does Jack like Little Jeanne? *Like like* her? Like *that*? But they just met!

Filomena stares at the ceiling. She feels a pang of pain in her heart. Then she laughs. If only she had told herself a few months ago that one day soon she'd be wearing pajamas embroidered with a princess's monogram in a fairy-tale castle and fretting about Jack Stalker dancing with another girl. She'd never have believed it. The absurdity of it all gives her a bit of solace. But thinking about Little Jeanne's head on Jack's shoulder still makes her heart feel a touch sore.

Just as Filomena's getting way too deep into a pity party, Gretel, looking luminous, bursts through the door, cheeks flushed.

"Isn't dancing divine?" Gretel gushes, shutting the door behind her and falling, sprawled out, on the bed. "I just love dancing. We don't do it enough!"

"I think I've done it enough for one day," Filomena says glumly.

Gretel's so caught up in her own happiness, she doesn't notice Filomena's tone. "Oh, but it's so fun!" she says.

Filomena lightens, feeling glad that at least Gretel had a good night.

"Are you all right?" Gretel asks, propping up on one elbow to look Filomena in the eye.

"Why wouldn't I be?" Filomena says, trying to be nonchalant.

"I saw Jack dancing with Little Jeanne, too, you know."

"So?" Filomena says. She's unable to make eye contact with Gretel.

"Come on, girl. Isn't there just a little something there between you? A little spark?" she teases, tickling Filomena's stomach lightly. Filomena laughs. Gretel continues, "You know he's always coming to you for advice, always asking your opinion on everything."

"I think he just respects my ideas," Filomena replies with a straight face.

"Well sure, so do I, but I don't get this special *look* in my eye whenever I talk to you," Gretel goes on. "You know, like you hold all the secrets to the world."

Gretel noticed a *look*? From Jack?

Though she's finding it hard to admit the truth, Filomena can't help but smile a huge grin at the thought of the *look* Gretel's talking about. She's never had a friend quite like Gretel.

"And come on—the way *you* look at *him*, too," teases Gretel. She fakes a swoon. "I mean, it's Jack Stalker, the Giant

Slayer! Winter Knight, Crown Prince of Vineland . . . What's not to like?"

Filomena plucks at a loose thread on her pillowcase. "I don't know. I mean, I guess when I read the Never After books, I kind of had a crush on him. But now it's so complicated. I mean, he's not just a fictional character to me anymore. He's my friend!"

"Oh, but that's the best!" Gretel says, throwing her hands in the air and falling backward on the bed again. "He's not just some imaginary boyfriend; he's real!" She gets serious for a second. "I mean, I know that we're saving the worlds and everything, but we're still allowed some fun. And if you have feelings for him, you should tell him."

"Should I, though? Doesn't that just ruin friendships?" asks Filomena.

"Or it makes them better," Gretel says wisely.

"I guess."

"Hey, you know what I just realized?" Gretel starts jumping up onto her feet so she's standing on the bed. "This is totally like a sleepover! We're having a sleepover right now!"

She starts jumping on the bed, and Filomena gets up and joins her.

"I've never actually been to a sleepover before," Filomena shares.

Gretel pauses jumping. "*What?!* How is that possible? Sleepovers are the best!"

"I've just never really had friends to do that with,"

Filomena says quietly. "I was bullied pretty hard at school by a bunch of literal trolls. It was sort of impossible to make friends."

Suddenly Filomena is wrapped in a tight hug.

"I hate trolls. Those Alfredos were rotten," Gretel says. "I'm so glad we met, Filomena. I'm so glad to be your friend."

Filomena feels light tears come to her eyes alongside a swell of love for Gretel.

"Plus"—Gretel pulls away with a huge grin on her face— "who else will be able to say their first sleepover was in a literal castle?"

All of a sudden, the door to their bedroom flies open. They whip around to see who it is.

Jack stands in the doorframe.

"Um, ever heard of knocking, Stalker?" Gretel says.

"I'm sorry." Jack blushes at the sight of them wrapped in a hug and standing on the bed. "I forgot my manners. But I have a good excuse. Because, uh, well . . ." He's clearly flustered.

"Spit it out!" Gretel says.

"The village is being attacked."

"How typical," Gretel huffs, and gets off the bed.

Though she'd never been to one until now so can't say for sure, Filomena has a pretty good idea that most middle school sleepovers aren't interrupted by a village attack.

CHAPTER SEVEN

SLUMBER PARTY CRASHER

F ilomena jumps off the bed. Though she knows Jack just said the village is under attack, all she can think is: *Did he overhear our conversation? He wouldn't have stood listening outside the door, would he?* Lily Licks, she hopes not.

"What's going on? Who is attacking the village, and where?" Gretel asks.

"We just got word that the Merry Greenwood Tavern is being ransacked by Robin Hood and his gang," Jack answers.

"All right, all right, give us a second to get out of these clothes." Gretel motions for Jack to leave.

"No time! Alistair, Riff, Little Jeanne, and Princess Jeanne left to help as soon as we heard. I came to get you, and we have to leave now!"

"Come on, Jack, we can't go fight in pajamas and a gown!" Gretel insists.

"Gretel, we don't have time!"

Sighing heavily, Gretel and Filomena follow Jack into the hallway. At the top of the stairs, Jack puts his arm out, motioning for them to stay back. The castle doors are creaking open.

Revealed in the entryway is none other than Robin Hood, who walks in chuckling.

Jack and Filomena look at each other and realize what's happening. Robin Hood thinks everyone in the castle went to the tavern to help. He knew if there was a crisis, they'd all run to assist.

Below, Robin starts grabbing gold coins and silver trinkets by the handful, shoving them into a sack. Silver candelabras, crystal goblets, jewel-encrusted vases—all are tossed into his bag.

Gretel, Jack, and Filomena watch in horror and silently try to figure out what to do. Jack motions with his arms, communicating that they need to run down and attack. He makes a face of surprise, indicating they need to take Robin . . . well, *by surprise* if they hope to overpower him. With her hands, Filomena tries to relay that they have no weapons! Gretel taps them each on the shoulder and points to four suits of armor that line the hallway like knights watching over the castle. Each suit has a sword.

They creep over to the suits and carefully, soundlessly, draw swords. But then Gretel knocks over one of the suits, sending a huge CRASH through the castle.

"Fiddlesticks!" she whispers.

"Who goes there?" Robin shouts from below, suddenly on guard.

It's now or never. Jack nods, and they all charge down the stairs with their weapons drawn. They surround Robin, their swords pointed at him. Filomena realizes that, in all the hubbub around Robin Hood, it's easy to forget he's just a teenage boy dressed all in black with slick dark hair and a sly smile.

Robin Hood laughs. "We have to stop meeting like this!" he says. "And are those truly necessary? I'm surrounded, aren't I? I give up; you win. Story over," he taunts.

Not one of the three laugh or smile. They all stand their ground, weapons at the ready.

"You know," Robin goes on, "I never realized how much I love the sight of a girl with a sword until now, seeing you two wield them." He bows his head to Filomena and Gretel. "I'd be lying if I said the same to you, though, Jack," he adds.

"What are you doing here, Hood?" Jack spits. Filomena can tell Jack's angry. Robin irritates him in a way she's never seen before.

Robin just grins. "I was hoping all you brave young heroes would race out to stop the village being ransacked. Isn't that the kind of thing you do? Save poor, helpless townsfolk?" He puts his hands in his pockets and pulls his shoulders back. It's as if he feels incredibly casual. As if three swords aren't pointed directly at him. "I guess you don't care as much as I thought since you're still here, lollygagging in your fancy pajamas," he sneers.

"We were just on our way!" Filomena shouts.

"Unfortunately, you seem to have ruined my little plan," Robin says, "but it was worth it, if only just to see you love-lies again." He winks at the girls.

"Ugh! Shut your face!" Gretel yells. "Targeting the White Rabbit's tavern just so you can steal from Princess Jeanne? Don't you already have enough?"

"I'll have you know, Gretel," Robin says, "that it's been years since I received an invitation to this castle! Don't you think that's a little rude? I mean, I do live in this kingdom. I'm a prominent figure, even. Princess Jeanne and I go way back! We used to be best friends. Bet you didn't know that. And yet, for years now, not one invite." Robin looks around the castle for a moment. "You know, it's not as nice as I remember."

"Oh right, because *your* castle is soooo great," Gretel says.

"Maybe you haven't been invited because you try to steal everything you see," Filomena says, motioning to his bag.

"Hmm. I suppose we're in a bit of a chicken-and-egg situation," Robin responds. "Did I start stealing because I stopped being invited, or was I not invited because of my sticky fingers? Something to ponder. Now if you'll excuse me, I think I've had my fill. I'll just be on my way." He starts toward the door.

"Oh no you don't," Jack says, placing his sword between Robin Hood and the exit.

In answer, Robin draws a blade of his own. But it's not just any sword; Robin is holding Jack's own Dragon's Tooth sword. It glints in the light of the candles. Filomena curses silently. If only Robin didn't have their Dragon's Tooth swords. When she still had one, she didn't fully appreciate its power. But now, with one being used against them, she certainly realizes its magnitude.

"Come on, Jack. Do you really want to die over a few silly gold fixtures?" Robin sneers. "I'm just taking a few trinkets. Princess Jeanne has so many. Think about it: the great, fantastic hero of Never After, Jack the Giant Stalker, dying over a few bobbles. That would be so embarrassing, don't you think?"

But instead of reacting, Jack is calm. He's not letting Robin Hood's taunts get to him this time.

"Come on, Stalker, show me what you've got," goads Robin.

"Gladly." With that, Jack lunges, but Robin's Dragon's Tooth sword cuts Jack's regular one in two, and the blade shatters to pieces.

Robin cackles with glee. "Oh, this is rich! I'm never giving this up! Did you like that, Stalker? Or should I say *Loser*? Oh yes. You heard me. Jack the Giant's Supper! Jack the Giant Loser of the Last Battle!" He laughs as he points the Dragon's Tooth sword directly at Jack's heart.

"NO!" screams Filomena.

"Leave him alone!" yells Gretel.

"Letting the girls save you, huh?" sneers Robin when Jack remains silent. "What? You've got nothing to say? Cat got your loser tongue?"

Jack shakes his head. "We might have lost the Last Battle, but we fought bravely. Unlike some . . . ," he says pointedly.

Robin wavers, turning slightly pale. "What are you talking about?"

"Oh, I remember you, Robin Hood. And not only from Cinderella's ball. There you were just one ogre sympathizer among many. Why would I take notice? It took me a while, but now I remember how I know you. Now I remember the battalion you served in. And I remember what you are: A deserter. A disgrace. A coward."

"Coward, am I?" Robin seethes. He steps forward, slashing madly.

Jack dodges and swerves, but the Dragon's Tooth sword is too sharp and Robin too fast; he lands a blow that slices open Jack's leg almost to the bone. This sends Jack crashing onto the knee of his other leg.

"JACK!" Filomena screams, and she and Gretel rush forward to defend him.

"I'm all right," Jack grunts, holding his hands up. "Stay

back!" He doesn't want his friends to get hurt; that would wound him more than the cut on his leg. He looks to Robin, cold with rage. "Don't hurt them," he warns, "or else."

Robin's chin lifts, his face arrogant. He positions his sword so the blade grazes Jack's throat. "Oh yeah? If you haven't noticed, I have the upper hand. So what are you going to do about it now, *loser*?"

Jack clenches his jaw and shuts his eyes, grimacing from the pain. Then he says one word. "This." And before Robin Hood can dodge or swerve, Jack's vines flash out of his wrists and grab the Dragon's Tooth sword at his throat. In seconds he's wrestled it cleanly out of Robin Hood's grasp and back into his own.

"Hey! That's not fair!" objects Robin, but he's slippery like an eel and manages to dance away before Jack's vines can return to trap him. Disarmed, he does what Robin Hood does best.

He flees.

"Give Princess Jeanne my best!" Robin yells as he runs out the doors.

Jack only shakes his head as he presses a hand to his bleeding leg. "Moron."

CHAPTER EIGHT

AN UNEXPECTED VISIT

Despite the softest of pillows and the warmest of beds, no one sleeps well at Northphalia Castle that night. The cut on Jack's leg is deep, and though the royal physicians do their best to make him comfortable, he still tosses and turns from the wound. Alistair whimpers for his missing pots in his sleep. Gretel worries over the state of her skin without her nighttime routine. Filomena keeps being awoken by nothing in particular, rather a general sense of unease. It certainly isn't the restful night that they all desperately need. And their new friends fare just as poorly. Riff has nightmares of being locked in the tower again, and Princess Jeanne refuses to accept that her old friend is working not just with her uncle but also with the ogres.

In the morning, they gather around the breakfast table in low spirits. Filomena can't help but feel like, after all that happened yesterday, they're back to square one. Still robbed, still searching for Robin Hood, still needing to retrieve Princess Jeanne's crown or else lose another kingdom to the reign of the ogres.

Little Jeanne walks into the breakfast room and takes stock of the low morale. She laughs. "Did someone die?"

Filomena doesn't find this funny.

"Tough crowd," Little Jeanne says, sitting down.

"How are you feeling?" Filomena asks Jack. She's worried about his leg. He arrived for breakfast with a pair of crutches. When Robin Hood slashed Jack's leg, Filomena's heart had stopped; she'd felt the pain, too, almost as if it had happened to her.

"I'm okay," Jack says with a strained smile.

"What did the doctors say?" asks Gretel.

"To not move for three months at least," he mumbles. "But obviously I can't do that."

"Oh no you don't," says Filomena. "You have to stay put."

"Yeah, you gotta let that heal, man," agrees Alistair. "You can't risk it. It's your health!"

Jack's mood darkens. "We'll see."

"You rest. We'll keep looking for the crown," Filomena says. "Right, guys?"

Riff and Princess Jeanne are subdued as well. Alistair reported that, while no one was injured during the ransacking of the Merry Greenwood Tavern, it hurt to see the cozy little pub damaged and terrorized. When they arrived to help, they'd found the tavern a complete ruin—windows smashed, tables and chairs overturned, patrons hiding in fear, and the White Rabbit shaking uncontrollably. Robin's goons robbed them of their coin and jewels and took every last penny from the till. It would take months to right the place.

Little Jeanne reaches for the last snozzleberry muffin without asking if anyone wants it. (*No manners, especially for a princess!* thinks Filomena. Filomena's own mother would die of embarrassment if Filomena did the same.) The young princess looks around at all the glum faces. "Maybe you should all stop for a while," she suggests.

"Stop?" Filomena furrows her brow.

"Yes, stop. You've been working so hard! Have you looked in a mirror lately? You guys have aged years since Robin Hood robbed you."

"Is it that bad? I mean, I know I don't have my moisturizer, but I didn't think anyone had noticed!" Gretel starts looking around for the nearest mirror with panic on her face.

"Uh, no offense," Little Jeanne adds.

"None taken," says Filomena coolly. "So I look fifteen? Big deal."

Gretel laughs at this. "Yeah, maybe now I can get into R-rated movies."

"You know what I mean," Little Jeanne continues. "Look what's happened to Jack! He needs to rest. How's he going to save Never After if he can't even run?"

"I can run," Jack mumbles. "Just not fast."

"Jack has to rest for sure," agrees Filomena. "But the rest of us can't. We'll keep looking."

"The crown isn't going anywhere," Little Jeanne says. "I mean, Uncle Richard won't be so stupid as to try putting it on while my sister is alive. And I don't think he's truly capable of murder."

"What's his plan, then?" asks Filomena, wondering—not for the first time—about Little Jeanne's angle. At dinner the previous night, the younger princess defended Robin Hood; today she's an apologist for King Richard.

"Probably just to have Jeanne agree to sign an abdication, relinquishing her rights to the crown and her kingdom," says Little Jeanne.

"I would never!" says Princess Jeanne hotly.

Little Jeanne shrugs. "You might have to."

"Never! This is my kingdom."

"But Uncle Richard has an army and almost all the land. You have one village that's loyal to you. That's it," says Little Jeanne.

"But once the crown is on my head, I *am* Northphalia's rightful ruler," Princess Jeanne argues. "It's the law!"

"Anyway," continues Little Jeanne, "like I was saying, it doesn't seem like the worst thing in the world to take a breather."

Alistair considers and turns to Filomena. "It's not good to get so tired that you can't properly defend yourself in battle."

"Plus you can stay here as long as you'd like," Little Jeanne says. "Right, sis?"

Princess Jeanne takes a sip of her espresso, her earlier agitation replaced by the airs of a consummate host. "Of course. I love company!"

Filomena can't believe this. Little Jeanne just wants them to give up! To have her sister abdicate the throne and the four of them take a break! Of course, Jack must rest. That's clear. Filomena's not going to let him put weight on that leg.

But as for the rest of them? Chill out? Just hang around the castle? That seems ludicrous. They have a kingdom to save from ogres!

Why doesn't Little Jeanne care about Princess Jeanne's kingdom? Isn't it her kingdom, too?

"You don't get it, Little Jeanne," Filomena says. "We have a mission to fulfill. We have a prophecy to keep in mind, and there's a lot to get done!" She looks to Jack for support. "Right, Jack?"

He sighs and winces from the pain in his leg. "I don't know. I'm feeling so foggy right now. I was going to argue, but maybe she has a point."

Filomena can't help feeling a little hurt. "So we just sit around here all day? Eating gumdrops and Hula-Hooping?"

"That actually sounds really nice," Alistair inserts.

"Gretel?" asks Filomena.

Gretel throws her hands up. "I'll do what everyone else wants to do."

"Well, I, for one, am tired." Alistair sighs. "We've been going nonstop ever since we first ran into Filomena." (All the way back in book one!)

"But . . . what about our quest?" Filomena asks, quietly now.

Jack limps over to the nearest chaise to elevate his leg. It's hard to see him so weak. "It will still be waiting for us when we're ready. Little Jeanne is right; the crown isn't going anywhere for a while. Richard won't make a move until he needs to. Trust me, I've been doing this a lot longer than you have."

Ouch. Filomena knows she's the newbie, but she kind of thought that Jack felt like they were on the same page. That they were a team. Aren't they? Now she doesn't feel so sure.

"Exactly," Little Jeanne says. "Relax, rest, and have a little fun. I mean, it's so nice having you here. It will be revitalizing, don't you think?"

Gretel and Alistair nod sheepishly, staring at their breakfasts to avoid eye contact with Filomena. Princess Jeanne and Riff don't say anything, but they look defeated as well. No one argues with Little Jeanne.

Filomena wishes she could talk privately with Jack,

Alistair, and Gretel. She feels like she's lost the rhythm and the tight alliance of her favorite foursome. She puts her head in her hands, resigned.

Just then, the front doors to the castle fly open. Everyone jumps up suddenly. Robin Hood? The henchmen? Ogres? Who goes there?!

No, none of those things. Something much, much better.

"Beatrice!" Gretel cries, running over to hug her cousin. "What are you doing here?" She pulls back to look at Beatrice. "Shouldn't you be on your honeymoon?"

Behind Beatrice, Byron, once beastly and now returned to his handsome princely form, steps into the room as well.

Filomena feels her heart lighten. Beatrice and Byron know exactly what's at stake! Maybe they can convince everyone that resting at this palace is silly.

"If it isn't the prince and princess of Wonderland!" Princess Jeanne singsongs. "Please, make yourselves at home. I won't hold it against you that I wasn't invited to your spectacular wedding."

But Beatrice and Byron don't appear able to join in on the joking—they look terribly morose.

"We were on our honeymoon, yes," Beatrice says in answer to Gretel's question. "But once we returned, we got a message." Turning to Filomena, she says, "We've been looking for you everywhere."

"For me? What kind of message?"

"Well, we're not sure exactly how it got through the

portal, but it looks like your father has figured out how to send messages from the mortal world."

Filomena's heart catches in her throat. "My dad? Is he okay? How did he do that?"

"We don't know really, but it seems he somehow knew that Wonderland was the last place you'd been. He must have sent the message before you left, but we didn't see it until we got back," replies Byron.

"What did it say? What's going on?" Filomena asks, raising her voice to a louder pitch than normal.

"Filomena, I'm so sorry," Beatrice says.

"Just tell me what's happening!" Why is her dad sending her messages in Never After? It can only mean something terrible has happened.

Beatrice sighs. She looks at Byron and then back at Filomena. Her pretty face is drawn and anxious. "I'm very sorry to tell you this, but your mother has fallen ill. It sounds quite serious, apparently."

Filomena grips the back of her chair to remain standing. She feels sick. Her mom is ill? "How serious?" She can feel tears start to form.

"I don't know, but I do think you should go back to the mortal world for now."

"Fil . . . ," Jack begins, starting to get up to go to her. "I'm so sorry."

"No . . . no, it's okay . . . ," she tells him. "You shouldn't move." She hides her face in her hands. She doesn't want to cry in front of everyone.

Gretel rushes over and envelops her in a hug. Alistair is there, too, holding her tightly. Her friends are with her.

She can't restrain herself any longer. She cries in their embrace. "Not my mom!" she wails.

Her mom. Her amazing mom.

She takes a deep breath, wipes her tears, and pulls away from her friends. Whatever they decide to do now, she knows only what she must do.

"I'm going home," she announces.

CHAPTER NINE

Home Sweet Home?

"Are you coming back?"

It's Jack.

After packing her possessions, Filomena said goodbye to everyone in the castle, including Jack. But he has followed her to the castle doors, even on his crutches.

She's still hurt that he took Little Jeanne's side at breakfast. It made her feel a bit of a fool. Maybe they weren't as tight as she assumed. She looks up at him and pushes her curls out of her face. "I don't know."

He nods. He understands.

"I hope so," she says.

In answer, Jack removes the Seeing Eye he wears around his neck, which is hard to do while balancing on crutches. Gruffly he hands it to Filomena. "Take it. When you need to use it, it will show you what you need to see."

Filomena looks down at the tiny object in her hands. It's one of Jack's most prized possessions. She wants to object, to tell him she's not worthy. But she doesn't. She puts it around her neck.

"Suits you," he says.

"Jack," she whispers, and takes his hand in hers. She has no words. She doesn't know what to say to him. His gift says more than she can.

He squeezes her hand, then releases her. "Go."

She squares her shoulders and walks out the door to a carriage that is waiting to take her to the nearest portal.

But when she turns around, Jack is still at the door, watching.

He raises a hand.

She does the same.

Then she climbs into the carriage, where Beatrice and Byron are already seated. She has a lump in her throat as she fingers the Seeing Eye around her neck.

Beatrice and Byron try to distract her with tales from their honeymoon, but all Filomena can feel is dread. She dreads the fact that she's leaving Never After while it's in crisis and Jack is hurt, and she dreads what she'll find when she crosses over into the mortal world. The portal spits her out onto the Hollywood Hills. One kingdom to another.

Filomena takes a breath and recalibrates. It always feels a bit hazy to switch between worlds. Looking out over Los Angeles, she thinks of all the starlets, film directors, and flashy celebrities roaming around the city right now. Not so different from Never After, perhaps. Both places where the imaginary becomes real, where legends and myths spread like wildfire, where there are good guys and bad guys.

"Mum? Mum! I'm home!" Filomena yells after bursting into her house. The cab ride felt like it took a thousand years. She's had butterflies of anxiety fluttering around her stomach ever since Beatrice and Byron told her what was going on. (Maybe more like chippermunks than butterflies. They feel heavier, more chaotic.)

No one is in the kitchen. There are no takeout boxes on the counters. She hears no jazz music (her mother's favorite) waltzing through the house. There's no mess at all, and mess is a telltale sign that her mom's near. It's all too orderly. The house would look like this only if Filomena's neat-and-tidy dad were in charge. Filomena rushes upstairs.

"Hello?" she cries.

She knocks on her parents' bedroom door.

"Come in," a weary voice says.

Filomena enters to see her mom lying in bed. Her dad is holding her mom's hand and sitting beside her. When he turns around, his face splits with a wide-open grin.

"You got my message! Thank goodness!"

He gets up and gives Filomena a huge hug, wrapping her tightly in his arms. She feels relief for the first time in days. Protected. Safe. She pulls back.

"Mum, are you okay?"

Filomena's mom smiles weakly, motioning for Filomena to give her a hug. "Hi, sweetie. I've been better." She laughs lightly.

"Mum, I can't believe this. What's going on? Beatrice and Byron told me that Dad sent a message saying you're sick?"

Bettina Jefferson looks at Carter Cho and smiles. "I told you not to bother her, Carter," she says.

"I knew she would want to know."

"How on earth did you get a message to her?" Bettina asks. She looks at Filomena. "I'm still understanding how all this Never After stuff works."

"I'm pretty good at solving mysteries, you know," Carter says.

Filomena laughs. Her dad *is* a mystery writer after all.

"I went to the portal we sent you off from, at the Hollywood sign. It turns out that if you don't want to actually go through the portal, you'll hear from an operator. I asked to get in touch with you, and the operator said the last place you were spotted was Wonderland's castle. So I sent a message."

"That's why Beatrice and Byron got it. That makes sense."

"'Wonderland's castle'?" Bettina asks. "As in *Alice in Wonderland*?"

Filomena wants to tell them all about her adventures, but she has only one thing on her mind right now. "What happened? Why are you sick?"

Her mother leans back on the pillows. She looks so pale to Filomena. So out of energy. Bettina is usually so vivacious, joking about her deadlines, dancing around the kitchen, poring over takeout menus. Now it looks like she hasn't eaten in days. She looks so frail, it's scary.

"It happened very suddenly, sweetie. One day I was feeling like my normal self, and the next day I just collapsed. We went to the doctor, but they aren't sure what's wrong yet."

Filomena feels her dad pet her arm. "They think it might be cancer," he says.

"Cancer?" Filomena buries her face into her mom's side. "No, no, no. This can't be happening, Mum." She starts to cry.

"My lovely girl, it's okay. Don't cry. We'll get through this. We can get through it together. I'm so lucky to have my support system here with me." Bettina smiles at them.

"I'll do anything to make you better, Mum. I'll make you soup. I'll learn how to make soup. I'll find a cure. I'll become a doctor. I'll do anything!"

Filomena's mom pats her head.

Suddenly Never After feels a thousand miles away. Nothing seems remotely as pressing as her mom's health. Maybe none of it will be important in the end—not getting Princess Jeanne's crown back, not helping Zera, nor defeating the ogres. This is Filomena's home, and these are her parents.

Her puppy, Adelina Jefferson-Cho, jumps up on the bed with them, and Filomena snuggles into her soft fur. Filomena has fought ogres, she's brandished swords, she's run for her life, she's rescued a prince from a curse. She's capable of meeting challenges that seem totally impossible, facing obstacles most people would never believe.

She can save her mom.

Chapter Ten
Filomena's Promise

I f there's one thing more shocking than the facts that Never After is a real place and Filomena is an actual princess, it's that Filomena's parents are making her go back to school now that she's home. She begged and pleaded, explaining that school feels so pointless with Mum sick, but they refused.

"If you're going off on all these quests and adventures in Never After, you have to go to school and learn. That's the deal," her mom had said before bed the previous night.

So despite everything—despite fighting Robin Hood and

wearing gowns and hopping portals—here she is, back at the same old middle school.

Though, she must admit, school is significantly less dreadful now that the Fettucine Alfredos, her once bullies, are history. So far, no one's made fun of her outfit (a combo of her purple combat boots and a purple dress), kids are actually saying hi to her in the hallways, and her books have yet to be knocked out of her hands. All in all, it's not too bad, being back.

It's almost the end of the day, and it's actually been a pretty good one. Filomena answered some questions in class, she scored a basket during gym class (has her hand-eye coordination improved?), and a group of girls even told her they dig her purple look—a style tip Filomena carried over from Princess Jeanne's castle.

Maggie Martin approaches her in the hallway before final period. "Hey, Filomena," she says.

Filomena has her guard up. The last time she and her ex–best friend spoke, Maggie had made fun of Filomena for still caring about the Never After series. What a laugh. Little did Maggie know, her so-called friends the Pasta Posse were *literally from* Never After.

"Hi, Maggie, how's it going?"

"I'm good. You seem so different today. What's going on with you?"

Filomena immediately feels self-conscious. "Different? How?"

"Like, just a different air about you. You nailed that book analysis in English class. That was sweet. Cool outfit by the way."

Filomena smiles and shrugs. "Thanks."

"Look, Filomena, I want to apologize. Those kids I was becoming friends with, they're total jerks. And I'm sorry I went along with it and didn't say anything. I was a coward. Now that they're gone, I realize how awful they were. Also, pretty weird that they all transferred schools at the same time, huh?"

"Yeah, definitely weird," Filomena says, trying not to laugh.

Even though Maggie is realizing her bad behavior only now that she isn't a part of the popular group anymore, Filomena still appreciates the apology. After all, Filomena understands what it's like to be under a spell, and in middle school, popularity is a pretty potent spell.

"So I was thinking . . . maybe we can hang out again?" Maggie asks shyly.

Filomena smiles. "I'd really like that, Maggie."

"You have algebra now, right? Want to walk together?"

Filomena and Maggie chat about how Maggie's joining the volleyball team, the upcoming school dance, and other things Filomena hasn't thought about in what feels like months. They get to Algebra One Honors and sit next to each other. Fighting with friends really is the worst. Filomena wonders if she'll ever be on good terms with her friends in both Never After *and* the mortal world. She and Maggie are just now starting to make up, and it reminds Filomena of how she left things with Gretel, Alistair, and Jack.

Those three were the first to ever help Filomena feel like a capable, cool girl. Around them she feels funny, brave, clever, like she can do anything, because . . . well, when she's with them, she sort of can! She can fight ogres and rescue queens and princes and cast spells and prevent the Prophecy coming true . . .

Oh fairies. She almost forgot about the Prophecy—the Prophecy that says if fairies' gifts fall into ogres' hands, it will mean the end of Never After as they know it. *The End of the Story*. It feels impossible to focus on algebra class now that it's come to mind. How can she pay attention when the fate of an entire world depends on her?

But maybe it doesn't depend on her . . . After all, Jack is taking Little Jeanne's advice now. Maybe they don't even need her anymore and she can just stay in North Pasadena and learn algebra forever. Major sigh.

Gretel always makes being biportal look so easy, but Filomena's having a hard time getting her head adjusted between worlds.

After school, Filomena walks home but finds her house empty. Empty? That's unusual. Her parents aren't really the kind to venture out and . . . Wait a minute. Now that Filomena's mom is sick, that *especially* doesn't make sense.

The home phone starts buzzing. Caller ID says it's her dad. She picks up.

"Hi, honey," Carter says. "Are you home okay?"

"Yeah, Dad, but where are you guys?"

"Your mom had a little, uh . . . accident, Filomena."

"What do you mean?"

"She was getting a glass of water while I was in my office working on my book, and she . . . well, honey, she collapsed. So I brought her to the hospital. I didn't want to trouble you on your first day back at school. The doctors are saying she's going to have to stay at the hospital for a while. Don't worry, though; everything is okay. I'll come pick you up in a few minutes, and we'll drive to the hospital together."

Filomena is speechless. This is so much worse than losing a battle. What was she thinking, sitting in algebra class, worrying about stupid prophecies and ogres and feeling jealous of Little Jeanne when, meanwhile, her mom was being hospitalized? Filomena feels so confused. She's pulled between two crises. What can she do?

She vows not to go back to Never After until her mom is cured.

Chapter Eleven
A Proposal of Sorts

Jack, Gretel, and Alistair are worried about Filomena and concerned about her mother. But Filomena is in the mortal world while they are in Never After. For now there's nothing to do but wait for Jack's leg to heal.

So after just a few nights at the Northphalian castle, a little bit of rest has transformed into a life of leisure. Little Jeanne has introduced them to her favorite activities. Mornings are spent practicing croquet skills, reciting poetry over French press coffee (or, in Alistair's case, hot cocoa), and oil painting. Every day there's teatime complete with crumpets, jams, spreads, and candies. In the evenings they play board games; their current favorite is Mansions and Mortals. Gretel is making everyone new outfits, and Alistair's really putting his marzipan where his mouth is—he's been cooking most of their meals. The castle chef is loving it (hello, paid vacation!).

But Jack is restless, so Riff keeps him updated on Robin Hood's whereabouts. The thief and his goons haven't been seen since the tavern ransacking, but they're sure to pop up again somewhere. Riff has resumed the search for the crown, too. He's looking all over the North to find it but with no luck.

In the meantime, as Little Jeanne predicted, an emissary from King Richard's court sends a short missive from her and Princess Jeanne's uncle.

> *Abdicate the throne,*
> *forget the crown,*
> *and keep your head.*

Princess Jeanne crumples the message in her sprite-manicured fingers. "Never!" she promises. "I'm not giving up my kingdom!"

"You show them," cheers Gretel.

"More fondue?" asks Alistair. He offers a tray holding a warming dish filled with bubbling melted cheese and a selection of fruits, chocolates, and baked goods.

"Oh, yes please," Gretel says eagerly, and chooses a crispy breadstick.

Princess Jeanne retires to her room for the evening. Having four heroes on her side hasn't quite worked out as she had hoped. Of course, she can't blame Jack for being injured, nor Filomena for having to return to her mom. Gretel and Alistair are plucky and energetic but, left to their own devices, entertain themselves rather than take the lead. Riff is searching, but it all seems futile. And now her uncle is offering her a way out. A way to keep her head on her shoulders.

She'd like to keep her head on her shoulders if she can.

Princess Jeanne has just sat by the windowsill so she can take in the lights of the village when she notices a familiar figure climbing the trellis below the window.

"Hey, Jeannie," Robin Hood says, his voice muffled through the glass. "Open up, will you?"

Princess Jeanne hesitates, but the scene warms her heart. Robin Hood used to come to her window like this all the time when they were kids. It's been a long while since they were last in this familiar position. She opens the window a crack, just wide enough to hear him but not for him to come in.

"Surprised to see me?" he says, sitting on the window ledge on the other side of the glass.

"What are you doing here, Robin? Haven't you stolen enough of my trinkets?"

"I'm not here for that, Jeannie."

"It's *Princess Jeanne*," she says.

"Oh, of course"—Robin bows his head mockingly—"Your Royal Highness."

Princess Jeanne rolls her eyes.

"Have you been enjoying my pranks?" Robin asks with a smile.

"Your *pranks*? Is that what you call terrorizing my kingdom?"

"I thought you'd find them funny." He shrugs.

"You thought I'd find locking up my best friend, frightening the villagers, breaking into my castle, and stealing my crown *funny*?"

"Come on, that guy's not your best friend. *I'm* your best friend."

"It's been a long time since that was true," Jeanne says softly.

"Well, I had to get your attention somehow. You have a darker sense of humor than you pretend, Jeanne."

They're both quiet for a moment. Why is he here? It's been so long since they last spoke face-to-face. She has to ask him. "Is it true, Robin? Are you really working with the ogres? Not just my uncle?"

Robin Hood squirms and doesn't answer.

"Why? I know we stopped being friends a long time ago, but I thought you still cared about me. How could you?" Jeanne can't stop her voice from reaching a fevered pitch of emotion. It hadn't hit her until now, how much Robin's betrayal hurts.

"Do you remember *why* we stopped being friends?" Robin says quietly. "It's because you thought I wasn't good enough to hang around with anymore once we grew up and stopped being kids. I'm just a scrappy boy from nowhere— not a prince, certainly—so what good could I do a princess?"

"That's not true!" she shouts. "You started acting out, Robin. Stealing, tricking people. You stopped being the Robin I knew."

But suddenly Jeanne feels sick to her stomach. Maybe part of what he's saying is true. A princess and a pauper . . . Could they have really stayed friends? It seemed impossible at the time, but now the idea didn't seem so strange.

"Do you remember what we said when we were kids?" he asks.

Princess Jeanne looks him in the eyes now. She'd forgotten how blue they are.

"We always said we'd run away together. Well, I have a plan. We can run away, still."

Her heart starts beating quickly. "Robin, I can't run away with you. I'm going to be queen."

"But you don't have your crown."

"Because you took it!"

"Did I, though?" asks Robin.

"If you didn't take it, who did?"

Robin shrugs. "Does it matter?"

"Yes, it does."

"But without it, you don't have to be queen anymore! You can be with me!"

That beating heart now drops into her stomach. She could leave it all behind, run away with Robin Hood. Is he serious? She can never tell. He doesn't act like this around anyone else. Serious. Earnest. Is he tricking her? Is this real? But she wants to be queen. (Doesn't she?) She does. If she's not queen, then King Richard will take over the North. And he'll ruin it; the ogres will ruin it. Running away with Robin Hood would be an act of complete selfishness. The ogres would be one step closer to taking all of Never After, and no matter how scared she might be, she can't let them do that. Not without a fight.

"Robin, I wish I could, but I can't." It's so hard to deny Robin. All their childhood promises are still alive in his heart.

Jeanne may be a princess, but she's no longer a child.

Robin Hood leans over, his eyes flashing. "It's that lunkhead, isn't it? That Sharif of Nottingham? Are you going to marry him? Is that it?"

"I don't know, Robin, but I know I'm not running away with you."

"The ogres will win, you know. You don't stand a chance. At least if you run away with me, we'll be free and happy somewhere."

"How can I be free and happy if my people are living in

fear and darkness?" She wants to make him understand, but she knows he never will.

"Fine then. Stay. I hope you get what you deserve," he bites.

"I can't, Robin. I just can't. You have to go."

He stares at her one final time. "Goodbye, Jeannie."

"Bye, Robin," she whispers.

Robin turns away, then motions over his shoulder. "And, um, good luck."

Jeanne watches him shimmy down the trellis and disappear, but even though her heart is heavy, something catches her eye.

Something large and terrifying and beating war drums.

An army marches north.

King Richard's army.

She gasps. If she won't abdicate, Richard will take the crown another way: by removing her head and placing the crown on his own.

It's too late.

Chapter Twelve

Mother Knows Best

After Filomena hangs up from her phone call with her dad, she slinks to the floor. *Mum is in the hospital?* This all makes no sense. Her mom is one of the healthiest people Filomena's ever met. And sure, maybe some of that is because Bettina's really intense about hand sanitizer and doesn't leave the house much, but she always makes jokes about her "strong English constitution." Filomena can't even remember her mom having the flu, let alone needing to go to the hospital.

She decides to put together a care package. It's exactly

the kind of thing that Gretel would suggest. Filomena feels a pang of missing Gretel but tries to push it away. How is it that, no matter which world she's in, she's missing someone? Being biportal definitely isn't as easy as it seems.

There are limited supplies in the house, and Filomena doesn't have a car, nor a driver's license come to think of it, nor a way to get to a shop and back in time to meet her dad. So she makes due with what's around: a packet of cookies in the pantry, some of her mother's favorite English breakfast tea, and a couple of Filomena's stuffed animals for some extra-plush support.

As she packs up her care package, she can't help but think of her friends. She never feels alone when she's with Jack, Alistair, and Gretel. But she feels so alone now.

For a moment Filomena lets herself wonder how they're doing, what they're doing, if they're safe and whole. She hopes Jack's leg is healing well. She fingers the Seeing Eye around her neck.

It will show you what you need to see, Jack told her.

She puts the Seeing Eye up to her face, looks through—and gasps.

An army! A huge, commanding, terrifying army is headed north.

King Richard is about to invade Northphalia and take the kingdom by force! She has to warn them! She has to help them!

But she can't! Her place is here. She has to stay and take care of her mom. She must be here for her mom.

Filomena's dad pulls up outside then, and she gets into the car with him. He smiles at her care package and pats her on the head. He looks in good spirits, despite it all.

At the hospital, Filomena throws herself onto her mom's bed.

"Mum, I've been thinking about you all day! I could barely focus at school, just thinking about how much I love you and how I hope you're okay. And what's going on now? Why are you in the hospital?"

Bettina pets Filomena's hair. "Sweet girl. It's okay. I just had a bit of an incident and wanted to check in with my doctors."

"Are you okay? What did your doctors say?"

Her mom sighs. "The good news is that I don't have cancer."

"That's amazing! That's incredible!" Filomena's heart swells. But Bettina doesn't share in her joy. "Why don't you seem happy about that?"

"The not-so-good news is that they don't know what's going on. They can't find anything they understand about this illness. It's like nothing they've seen before."

"But how can that be possible? We need to go to a better hospital! We need to get better doctors!"

From his place standing in the doorframe, Carter speaks: "Filomena, we've got great doctors. It's not that, honey."

Filomena feels tears welling in her eyes. She feels so helpless.

"I brought you something, Mum," she says. She lifts the care package onto her mom's bed, emptying out the cookies and tea and stuffed animals and all the other comforts of home.

Bettina looks at her with so much love that now *her* eyes start to tear up. "Filomena, you are the most caring daughter a mother could ever hope for. Thank you for bringing me these . . . but I've been thinking about something."

"What, Mum?"

"You're worried about your friends, aren't you?" her mother asks.

Filomena thinks of what she saw in the Seeing Eye.

"I don't understand everything that goes on in that place, but I know it's dangerous. And that they need you," Bettina tells her. "They do, don't they?"

Filomena nods.

"So here's the thing. We are so proud of you and all the brave things you've accomplished. There's nothing you can do for me here, sweetie. Your dad will take care of me, and I'll take care of myself. You need to go help your friends. You'll just be worried sick if you stay here."

At this, Filomena starts to cry. She knows her mother's right—there's nothing Filomena can do for her—but feeling unable to help her mom makes Filomena feel like everything is out of control. On the surface it seems ludicrous to leave her mother when she's suffering. But she *is* less useful here, and she can be useful somewhere else. She can help prevent Never After's suffering, even. But she can't prevent her mother's, not even if she stays.

"I bet that by the time you come back, we'll have things more figured out. Right?" Bettina says, looking to Carter.

To Filomena, he says, "Your mother's right. Of course we want you here; we always want you here. We know you and we know you're thinking about everything going on in Never After. You should be there to help your friends."

Filomena realizes that if her parents—the most protective, cautious parents in the worlds—are urging her to do this, to take this risk, then it's worth listening.

Her mother looks at her, wiping tears from her eyes.

"Never After needs you, Filomena."

CHAPTER THIRTEEN
FILOMENA RETURNS

When Filomena returns to Northphalia, she finds the gorgeous Northern castle has been turned into a battle fortress. Riff is rallying troops, ordering men to their stations, and preparing to evacuate women and children.

"You're back!" cries Gretel, giving Filomena a hug. "And not one second too late!"

"What's the plan?" she asks.

Jack walks up, his stride purposeful. His leg has almost completely healed. "How's your mom?"

"She's okay," Filomena tells him. "What are we going to do?"

"Riff is going to hold the castle," Jack tells her.

"I'll never surrender," says Princess Jeanne. "If Richard wants the crown, he'll have to take my head."

Little Jeanne is uncharacteristically silent.

Filomena hopes they know what they're getting into. That army looks terrifying. But she turns her attention back to Jack, who has more to tell her.

"Robin Hood was here a few nights ago, and Alistair, Gretel, and I followed him into Sherwood Forest."

"We got our stuff back!" crows Alistair, and hands Filomena her pack.

"My books!" She smiles at the sight of them all. She looks at her friends with tears in her eyes. "Thank you!"

"And we got our Dragon's Tooth swords and everything," adds Gretel, whose face is not as shiny as before. She must have retrieved her skincare, too.

"How?" asks Filomena, awed.

"Robin's not the only one who can be stealthy," says Gretel, nodding toward Jack. "Helps if you have vines to snatch things away with, too."

"We got another message from Snow Country," says Jack grimly. "Zera was captured. There's no time to waste."

★ ★ ★

As they're saying goodbye to Princess Jeanne, Little Jeanne, and Riff, Beatrice and Byron walk into the room.

"Wait, have you guys been here this whole time?" Alistair asks, confused.

"No, Alistair." Beatrice smiles, a bit sadly. "We went to Wonderland. But when we got there, something very grave had happened."

"More bad news?" Gretel says. She's looking a bit frightened.

Beatrice takes a deep breath. "Prince Charlie has been turned into a frog."

Everyone gasps.

"Poor Hori!" Gretel shrieks. "How awful!"

At this point, Filomena doesn't know whether to laugh or cry. A frog? Like in the fairy tale? Wait . . . Of course. If Beatrice is from *Beauty and the Beast*, then this must be Hori's turn to live out a fairy tale . . . The Princess and the Frog. It looks like Filomena will have to include this in the thirteenth Never After installment as well.

She flips through the Never After books just in case she sees something that might come in handy. She turns to the page written with the Prophecy. She almost doesn't read it—it's just too scary—but then she notices two *new* final lines have appeared. How did that happen? And when?

Thirteen fairies to this world were born.
Thirteen fairies of ogres' scorn.

Thirteen blessings the fairies gave;
All the gifts that ogres crave.
To keep fairies' gifts out of ogres' hands,
Only the League of Seven can save the lands . . .

Rose Red and Snow White

Magic mirror on the wall,

Can our heroes answer the fairies' call?

One fairy pleads for help; the other is lost.

Who is ready to pay the cost?

A daughter appears with hair red as rose;

She creates her own mirror and makes her own clothes.

In the land of snow, things are not as they seem,

And what happens when you underestimate a queen?

Magic mirror on the wall,
the stakes have risen; will they ever fall?
Magic mirror, does danger abound?
And can the League of Seven be found?

PART TWO

Wherein . . .

Our group of four searches for the
League of Seven.

Everyone tries out true love's kiss.

And fairies and mirrors abound.

CHAPTER FOURTEEN

ARE WE THERE YET?

"Seven, seven, seven," Alistair ponders. "Who do I know that runs in a group of seven?"

The gang is on the road again. Filomena and her friends bade farewell to the Northphalian castle and are back on the road to Snow Country. Filomena, Gretel, Alistair, and Jack, now with new additions Beatrice and Byron. They're walking from Northphalia to Snow Country as the air grows colder and colder.

Filomena's quite glad to have Beatrice and Byron joining them. Nothing bonds two girls like spending the night in fear of being eaten by a beast, so count her and Beatrice bonded for life. And as a real added bonus, the beast in question turned out to be the utmost gentleman. Having her friends Beatrice and Byron with them is bolstering Filomena's spirit, even if she's still feeling pretty discouraged by what they're up against.

"What does everyone think of their outfits?" Gretel says in high spirits.

Even without her special scissors, Gretel spent a lot of downtime in the castle creating full weatherproof wardrobes for Filomena, Jack, Alistair, and herself.

"They're amazing, Gretel," Filomena says. "I love my fur collar."

"And I love my earmuffs!" Alistair chirps, touching the cream-colored puffs that reside over his ears.

Beatrice smiles. "Jack, that leather looks nice on you." Filomena has to agree. Gretel made Jack a shearling-lined leather jacket that really fits the whole rugged hero look.

"I guess you weren't really being so lazy in the castle after all, huh, Gretel?" Filomena teases.

"Oh please, making these outfits was like therapy, I've missed sewing so much. Princess Jeanne set me up with a whole design space. I could have made an entire winter collection if I'd really pushed myself. But I figured it's better to have one outfit each. It's not like we have a valet to carry our bags to Snow Country!"

Everyone laughs at this, and even Jack joins in. It's a relief to laugh despite knowing they're leaving friends to an uncertain fate. But Riff promised to keep Princess Jeanne and the kingdom safe, and they have to trust that he can stay true to his word. For now, they're back in their comfort zone: on their way to the next adventure together.

"You know, Princess Jeanne may have seemed spoiled at first, but she really grows on you, don't you think?" Gretel says. "She gave me a ton of materials for all our outfits, and it was pretty nice of her to let us stay at the castle for so long. And she's so brave not to abdicate her throne!"

"She provided basically every ingredient I asked for! Even ones that had to be imported from outside Northphalia!" Alistair adds.

"You've gotten quite great at cooking, Ali, haven't you?" Jack says.

"Yeah, turns out I like food so much that I actually enjoy making it! I also realized that if you make your own food, you can have *anything* you want. Anything you can think of!" Alistair starts drooling a bit, dreaming up his next concoction.

"Unfortunately our mission seems to dictate that you likely won't have access to a castle-sized kitchen for the next while," Filomena points out.

"Not to gossip, but I'm kind of glad we're away from Little Jeanne," Gretel whispers to Filomena. "Something about that girl was starting to rub me the wrong way."

Filomena nods silently. She's ready to not think about

Little Jeanne anymore and especially to not think about Little Jeanne with her head on Jack's shoulder . . . dancing . . . Ugh! But she has to agree with Gretel that Princess Jeanne really grows on a person. Filomena will miss her.

"Princess Jeanne is kind of surprisingly a homebody, don't you think?" Alistair inserts.

"She'll make a good queen if that's the case," Byron says. "Hopefully she'll get the chance."

"Just another addition to our list. Help Zera, find Princess Jeanne's crown, figure out what this League of Seven thing is all about, turn Charlie back into a prince, and somehow prevent the ogres from taking over Never After. Easy little to-do list," says Filomena with a wry smile.

"Speaking of the League of Seven," Alistair says, "I'm seriously trying to rack my brain here. Who do we know that hangs out in a group of seven?"

Before they left Northphalia's castle, Filomena filled in everyone on the updated Prophecy. They all agreed that they needed to find this mysterious League of Seven if they were to stop the ogres from taking over Never After. So now their Snow Country mission isn't only about finding and helping Zera; it's also about finding this League of Seven so they can save Never After. They've been brainstorming but still have come up with nothing.

"What do you think the League of Seven is like?" Gretel wonders.

"I bet they're fierce warriors," Filomena says.

"Yeah, they know all the good fighting moves," Alistair adds.

"I bet they have really cool outfits," Gretel says.

"It's weird that we've never heard of them before now," Jack says. "You'd think if a group of fierce warriors was wandering Never After, we'd know."

"Are you sure the books don't say anything else about them, Filomena?" Byron asks.

"Nope. Just the one says that to keep fairies' gifts from ogres' hands, 'only the League of Seven can save the lands.'"

They all ponder this.

"Seven, seven . . . ," Alistair repeats, muttering.

"I love that prophecies are always in rhyme," Byron says. "It's quite sophisticated."

"You like poetry, Byron?" Alistair asks.

"Oh yes, I love it. I like the Romantic poets especially. Keats, Wordsworth, all those gentlemen."

"Romantic poetry? Like 'roses are red, violets are blue,' that kind of thing?" Alistair asks.

Byron laughs. "Sure, that kind of thing."

Suddenly Beatrice stops in her tracks and they all pile up behind her. "Rose Red!" Beatrice exclaims.

Alistair looks at her. "Yeah, Beatrice, that's the first line. 'Roses are red.'" He says this slowly, like she hasn't understood.

"No, no, you just reminded me of my cousin, Rose Red! She lives in Snow Country."

"I don't think I've ever met our cousin Rose Red," Gretel says.

"Jeez, Gretel," Alistair jokes, "how many cousins do you have?"

Filomena frowns, thinking. *Rose Red . . .* That rings a bell. She tries to remember what she learned about Rose Red in the Never After books. They all start walking again.

"Rose Red is friends with the famous dwarves of Snow Country," Beatrice explains. "And if I'm not mistaken, there are seven of them."

"Seven!" Jack exclaims. "Do you think they could be . . . ?"

"It's worth a shot, I say," Beatrice replies. "Plus you'll all like Rose Red. She's cool."

Snow Country, Rose Red . . . Something clicks in Filomena's head. "Beatrice, is Rose Red the sister of Snow White?"

"Oh, no. Rose Red is Snow White's daughter!" Beatrice says.

"Wait a minute," Jack says, "I just remembered: Isn't Colette's nickname . . . Snow White? It is, isn't it?"

Snow Country. Snow White. Rose Red. For some reason, Filomena can picture only blood on snow. But she tries to shake the vision away.

CHAPTER FIFTEEN

HEIGH-HO, HEIGH-HO, TO SNOW COUNTRY WE GO

"Next time, I'm totally adding like two more layers of fleece to our jackets," Gretel says, shivering.

"Is it just me or did it drop like ten degrees in the last ten steps?" Alistair adds.

"Drama queens!" Filomena laughs. "After all we've been through, we can't let our downfall be the cold, can we?"

Though she's trying to keep spirits high, Filomena has to

admit that the cold is getting a bit out of hand. And the sun is starting to set on the snowy landscape.

"We're almost at the border of Snow Country," Jack says. "Once we cross over, I say we find somewhere to rest and call it a night."

"You know what invention would be really great for Never After?" Gretel asks. "A service that, when you're on a quest, you can use to book a room to stay in ahead of time. You know, Fil, like in the mortal world? Nice elves and woodland creatures could rent out their spare rooms for weary travelers like us!"

"And what money would we use to pay for that? Do you have a stack of gold lying around, Gretel? Have you been holding out on us?" Jack laughs.

"They should pay *us!*" Gretel adds. "We're saving their butts from the ogres! If I ever run for prime minister of any kingdom, I'm totally going to use that in my platform. *Free room and board for heroes!*"

Filomena chuckles.

"That would be a popular campaign, but only if the ogres weren't in power. And eventually, hopefully, there won't be a need for heroes anymore," Beatrice says.

Jack looks uncomfortable.

"What is it, Jack?" Filomena asks.

"I always feel weird about the title *hero*. Don't you? It just feels presumptuous."

Byron pipes in: "For what it's worth, from where I'm standing, rescuing me from a curse and returning my mother and me to our real forms are pretty heroic acts. Especially when risking your life to do so." Byron does a formal little bow.

Jack is ready to change the subject. He shivers. "So, Byron and Beatrice, you went to Bali for your honeymoon, right? It's hot there, isn't it? Can you tell us about it? Describe it in very precise detail. Just how warm was it?"

They all laugh, and Beatrice and Byron gladly tell them about Bali.

An hour or so later, everyone is deep in daydreams of hot sandy beaches and luscious fruit drinks. They can almost forget the frigid temperatures they're walking through. But the ground is gradually becoming more and more packed with snow. The sun is half-set now, just a blazing semicircle on the horizon. Before them, as far as the eye can see, are rolling hills covered with glistening white blankets of snow. Pine trees the size of buildings stretch upward, grand and evergreen.

"It's so beautiful," Filomena whispers.

Jack smiles at her. "Welcome to Snow Country."

They soon spy a snowy pathway that snakes between the rows of pines. They begin to follow it, but sharp icicles suddenly stick out over the path from either side, blocking the way.

"What the . . . ?" Alistair starts.

A voice echoes loudly through the trees. "WHO GOES THERE?" it booms. "AND WHAT INTENTIONS HAVE YOU IN ENTERING SNOW COUNTRY?"

The group all looks at one another. *What now?*

Jack steps forward, a hand resting lightly on the hilt of his Dragon's Tooth sword. "We come to Snow Country in peace. We've been summoned by allies." Jack is unsure if he should mention exactly *which* allies. After all, he has no idea who this voice belongs to. And, these days, there are many sides in Never After.

Several voices start whispering to one another through the trees. They exchange expressions of confusion. Everyone is on guard, hands on sword hilts, ready to fight if necessary. Filomena catches a few phrases, like *Dragon's Tooth sword* and *cool earmuffs* and *princess*. Then the voices all hush.

Jack looks to Filomena and they exchange a silent agreement: They're ready for combat. Suddenly from either side of the pathway emerge several huge figures, each wearing a pointed velvet hat. Filomena tenses. Giants!

"ATTACK!" one says.

Before they can regain their bearings, the group of travelers is ambushed. The giants' weapons of choice are icicles, which are surprisingly sharp. Every one of them is suddenly engaged in one-to-one combat and has to stretch high in order to fight properly.

"Wait!" Beatrice cries, midswing against an icicle. "We aren't invaders! We're just looking for my cousin Rose Red!"

As soon as Beatrice utters those words, the giants drop their icicles and start smiling. Jack, however, is caught up in the fight and bodychecks one giant even after they've already withdrawn their weapon.

"Hey! What the heck, man?" the giant yells, though Jack barely bumped their hip.

"Oh, my apologies." Jack reddens, now seeing that everyone else has finished fighting.

Beatrice continues her plea: "You don't happen to know seven dwarves who live with my cousin Rose Red, do you?"

A giant, this one in a yellow hat, chimes in, scratching his head. "Did you just say DWARVES who live with Rose Red? Why, that be us!"

"Dwarves? But you're giants!" Alistair points out.

"Exactly!" says the leader. "We're Dwayne's Army of Really Very Extra-Large Soldiers. Or, you know, DWARVES for short."

"Who's Dwayne?"

"Me," says one. "But they call me Cap."

These huge giants live with Rose Red? Filomena counts: There are seven of them. Can it be? She gives Jack a look, and he shrugs. Then she thinks back to all the other times she's encountered fairy-tale figures. They're almost never what she's been led to believe. So the seven dwarves are actually . . . seven giants?

"You're Rose Red's family?" one of the giants asks.

"Well, just two of us," Beatrice says, motioning to herself and Gretel. "But the rest of these people are our dear friends, and we're all traveling together! We actually came to Snow Country partly to find Rose Red."

The giants look at one another. "Counsel!" one in a red hat shouts. They huddle together and begin whispering feverishly. It's a charming sight, these seven creatures, each eleven feet tall and with a cute velvet hat in a different color, deliberating. Filomena catches the words *hungry* and *fire*. She's not sure if these words are a good sign or not.

The giants unfurl from their cluster and straighten, then size up Filomena and the group. "We aren't sure about you lot," says a giant in a purple hat and with a low, gruff voice. "It's hard to trust travelers these days."

"You look quite cold," Gretel says. "I can make you all some nice warm clothes, if you'd like."

The giants look at one another, considering, seemingly pleased by this offer.

"Nice, Gretel," Jack says. "Who knew your seamstress skills could be a bartering tool?"

Gretel realizes something: "Oh, not that Rose Red isn't already making you warm clothes. I've never met her, but I'm sure she's quite good with needle and thread."

At this, the giants bust out laughing. They laugh so hard, tears stream from their eyes. Gretel looks to the group as if to ask, *What did I say?*

The giant in the yellow hat wipes his eyes. "Oh no, dear, Rose Red couldn't sew a stitch if her life depended on it!"

"Well then," Gretel continues, "we need a place to stay tonight, and we'd really like to see Rose Red. If you take us to her, I'll be glad to make you some proper winter coats."

Several of the giants are looking at the giant in the red hat—*Dwayne, aka Cap*, Filomena thinks—and nodding encouragingly.

"Come on, Cap," one says shyly. "You know we're freezin' out here on our patrol shifts."

Cap seems to consider this. "All right. But we need to be absolutely certain of which side you're on. If you know what I mean."

Filomena gets an idea. It seems risky, but she can see actual ice crystals starting to form on Alistair's eyelashes. They need to get inside pronto. And if they're going to trust these giants enough to sleep at their house, then they have to be trustworthy enough and show their alliances.

It's decided, then. Filomena takes a moment to flash a light on her forehead and mutter the words her aunt taught her, and then steps forward to let the mark of Carabosse shine from her forehead. The moon and the stars that surround it glow brightly and and cast a warm light onto the giants. They look at her in awe.

"Carabosse," the yellow-hatted giant says softly.

"All right, all right, that's enough." Cap waves at her. "Turn that thing off. We get it—you're with the fairies. Good, good. Well, on to home, then! Our shift's over, it's almost nightfall, and you're our final travelers for the day. Let's get you lot cozied up by the fire."

The kids almost faint at hearing that last sentence. Filomena laughs to herself, thinking how fire is one of those funny, remarkable things. It's terrifying when launched by an ogre but sounds absolutely divine when offered by a gentle giant or, you know, a member of Dwayne's Army of Really Very Extra-Large Soldiers.

CHAPTER SIXTEEN

INTRODUCING ROSE RED!

"You know, guys," Alistair says, "I've come to a conclusion: I think I'm done with being ambushed. I think I'll take a break from it."

Filomena and Jack laugh as they walk next to Alistair. The seven giants are leading the way in front, with Beatrice, Byron, and Gretel behind.

"Unfortunately, Ali, I don't think we have much of a choice," Gretel pipes up.

"That was actually one of the more pleasant ambushes I've experienced," Jack says.

Filomena still isn't quite sure what the deal is with these giants. She's put together that they're the famous seven "dwarves" she heard about, but of course in translation: The mortal fairy tales forgot to explain that DWARVES is an acronym. The red-hatted giant is Cap, who appears to be the pseudo leader. The yellow-hatted giant introduced himself as Joyful, and the giant Jack bodychecked is Crabby. So the other giants are presumably Slumber, Shy, Sniffles, and Silly. As one can imagine, it's quite easy to guess who is who. But these giants are far from miners who sing about work; rather, they are the border patrol of Snow Country. They keep the kingdom safe from ogres.

"Miners? Why would they mine coal? We don't even use coal in Never After! So bad for the environment," Jack says when Filomena asks.

She busts out laughing. "You guys care about the environment in Never After?"

He smiles. "Of course! Mother Nature is the greatest power of all!"

She's impressed. Jack the Giant Environmentalist. Who knew?

"Is this another one of your mortal world mix-ups?" Jack asks her.

"It must be. In the mortal world, the story goes like this: Snow White is super beautiful, and the Evil Queen is jealous. The Evil Queen's Magic Mirror tells her that Snow White is the fairest in the land, so the queen sends the Huntsman to kill her off. But the Huntsman feels bad for Snow White, so he lets her escape into the forest, where she eventually finds and befriends seven dwarves—in our stories they're actual dwarves—and basically does their laundry and cooks for them."

Jack's eyes have widened in disbelief. "Are you serious? So in your world, Snow White is so pretty, she gets punished, and then she's just happy to do chores all day? That's messed up."

Filomena considers this. "I guess I never really thought about it like that. But you're right, that is messed up."

"Classic mortal world," Jack says, rolling his eyes.

"Hey, it's not the mortal world's fault that ogres have been feeding us the wrong stories!" she says. She does like the mortal world after all, even with its many faults.

"True, but you guys believe them!"

"Okay, okay, let's call a truce," Filomena says, bumping Jack's shoulder. "Tell me the real story. The Never After version."

Jack sighs. "Once again, I think we're sort of living it. But from what I know, Colette fled to Snow Country some years ago, after the Last Battle. She's the fiercest warrior of the thirteen fairies. She has hair dark as night and skin white as snow, so that's why she was nicknamed Snow White. But Snow White is also what she called her sword, since it was made from starlight."

Filomena nods, following along so far. Jack continues, "I'm not sure exactly how she ended up befriending the giants, but I'm guessing it's some variation on the story you told. She must have married some sort of prince and had Rose Red. But we had no idea she was in Snow Country until Zera sent the message saying she found her and needs help. Maybe Rose Red will know more." They fall silent for a bit as they continue walking.

Filomena is amazed by the beauty of Snow Country in twilight. The hills stretch far in all directions and are covered in snow. As they walk the path, she sees little cottages here and there through patches of trees, each one more adorable than the last. In the distance she can see a village warmly lit with glowing windows. Farther still is a castle. She'll never tire of the thrill of seeing a real castle in the distance.

Jack remembers Filomena's excitement at the idea of seeing snow. "Is it as magical as you hoped?" he asks her.

"It's everything I dreamed snow would be! Although I could use that fire soon."

Just then, the giants stop at a large stone cottage to the right of the path. "We're here, everyone!" Joyful calls out.

"Finally," moans Slumber.

They all file through the gate and toward the cottage. It appears to be a bungalow but is also incredibly tall. *Well, it does have to fit seven giants,* Filomena realizes. It has a thatched straw roof. It looks so charming. Filomena can almost smell a toasty fire and cookies baking in an oven. She smiles at Alistair and Gretel. After a long day of walking, it feels excellent to finally arrive at a warm place to rest.

But when they walk into the cottage, it's not cookies that Filomena smells. The cottage has an immensely high ceiling and is certainly warm and cozy, but the smell is distinctly chemical. Burnt chemicals, even.

"Good lord," Byron whispers to Beatrice, plugging his nose. "What on earth is that stench?"

Sniffles, predictably, sneezes.

"Rose Red, we're home!" Crabby yells.

"Just a second! I'm in the middle of something!" a voice answers from above.

Aren't we in a one-story cottage? Filomena looks up. A loft is built over the kitchen. Smoke is pouring from the loft platform.

"Rosie, are you experimenting again? I swear to fairies, if the roof catches fire again . . . I'm not cleaning it up!" Cap yells up to her.

"Don't worry, I have everything under control!" the voice—Rose Red—says. This is followed by a short scream. "All good!" she says after.

Joyful takes on the role of host. "Sit, sit!" He motions Filomena and company toward enormous plush couches by the fireplace. "Warm yourselves! We'll get supper ready."

"I know it's cold," Silly says to Cap, "but I'm opening a window. That smell is going to knock us all out."

"Experimenting again, always experimenting," Cap mutters as he walks to the kitchen.

Taking off their Gretel-made outerwear, the gang sits on the couches at their new resting spot. Since the furniture is giant-sized, there's more than enough room for all of them and probably for everyone they've ever met, too.

Alistair wiggles his toes in front of the fire. "Now this I could get used to," he says, leaning back with his hands behind his head.

Beatrice and Byron are cuddled up on the fur rug in front of the fireplace. Filomena loves them, except *ugh* they're so cutesy. She supposes that one day that kind of thing might appeal to her, cuddling or whatever . . . For now she looks away. She loves Beatrice and Byron, but get a room much?

She puts up her feet and stretches. Goodness, she is hungry. When did they last eat? She can't remember.

Just as her stomach is about to let out a rumble, Rose Red comes climbing down the ladder that leads to the loft. Rose Red is indeed a redhead with heavy smatterings of freckles on her face, chest, and arms. She looks the same age as Filomena, maybe one year older. She has on supercool glasses: big lenses with thin frames that appear to change color.

"Hi. Who are you guys?" she asks bluntly.

Beatrice stands up. "Hey, Rose Red. I know we haven't met before, but I'm Beatrice, and this is Gretel," she says, pointing to Gretel, who pushes Filomena's feet off her lap and waves. "We're your cousins."

Rose Red's face brightens. "No way! That's majorly rad. I think my mom mentioned something about cousins once, but I never thought to visit you guys. Thanks for coming over! I think I have a DNA test somewhere in the attic office; we can take it if you want to find out for sure."

Beatrice laughs, and Gretel smiles.

"I'm pretty positive we're blood relatives," Beatrice says, "but maybe another time."

"What were you doing up there?" Alistair chimes in from the couch.

"Oh yeah, sorry about the smell. I've been working for weeks, trying to figure out how to create a talking mirror. Or a magic mirror? Not sure what the official term is these days."

Jack perks up, interested. "You're trying to make one? I didn't even know they could be made."

"Well, I don't have proof that they can be just yet, but I'm working on it," Rose Red replies.

Filomena's playing catch-up here. "Are there a lot of talking mirrors in Never After?" she asks the group.

"Only thirteen," Jack answers. "Long ago, each fairy animated one as a gift to the kingdoms. They were a great way to communicate across Never After. They had very temperamental personalities, but if the mirror liked you, you could use it as a sort of portal to talk to someone standing in front of another mirror."

"Like FaceTime!" Filomena says.

"Face time?" Rose Red asks.

"Yeah, it's this thing in the mortal world. You can video chat with someone on your cell phone."

Rose Red shrugs. "I have no idea what any of those words mean."

Filomena feels shy then. She figures she can explain Face-Time later. Sensing this, Jack picks up where he left off.

"And they're not only used to communicate to other people; you can talk to the mirrors themselves. They're quite fun to chat with. They're blunt, but if you want someone to tell it to you straight, a mirror is the one to do it. They know a lot, too, of course. They have some sort of mirror world capability to know the truth of our world. And that's another thing: They can speak only truth. But the ogres have taken control of most of them. Actually, come to think of it, I might be wrong, but I heard the last non-ogre-possessed talking mirror is here . . ."

"In this room?!" Alistair jumps up, excited.

"No, in Snow Country." Jack turns to Rose Red. "Isn't that right?"

"Queen Christina has it," she answers. Filomena can't tell whether this is a good thing or not. "So anyway, like you say, Jack, since talking mirrors tell only truth, I figured I'd try to infuse my prototype with some truth serum I acquired. That's what the smell is." She waves her hands through the air.

Alistair sniffs. "Ah, the smell of truth."

From the kitchen, the giants bellow their readiness.

"Dinner's about to be served!" Joyful shouts.

"Yeah, so get your butts to the table," Crabby says.

"You guys hungry?" Rose Red asks.

The table is packed with people. Well, people and giants. On one side sit the seven giants in massive chairs, and on the other side sit five of the humans—Filomena, Jack, Gretel, Alistair, and Byron—on a bench far too long for them. At each end of the table are Beatrice and Rose Red. Everyone passes around plates and bowls of fabulously warm curries.

"So . . . not that I'm not glad my long-lost cousins have come for a visit," Rose Red starts, "but since you seem to have brought an entourage with you, I presume there's another reason you're here."

"You presume correctly, Rose Red," Jack starts. "I'm Jack, by the way—Jack the Giant Stalker. These are Alistair Bartholomew Barnaby and Filomena Jefferson-Cho of North Pasadena."

"Before you ask," Filomena chimes in, "yes, I'm a mortal, but I'm also the daughter of Rosanna, who I never met, and a niece of Carabosse; I have the mark of the thirteenth fairy; Jack and I are fairy gifts; Gretel's biportal; Byron used to be a beast, but we broke his curse; and Beatrice is the not-so-wicked stepsister of Cinderella and is now married to Byron, so they're the prince and princess of Wonderland." She gasps for air after saying all that in one breath.

"You're getting really good at that, Fil," Alistair says.

"You're the daughter of Rosanna?" Rose Red asks. "Doesn't that make us cousins as well?"

"Licking lilies, are all girls in Never After cousins?" Alistair shouts, throwing his hands up.

"I guess so!" Filomena smiles. "Cousins on a different side of the family than Beatrice and Gretel, I suppose."

"Not to break up the family reunion," Jack says, "but you're right, Rose Red: There is another reason why we're here."

"Please, call me Rosie. Rose Red is *so* medieval. My mom's into classic names."

"Rosie. Got it. You see, the fairy Zera is an old friend of mine, and when we were in Wonderland, she called us and requested our help, asking that we come to Snow Country. We got slightly delayed by a week or so, but we're here now. Beatrice thinks you might be able to help us find Zera."

Rosie nods. "That's what I thought. I saw Zera not too long ago. She came to visit me when she got to Snow Country and couldn't find my mom. I have no idea where my mom is, either. I haven't seen her in years, so I wasn't much help," she says softly.

"We got a message from Zera, she said she found Colette, we thought you would know where they are," says Jack. "Zera was asking for help. It sounded desperate."

Rosie looks troubled. "Aunt Zera found my mom? But I haven't heard anything."

"You don't know where they are?" asks Filomena.

Rosie shakes her head. "Not a clue. But before Zera left to look for her, she did tell me something important." Rosie took a deep breath before speaking again. "She said she wanted to be honest with me, to be realistic about the stakes she and I are up against. She said it might possibly be the last time I'd see her—you never know what might happen these days in Never After—and she needed me to pass on a message. I think she probably wanted me to give it to you."

Everyone is silent at the table, all eating paused. Filomena holds her breath.

"So she told me the ogres want total control of Never After. And they aren't far from getting it. I'm sure you know that the ogres can't take over completely as long as the fairies are alive." Everyone nods. "Well, the fairies worried that if they were all hunted down, it would leave Never After too vulnerable. So Zera told me they put in a safeguard."

"A safeguard?" Alistair repeats.

"Yes, so even if they are all killed—fairies forbid—there will still be hope for Never After. The safeguard is a collective spell they cemented. It's very powerful. Zera said that as long as the three major kingdoms of Westphalia, Eastphalia, and Northphalia have rightful rulers, then Never After can stand. Even without the fairies."

Another silence falls over the table. It's good news, sort

of, but of the heaviest kind. Filomena once again feels the weight of the worlds descend onto their shoulders.

"But how do the rightful rulers get on the thrones?" Gretel asks.

Filomena puts the puzzle pieces together. "Rosie," she says, "do you know about the Prophecy? Well, it just got updated. I'm not sure how, but I think it has to do with Carabosse's magic. She's so powerful, she can prophesize even after death, I suppose. And the Prophecy now says that to keep Never After and the fairies' gifts out of the ogres' hands, *only the League of Seven can save the lands.*"

"That's another reason why we're here, actually," says Gretel. "We think *you* might be the League of Seven."

"Me?" Rosie asks. "Me alone?"

"No, not you, actually. *Them,*" Gretel says, and motions to the giants.

The giants all freeze midbite, looking up from their curry. Then they start laughing hysterically, as does Rosie. Filomena is confused. But she's glad for the change of mood.

"You thought—" Rosie starts, gasping for air between fits of laughter. "You thought—HA! You thought these giants might be the heroes to save Never After from the ogres?"

Cap guffaws. "Us! Heroes!"

"Can you imagine?" Joyful chuckles.

"I don't think it's such a crazy idea!" Filomena backs Gretel up. "You're huge! And you're the border patrol, after all. You do wonders with those icicles."

"Speaking of which, I've been meaning to tell you guys," Rosie says, looking at the giants, "you really shouldn't use weapons that melt. One gust of an Ogre's Wrath and you're weaponless!"

Cap nods and then speaks directly to Filomena: "We may be large, but we're gentle. We don't attack unless it's to defend. It's part of our nature. I'm sorry to say we aren't the seven you're looking for."

"All right, so if you're not the League of Seven," Jack says, "then who is?"

The table ceases laughing and ponders this for a moment.

"I can't say I have the faintest idea," Rosie says, "but I'll be more than glad to join you and help you find out."

CHAPTER SEVENTEEN

HORTENSE'S MARRIAGE BLUES

Miles and miles away from the quaint cottages of Snow Country, Hortense sits in her palace bedroom. She and Charlie have returned from their honeymoon and are back in Eastphalia, but things have not gone exactly as she expected.

Having grown up at Rosewood Manor in Eastphalia, Hortense is glad she didn't have to move far once she married Prince Charlie. However, his castle is a far cry from her beautiful country estate with its horses and gardens and two-story house.

The castle really is a palace, and all the grandeur of princessdom comes with it. She imagines that people who know her probably think she's living a fairy tale now. But in reality she's trapped in a nightmare.

It was horrible, how it all happened. First of all: Though she loves adventure, it wasn't like her and Charlie's honeymoon to the Deep was exactly relaxing. They had to pass all the dragons' tests in order to get the Dragon's Tooth swords, and the dragons weren't exactly pleased by their visit.

Hortense giggles to herself, remembering how the dragons reacted when she and Charlie showed up.

"Is this Jack the Giant Stalker's doing?" they'd growled. "Is he going around bragging about passing our tests? This is not a tourist attraction! This is SCARY! This is DEADLY!"

(After hearing this, Hortense made sure she and Charlie didn't mention they were on their honeymoon. She figured the dragons would not be thrilled at the idea of the Deep becoming a honeymoon destination.)

But after proving themselves worthy—and that they were very scared and taking this very seriously—she and Prince Charlie passed the tests (thank fairies) and received their Dragon's Tooth swords as rewards. They also had to promise not to tell anyone to do the same.

So needless to say, the honeymoon wasn't exactly relaxing. On the journey back, Hortense had looked forward to spending a few days sleeping, wandering around the castle, maybe hunting a little with her bow and arrows, riding her horse, and generally getting her bearings before really entering her responsibilities as princess of Eastphalia.

Well, that dream was certainly cut short.

They'd barely returned home when an old woman knocked on the grand castle doors. Hortense had been automatically suspicious. How did this woman get past the guards at the gate without questioning? The guards would have at least notified them of a visitor had they seen her. Second of all, Hortense had remembered that Gretel and Filomena were always going on about how, in the mortal versions of Never After stories, little old women are often villains in disguise. (This seems really unfair to little old women, who are generally very nice.) But still, it gave Hortense pause, even if she was being prejudiced.

She'd told all this to Charlie, but he's such a sweet and trusting boy that he'd called nonsense, and when the little old lady asked to see him, he went gladly. Hortense was all like, *Fine! Don't listen to me!* and stayed in their bedroom. Was it their first marital spat? She'd been mulling this over when she realized Charlie had been gone for a very long time. She'd gone downstairs to see what was going on, whether Charlie had been hoodwinked into a pyramid scheme and was ready to start selling sunflower suns around Never After.

But he was nowhere to be found. Nowhere at all.

Hortense had called out for Charlie and walked the

whole of the castle grounds. Finally she went to sit by the pond she and Charlie often liked to visit with books in the afternoons.

A croaking had sounded loudly from the pond, and a particularly cute frog jumped right into her lap. "Hortense?" it had croaked.

A talking frog! Surely it wasn't the strangest thing she'd seen in Never After, but it surprised her nonetheless.

"Hortense, it's me, Charlie!" it had said, looking up at her with its big froggy eyes.

This was not exactly how Hortense had envisioned starting her life as a married woman.

It's been days, and she's tried everything she can think of to transform Charlie from frog prince back to human prince. She'd immediately sent word to Beatrice, of course, who rushed to tell their friends Gretel, Jack, Filomena, and Alistair. If anyone can help them out of this bind, Hortense was sure it's those four.

But she understands there are other pressing matters at hand in Never After, and Beatrice and Byron were gone to find Zera with the four, leaving Hortense alone with her frog prince. She sighs loudly, thinking about it all.

"Are you sighing about me being a frog, Hori?" Charlie says. He's sitting on a pillow on their bed.

"I'm just glad you can still talk," Hortense answers. "But

yes, I am. I'm trying to think of what might break this spell. I mean, certainly it's the ogres' doing, don't you think?"

"Unless a random old woman really has it in for us, then yes, I'd have to guess this has something to do with the ogres."

"Filomena told me that in fairy tales in the mortal world, true love and true love's kiss are often what break spells. Shall we try that?"

"Are you willing to kiss a frog?" Charlie croaks. His tongue flies out of his mouth, stretching to the window, and grabs hold of a small bug, then snaps back. He swallows the insect. "Apologies, love," he ribbits. "It's animal instinct. It appears I can't help it."

"Oof," Hortense says, trying not to be repulsed.

She takes a breath and goes over to Charlie. She picks him up in her hand, looks into his froggy eyes, and tries her best not to be totally freaked out that the love of her life, her dashing Prince Charming, can quite literally fit in the palm of her hand.

She purses her lips and gives him a smooch.

She waits.

She peeks, cracking one eye open just the slightest bit. Nope, still a frog.

"Do you think we have to, um, do more?" she asks.

"I can't imagine it's true love's *French* kiss, can you?" Charlie ribbits in reply.

"I guess we're lucky that Eastphalia doesn't follow its old

French court rules," Hortense teases. "Didn't they eat frog legs?"

Frog prince Charlie sticks out one of his froggy legs. "It does look rather appealing, doesn't it?" he says. "Sautéed with a bit of butter?"

At least he still has a good sense of humor.

Just for kicks, Hortense tries one final kiss. But all she gets is toad slime.

Chapter Eighteen

Pleasantries with the Prime Minister

The next day Hortense tries to go hunting. Though it's usually an activity that brings her much joy, today she finds it lacking luster. Plus, hunting does seem different when your beloved has been turned into an animal. She may be a fearless huntress who shoots rabbits for dinner, but she's certainly not trying to hunt cursed humans!

First Byron is turned into a beast, and now this? What is

with the evil queen Olga and turning boys into animals? That lady needs to lighten up.

Hortense is also having a hard time enjoying hunting because she's terrified that she'll accidentally step on a frog. Charlie has assured her that frogs have very alert senses and that if he were hanging out in the grass and some human was walking around, he'd catch on and jump out of the way before being stepped on. But still she worries.

Hortense comes back to the castle to change, but before she can get to her room, a castle page comes up to her. *Lily Licks,* she curses. She's been trying to avoid members of the court and the castle staff as best she can. She and Charlie agreed that they shouldn't tell anyone about the curse. They need to learn more first, and they don't want to risk word getting out and something going awry. She and Charlie don't know why Charlie's been cursed, and if the citizens of Eastphalia find out their prince is now a frog, who knows what will happen?

The only people who know, of course, are Beatrice, Byron, Jack, Filomena, Alistair, and Gretel. Beatrice told her that Princess Jeanne of Northphalia was also present for the news since they were at her castle. This initially worried Hortense; she's never met Princess Jeanne. But Charlie assured Hortense that, despite Jeanne's spoiled nature, she's actually quite lovely. Charlie and Princess Jeanne knew each other as children and as the royalty of neighboring kingdoms. They often played together in courtyards while their parents went over kingdom-related business. Hortense just hopes Charlie's right to trust Jeanne. Though, if Filomena and Jack trusted Jeanne enough to stay at her castle, then that seems as good an assurance as any.

"Princess Hortense!" the page calls to her. "May I have a word with you?"

"I'm afraid I'm just off to change," Hori replies. She's nervous about what the page might ask her.

"It's very important, Princess. There's a visitor."

A visitor. They haven't had a visitor since the little old lady, if one can even call her a visitor. Hori has brushed off any visitations to the castle until she can get this curse under control.

She walks over to the page, who is standing at attention. "Who is the visitor?" she asks.

The page looks at her nervously. "It's the prime minister, Your Highness," he says, quivering.

Hori sighs deeply. "All right, I'll see what this is about. Where is he?"

"In the receiving room, Your Highness."

"Please, John, how many times have I told you to call me Hortense?" she says, patting John's shoulder.

Hortense walks into the receiving room while taking off her white leather hunting gloves. The prime minister rises from his place on the couch and bows to her.

"Your Highness," he says.

"I thought you're supposed to address only queens as 'Your Highness'?"

"I believe it's appropriate to address a princess by such a title. If I were speaking to your mother-in-law, I would say 'Your Royal Highness.'"

"Hmm." Hori sits on the couch opposite the prime minister. "I suppose I'm not really one for outdated formalities."

"It's a shame your mother-in-law can't join us today," the prime minister says, "but it seems she is otherwise occupied. She set up this meeting for us."

"That was nice of her," Hortense responds.

How Hortense dislikes this man! He's always given her definitely creepy energy, but it seems no one else has picked up on this. Nobody wants to rock the boat, apparently. Hori's gotten into many arguments with Prince Charlie's parents over things the prime minister has done. He's constantly cutting palace support to the poorer regions of Eastphalia, which Hortense thinks is despicable.

He sits across from her now with his thinning, mousy hair and his creepy blue-and-white pinstriped suit, crossing his legs and grinning his greasy grin at her. She scowls back.

John comes in and offers them tea.

"A cup of English breakfast, please," the prime minister asks.

"*Dohwa-cha* for me, John, thank you," Hori says.

"*Dohwa-cha*?" the prime minister asks. "What is that?"

"It's peach blossom tea, sir," John replies.

"Oh, that sounds delightful. I'll have that, too," he says. John bows and leaves the room. "When in Rome," the prime minister says, winking at Hortense.

She gives a sarcastic smile, grimacing inside.

"So this is quite the outfit you have on, isn't it?" he says. "What's the occasion? Going off to war?"

"Do you think princesses just lounge around in gowns all day, Prime Minister?" Hortense says, smiling her best sweet-princess smile.

"Of course I'd never think such a thing of you, Princess Hortense. Tell me, is this your typical daywear, then?"

"I was out hunting, actually. I quite like to shoot a bow and arrows. Been doing it since I was a young girl at Rose-wood Manor," she responds.

"Are you any good?" he asks condescendingly.

She sighs lightly. "Let's just say if an apple were sitting on your head right now, I'd have no trouble shooting it off. Now, let's get down to business, Prime Minister. Why have you come to pay me a visit?"

"Getting into it before our tea has even arrived? Are you in a rush, Hortense?"

"I just don't want to hold you up from what I'm sure is a very busy schedule. Lots of funding to cut and all that! Lots of poor families to turn out onto the street, isn't that right? Or perhaps today's task is more focused on planning the monthly parliamentary party." Hortense knows Charlie would chastise her if he were here. He thinks it's important to maintain a diplomatic relationship with the prime minister, even if they disagree. *We'll have more influence that way,* he's always saying to Hortense. And perhaps he's correct. But Charlie isn't here right now. He's upstairs being a frog.

John reappears with a tea tray. Hori takes her cup, hoping it might calm her. She hasn't even heard what the prime minister has to say yet, and already her blood is boiling. Is being a princess always this unnerving?

"I see we're not interested in playing nice," the prime minister responds, still smiling. "That's fine by me. I'll get into it, then." He picks up his teacup and takes a sip. "Divine! I'll have to get some of this for my next party, as you say." The prime minister gives a short, stilted laugh.

Hortense smiles mockingly.

"The reason I've come to see you," he says, "is because no one has heard from Prince Charlie in a while. I don't know if he's out gallivanting around Never After or what, but at some point he has to take on his responsibilities as a prince, and take them seriously."

"He's not out gallivanting," Hortense says.

"Oh really? I thought he might be off betting on centaur races or something of that nature. That's good to hear. So where is he?"

Hortense pauses, unsure what to say. "He's away on business."

"Not royal business, I presume, or I'd likely know about it. But no matter—he's away all right. The fact still stands that if Prince Charlie is not crowned king of Eastphalia before the summer solstice, then the kingdom will be forfeit to Queen Olga and Cinderella."

Hortense nearly drops her tea. "Excuse me? Why would that be? How could that be? That doesn't make any sense."

"There are a few things about royal business that I'm sure you don't quite understand, Princess Hortense, and I suppose this is one of them. You married *into* royalty, after all. It's expected that you won't understand all the goings-on."

If Hortense were a dragon, fire would be coming out her nostrils and smoke out her ears right about now. "I may not have been born into royalty, but I understand basic logic. Can you tell me, why forfeit the kingdom to two people with absolutely no claim to the throne and nothing to do with Eastphalia?"

"Look, Hortense, I'm not in charge here. I don't make the royal rules, nor do I care to act against ancient clauses and treaties created by the fairies. If it were up to me, there would be no royal families at all. No offense. I just think the monarchy is a bit outdated. However, I have no way of stopping it, and thus I must work with the system at hand."

"Speaking of outdated, isn't it rumored that you rigged your last election?"

"Let's not be cruel, shall we? I understand you're upset, but if you can get your prince back to Eastphalia before the summer solstice, then you have nothing to worry about, all right? I don't see why you're getting so worked up." The prime minister stands to leave. "That's all I came to tell you, Hortense. You and I may not see eye to eye on everything, but I think you can understand what you must do. Best of luck finding Charlie, and I'll see you at the summer solstice."

He begins to walk out, but then turns back around. "*Dohwa-cha*, was it? I simply must get some of that." He has the temerity to whistle as he makes his way out of the office, through the castle, and out the front doors.

Hortense stands in the receiving room, staring after him, shocked. There is something very odd about the way he acted. He couldn't be . . . could he?

Could the prime minister of Eastphalia be siding with the ogres?

CHAPTER NINETEEN

DIVIDE AND CONQUER

Filomena has to give it up to the giants: They sure do know how to keep their cottage cozy. After the cold glamour and grandeur of the Northphalian palace, being at the giants' homey cabin helps her feel a sense of calm. It's like she's on a grand tour of the cutest places to stay in the Never After kingdoms! Except, of course, her tour involves fighting for her life at every turn.

Filomena sits down at the long wooden table. She takes a sip of hot cocoa. "Thanks for cooking, Alistair," she says. Alistair has whipped up breakfast for everyone.

After their curry dinner the previous night, Filomena, Jack, and their friends decided it makes the most sense to stay at the cottage while they plan how to find Zera and search for the League of Seven.

The giants, being the gentlemen they are, agreed to stay at their girlfriends' cottage until Filomena and her crew leave. Luckily their girlfriends all live together in the cottage across the path. How convenient!

"Hey, no problem, Fil," Alistair replies. "I'm loving this kitchen! Everything's made of wood!"

Gretel takes a bite of pancake. "Fil, don't you think that if there was TV in Never After, Alistair would have a cooking show?"

"Totally, he could tour every kitchen in the land and make different dishes in each!" One of Filomena's favorite facts about Gretel: She's biportal. Filomena feels a little more sane knowing someone else gets how weird it is to occupy two worlds.

"You two are so funny with your mortal world stuff. I never have the slightest idea what you're saying," Rosie chimes in. She's buttering toast.

"I bet you'd love the Discovery Channel, Rosie." Gretel laughs. "If you come visit me in the mortal world, we'll totally binge it."

Jack walks over to the table carrying a plate of food. "I have to say, staying at this cottage sure feels a lot more normal to me than staying at Princess Jeanne's castle," he says, taking a seat beside Filomena. "Not that it wasn't cool. But silk pajamas and a four-poster bed? That was intense."

"Yeah, the beds here are great!" Alistair enthuses from the kitchen.

"I concur," Byron says, sitting down at the table with a cup of coffee. "Finally a bed that fits me properly! I'll have to get myself a giant-sized bed when all this is over."

Filomena notices that Jack is sitting very close, so close that they're almost touching. He turns and smiles at her. "How did you sleep, Fil?" he asks in a soft voice only she can hear.

"Pretty well. Gretel doesn't snore, so that's a plus."

He laughs. Their arms bump as they butter their toast and pick up their teacups. Each time, Filomena gets a little jolt.

"You know," Jack says, "I was thinking, maybe, we never really—" Suddenly he blushes a bit, covering it with a cough.

"What?" she asks, her heartbeat speeding up.

He takes a deep breath. Is Jack the Giant Stalker nervous?

Suddenly everyone sitting around the table is paying attention to them.

"Uh, never mind," says Jack.

Filomena tries not to look too disappointed.

The group turns its attention to Gretel, who's asking Rosie about the interior decor. "So, Rosie," Gretel's saying, "I have to ask: Are you responsible for all the doilies around here?"

Rosie grimaces, then laughs. "No way! This cottage is *so*

not my taste. The giants chose all this. If it were up to me, I'd live in a totally minimalist house. Just the essentials. Maybe some nice plants. No doilies on every table, no fuzzy throw pillows with cutesy sayings everywhere, and definitely no flowery curtains!"

"I don't know, I kind of like it," says Alistair.

"Well, I am pretty much a guest here, so it's not my place to critique. But when I move out, I'm totally changing my decor scheme."

Filomena's liking Rosie more and more as she gets to know her. Rosie feels kindred, somehow.

"So what's our plan for today?" Gretel asks the table, changing the subject to more serious matters.

Jack seems ready to get into it; he has a plan fully formed. "I'm thinking we can split up today. Some of us can go out exploring, get the lay of the land around Snow Country, and talk to people in town. See if anyone knows anything about Zera's whereabouts."

"I can't do that, unfortunately," Rosie says. "I can't really go too far from the cottage these days."

"That's all right," Jack responds. "I was thinking I'll go. I have some allies from old times around here. I'm sure I can seek them out."

"We'll go with you, Jack," Beatrice volunteers. "Since Byron and I are Prince and Princess now, I think it'd be good to get to know as many people in neighboring kingdoms as possible."

"Great, it's set," Jack replies.

"And what should we do here, Jack? Twiddle our thumbs? Play with cootie catchers?" Gretel teases.

"I was thinking Filomena might have an idea of what to do, actually," Jack says, looking at Filomena.

It feels good to be Jack's right hand again. Or maybe Jack's her right hand . . . They're each other's right hands? Is that anatomically possible? Either way, it feels good to be a team again. And maybe even more than just a team. Maybe . . . Filomena's mind drifts to what Jack wanted to ask her. But wait—right now she has a mission to focus on!

Filomena considers the task at hand for the moment. She still thinks they need to find the League of Seven before they can do much else. The Prophecy docs say only the League can save Never After, after all. Without the League of Seven, they stand no chance against the ogres.

"We'll work on the League of Seven issue," she says.

"All right, everyone," Jack announces. "Eat up. We're all going to need our energy today."

After Jack, Byron, and Beatrice leave to go exploring for the day, Rosie leads them to her attic office. "Come on," she tells the rest.

"Ooh, we can do our brainstorming up here?" Filomena says, climbing up the ladder.

"Whoa, I don't know that I've ever climbed a ladder

before," Alistair says. "This is kind of freaky! Is there any other way up?"

Gretel laughs.

"Alistair, I've seen you literally stab ogres in the heart, and you're afraid of climbing a one-story ladder? You can't be serious."

"Hey, everyone's got something, all right? Heights are not my strong suit!"

Before Alistair can protest too much, Filomena and Gretel push his butt up the ladder. They all climb onto the loft platform.

It looks like a whole different world up here! Filomena surveys papers scrawled with calculations, odd-shaped bottles containing metallic or colored translucent liquids, drawing boards and drafting tables, and . . . are those mannequins?

Alistair walks around Rosie's laboratory, inspecting everything. "What's this?" he says, holding up a shimmering net.

"Oh, it's this trapping device I'm working on for the giants' border patrol. The net is made of superstrong, sticky fabric spun from silver. I got it from Rumpelstiltskin's sister. He spins gold; she spins silver—family business. I had to promise to give her my firstborn child, but I don't even want kids, so that was an easy bargain!"

Filomena's in awe of Rosie—the life she's lived!

"Rosie, you didn't tell us you're, like, a genius!" Gretel proclaims.

Rosie laughs. "I certainly wouldn't call myself a genius. If I was a genius, I wouldn't have worked on this stupid magic mirror for weeks with barely any progress."

"Speaking of," Alistair says, "what's with you and talking mirrors, anyway? Why are you trying to make one?"

"I'm sort of obsessed with them," Rosie explains. "They're very ancient, you know. Usually you have to develop a real relationship with one to get it to engage with you at all, but I guess the ogres forced their hand. I'm not sure how."

"Why do the ogres have them?" Filomena asks.

"Talking mirrors are very powerful. Like Jack told you, they know all about our world and can speak only truth. When that power gets into the wrong hands, it can be dangerous, taken advantage of. You can imagine what the ogres might want to use them for."

Gretel, distracted, has wandered over to the row of mannequins. Fabric scraps are all over them. "What's up with these, Rosie? Are you into fashion design, too?"

"No, no, this is more an experiment than a fashion project," Rosie answers.

"What kind of experiment?" Filomena questions. She hopes they're not being too nosy. But she has a feeling Rose Red is holding back.

Rose Red sighs. "I guess I should tell you guys a few things." They all sit in a circle on the floor. "Do you know who the ruler of Snow Country is right now?" Rosie asks.

They shake their heads. Even Alistair seems confused.

"It's Queen Christina," Rosie goes on. "She's a horrible queen. Cruel. Always so threatened by anyone who seems even a little bit powerful. I suspect she's in cahoots with the ogres, though I haven't been able to prove it yet. And I can't be totally sure, but I have a strong suspicion that my mother's disappearance has a lot to do with Queen Christina."

Filomena gets a sinking feeling in her stomach. Another kingdom ruled by cruelty?

"What you also don't know about me is that I have a lot of brothers. Had. Have?" Rosie sighs. "They're older than me. They're my dad's sons. I guess they're more half brothers? But as my dad says, there's no such thing as half-loved. They're my brothers! My mom is their stepmother. Well, that's the whole thing. So I've been obsessed with talking mirrors for a long time, mostly because they seem like the most straightforward way to find out where my mother is."

Sadness sweeps over Filomena. So much is going on that it's been a moment since she's thought about her own mother. Filomena thinks of her now, wonders if she's still in the hospital or if she's been allowed to return home yet. She hopes her mother is at home, in bed with a good book and a steaming hot cup of tea. Fil sympathizes so much with Rosie. Losing a mother . . . It's something she doesn't want to even imagine.

Rosie keeps telling her story: "After my mother had been gone for a while and none of us could figure out where she was and what happened to her, I decided we should sneak into Queen Christina's castle and steal her talking mirror. If we could just ask it where my mother is . . ."

Gretel pats Rosie on the shoulder. She's starting to tear up. "It's okay, Rosie, you don't have to tell us about this right now if you don't want to," she says.

"No, I have to," Rosie responds, taking a deep breath. "I was keeping watch. My brothers were going to grab the mirror off the wall. I thought that if talking mirrors tell only truth, then they must also have a sense of justice. They'd be on our side. We even chose a day when Queen Christina was away. She was at Cinderella's ball actually."

Gretel's, Alistair's, and Filomena's eyes widen, realizing they'd been in the same room with this queen.

"But it didn't matter that she was gone," Rosie says. "Her horrible minions captured my brothers, and I couldn't warn them. I didn't even see them. The minions kept my brothers in Christina's dungeon, and every day I would go to check on them. I'd sneak up to this one tiny window that looks into the dungeon. The day Christina got back from Wonderland . . . It was horrible."

Rosie looks so shaken up, Filomena wants to ask her to stop talking, stop telling the story, stop reliving it. But she knows, somehow, that she needs to hear the end.

"Queen Christina turned my brothers into swans. She cursed them. I had to watch them transform from boys to swans, and it was so awful to see them contorting like that. They were in so much pain." Rosie wipes her tears away, remembering. "But she let them go. She turned them into swans and then let them fly away. I thought that was so odd. But when I think about it now, it makes sense. She captured their personhood, so they'll be trapped no matter where they go. And it's all my fault. I was supposed to keep watch, but I failed them." As Rosie says this, she stands up to touch the strange fabric scraps hanging off the mannequins. "After that, I decided that if I couldn't access an existing talking mirror, I'd make one. I'd find a way. So I went to visit the Winter Witch."

Alistair gasps. "That's very dangerous, Rosie!"

"Who is the Winter Witch?" Filomena asks, puzzled. She has a vague buzzing of memory. The Winter Witch is mentioned somewhere in the Never After books . . .

"She's a very unpredictable old witch who lives on the mountain in Snow Country," Rosie explains to Filomena. "It's impossible to tell whose side she's on or who she favors. She has no allegiances, and she's very powerful. She never leaves her cave."

"Visiting her means risking your life," Alistair says. "I've heard of people who went to see her and never came back. If she doesn't agree with whatever it is that you seek, you're a goner."

"Well, that's chilling," Gretel says.

"So you risked your life like that?" Filomena says.

"I did, and even with her gifts, still nothing!" Rosie yells in frustration.

"What happened?" Filomena asks. She has to know.

"I told her why I was there, that I'm searching for a way to create a talking mirror and that my brothers are cursed. At first I thought she would kill me on the spot; after all, it is incredibly presumptuous to try to create one of the most ancient powers in Never After from scratch." Rosie laughs at herself, cooling her tears. "But she said she liked my pluck, or something like that. She gave me a truth serum she created—an incredibly powerful substance, very rare. I'm not sure if even the fairies can make truth serum. And she also told me a way to reverse the curse on my brothers."

"Wow! That's incredible!" Alistair says.

"It would be, if I could ever bloody figure out how to do it." Rosie sits back down in a huff.

"So what is it? How do you reverse the curse?"

"I have to make shirts for them out of star flowers."

"That's it? You just have to make shirts?" Alistair says.

"That, and I have to put the shirts on them. But star flowers are incredibly delicate and hard to find. Whenever I pick them, I accidentally ruin them. I'll finish three shirts, but by the time I'm on the fourth, the first three are wilted and falling apart."

Filomena looks over at Gretel, who is absolutely beaming.

"Rosie, Rosie, Rosie," Gretel says, grinning. "Aren't you lucky that your dear cousin Gretel happens to be an expert seamstress?"

CHAPTER TWENTY

GRETEL'S CURSE—
BREAKING ASSEMBLY LINE

G retel is totally in her element. She's pacing around the loft, surveying the materials at hand. Filomena loves to see her friends so expertly doing what they do best. It makes her wonder what exactly it is that she does best.

Despite Rosie's protesting, Gretel finally got her to agree to let them help.

"Aren't we supposed to be figuring out this League of Seven thing? Not making T-shirts?" Rosie says.

"Of course, but who says we can't do both?" Gretel says, smiling. "We can brainstorm while we sew. That's one of the best things about sewing: You can think and talk about other things while you do it. Now look, your problem is that you aren't able to sew fast enough to keep all the flowers fresh. As soon as they wilt, the shirts become limp and break apart, right?"

"Right. And then I can't get them on my brothers fast enough, and it's the most frustrating thing in all the worlds."

"So I think what we need to do is dry the flowers. That witch never said the flowers had to be fresh, did she?"

Filomena grins. "Aha! A loophole!"

"So we'll collect them, dry them, and sew them promptly. Plus, with four of us sewing, it'll go way faster."

The four go out to a patch of star flowers that Rosie found in the forest and start picking as many as they can gather.

"Wait!" Gretel says, slapping Alistair's hand as he tries to pluck a flower. "We shouldn't pick *all* of them. Just in case we mess up and need backup."

They go back to the cottage. Alistair lays the flowers out on baking sheets to dry in the oven. Once the blooms have dried, the friends go up to Rosie's loft again.

"So how many shirts are we making?" Gretel says, laying out the flowers carefully.

"Seven."

Filomena's and Alistair's heads nearly snap off, they turn to look at each other so fast.

"Seven?" Filomena asks.

"Seven," Rosie confirms.

"The League of Seven!" Filomena and Alistair say at once, jumping up and down.

But Rosie doesn't look quite so excited. "I don't know, guys . . ."

"This is perfect, this is fate!" Filomena says. "I can't wait to tell Jack." Once she calms down, though, she realizes Rosie is skeptical. "You're not excited about your brothers being the League of Seven?" Filomena asks.

"It's not that . . . ," Rosie says. "I mean, my brothers are brave and all . . . but, well, you'll see."

Filomena's confused. Why isn't Rosie excited by this? They're one step closer to saving Never After!

"Well, whether they're the League of Seven or not, we're still going to reverse the curse," Gretel says. "But seriously, Rosie, it feels like too much of a coincidence. Seven brothers, seven heroes?"

Rosie says nothing, only shrugs, and Filomena holds on to hope.

A few hours later, they're still working away. The delicate business of sewing these flowers into shirts is no joke. Gretel keeps saying that if these turn out well, they can sell them off as one-of-a-kinds, as long as the brothers don't need them for life.

Alistair is clearly growing weary. "Why is it that the cures to curses are always so time intensive?" he whines.

"I think because if they weren't," Filomena ventures, "then everyone would be able to reverse them."

"You make a good point, Seamstress Filomena."

Gretel's way further on her shirt than the others, and Filomena sees she's not even looking at her hands as she sews. Gretel's staring at Rosie's glasses instead.

"What?" Rosie says, smiling shyly.

"Your glasses are to die for! I'm obsessed. How do they change color like that?"

"I developed them myself, actually. After the whole mirror thing was a total bust, I had to entertain myself somehow. So I started inventing things."

Had to entertain herself? Wait, didn't Rosie say something this morning about not being able to go far from the cottage?

"Rosie, are you trapped here?"

"Sort of. But not by the giants! Don't worry. It's just . . . I think Queen Christina either doesn't know about me or thinks I was turned into a swan with my brothers. Either way, I don't want to risk her finding out that her curse didn't reach the whole family. And if I get turned into a swan, who will save my brothers?"

"So you've just been hanging out at the cottage the whole time your brothers have been swans?" Alistair asks incredulously.

"Pretty much. That's why I was so excited when you guys came! Finally some new company! I love those big ol' guys, but conversations with giants can get pretty repetitive. It's always *girlfriend* this, *new tea cozy* that."

How awful! At least when Filomena was sort of trapped in her house in North Pasadena (her parents are *really* overprotective, remember?) she had takeout and movies and books. Rosie literally had to invent stuff to keep herself entertained! Necessity really is the mother of invention.

"Speaking of conversation, Filomena, I know you gave me your whole rundown quickly at dinner, but what's it like going between here and the mortal world?" Rosie asks.

"To be honest, it's pretty weird," Filomena says. She hasn't really articulated this out loud to anyone. It's all happening so fast. "I was actually back in the mortal world recently," she continues, "because I found out my mom is sick."

Gretel and Alistair look at Filomena sadly. No one has really talked about this since Filomena returned.

"I'm so sorry to hear that," Rosie says. "I know it's not quite the same, but having a missing mom isn't great, either. So I kind of know a little of what you're going through. Always worrying."

Alistair looks at his hands sadly. "Me too, Fil. I'm sorry I've never brought it up. I know it must be really hard." He looks at Rosie. "My parents both died," he says quietly. Gretel puts her head on his shoulder.

Rosie sighs looking at their sad faces. "It sucks to be a kid and worry about your parents," she says. "Do you know what your mom is sick with, Filomena?"

"That's the weird thing. The doctors have no idea. They say it's like nothing they've ever seen before. I feel guilty; part of me hasn't thought about it much while I've been here. There's so much going on. But every night before I fall asleep, it's all I can think about. I just stare at the ceiling and wonder how she's doing, if she feels horrible, if she feels better, if she's eating. If my dad's giving her enough hugs and cookies." Filomena tears up a bit.

"I know that feeling," Rosie says. "Remind me to give you some of my special tea tonight. It makes falling asleep easier."

"Hey, you know what we need?" Alistair says. "A GROUP HUG!"

Filomena wipes her tears and laughs a little. They all lean in for a group hug.

"This is cool," Rosie says.

"We learned it from Filomena," Alistair replies. "I love them now! Best thing I've learned from the mortal world since cheeseburgers."

"Wow, FaceTime, TV, cheeseburgers . . . When I come to visit the mortal world, there'll be a lot of things you'll have to show me," Rosie says, bumping Gretel's shoulder.

"Hey, guys," Gretel says, and holds up the shirt she's working on. "It looks like we're close to being finished!"

"That's good," Filomena says, "because it sounds like Jack, Byron, and Beatrice just got back!"

CHAPTER TWENTY-ONE

JACK HAS A GIANT PROBLEM

"Going down is even worse than going up!" Alistair yells from the ladder leading to Rosie's loft. Filomena realizes she probably should have gone down after him. He's the last person to climb down the ladder, and at this rate he could be up there all night.

"Come on, Alistair, you can do it!" Gretel encourages.

"Man, what's your problem? You're only, like, five feet off the floor," Jack says. He's clearly frustrated. When they returned, Filomena immediately noticed that he, Byron, and Beatrice had a grave air about them. They're sitting at the long wooden dining table, waiting for Alistair to join.

Byron gets up and, like the tall, brawny gentleman he is, lifts Alistair from the ladder and places him softly on one of the benches at the table.

Alistair blushes. "Gee, heh, got yourself a strong one there, Beatrice."

"I think some of my beastly strength stayed in my system." Byron laughs, flexing an arm. "I definitely wasn't this strong before."

Filomena can tell that Jack is not in a joking mood. "So how'd it go, guys?" she asks after they are all seated.

Jack puts his head in his hands and says nothing.

Beatrice looks at him and decides to speak. "We found out where Zera is," she says. All the faces at the table lift toward hers, so hopeful. "Like the message said, the enemy discovered their location and they were under attack. Well, she's been captured."

Now Filomena understands Jack's demeanor. It's the worst *I told you so* of all time. They're too late.

Or are they? Internalizing this information, Filomena feels her brain go into hyper-planning mode. As long as Zera is alive, they can fix this . . . There's a chance.

"Where is she? Did you find out who captured her?" she asks.

From behind his hands, Jack speaks. "Queen Christina.

Zera is trapped in her castle. In the dungeon, probably."
He's almost emotionless while saying this, which scares
Filomena more than anything. He's not crying, not angry.
Just blank.

"Okay, well, as long as we know where she is, we can
rescue her," Filomena says. "Am I right?" The table is silent.
"I said," she says louder, standing up, *am I right?"*

"Yeah!" they all cheer. All except Jack.

"Clearly we have to go get Zera," Beatrice says, "but what
do we do about the League of Seven situation?"

"We have news on that front, too, actually," Gretel shares.
"Turns out Rosie has seven brothers. Isn't that right, Rosie?"

Rosie looks hesitant to speak. "I do, yeah. They were
cursed by Queen Christina. She turned them into swans.
That's what we were working on today."

"The Winter Witch told Rosie that she has to make her
brothers shirts out of star flowers in order to reverse the
curse!" Alistair tells them.

"You went to the Winter Witch?" Jack says, suddenly
looking up from his hands. "That's incredibly dangerous."

"Trust me, I've been told," Rosie replies. "But I had
no choice. Anyway, these three think my brothers are the
League of Seven."

"That's great!" Beatrice exclaims. "So first we reverse the
curse on your brothers, then we rescue Zera."

"Wow, I can't wait to meet the League of Seven," Alistair
says dreamily.

Rosie just laughs nervously.

Jack still looks blank, but now it seems to Filomena that he looks a little angry, too. "I'm not so sure about this whole League of Seven thing," he says.

"What do you mean, Jack?" Gretel asks.

"I just don't like the idea that we have to wait around for these seven warriors to come save us."

"I feel some relief, honestly," Alistair says. "Knowing there are seven brave warriors out there takes some of the pressure off!"

"But we don't even know who they are," Jack says. "How are we supposed to trust them? How do we know they're the ones to save us? Why can't we just do this ourselves?"

Filomena tries to put her hand on Jack's shoulder, but he shrugs her off.

"Jack," she says, stern now, "you know why. The Prophecy says the League of Seven is the only way to save Never After. This is bigger than us; we have to find them. And so far it seems like Rosie's seven brothers are our best bet. I think we should at least *try* to help Rosie break the curse. Then we can go with the League of Seven to rescue Zera."

"Fine."

Everyone quiets. It seems there's not much to say, but a foul mood has certainly descended after finding out about Zera's capture. Jack walks over to the couch and sits down, staring into the fire.

"Why don't Byron, Rosie, and I make dinner?" Beatrice offers. "You four go unwind."

On the couches, it's quiet. Alistair breaks the silence, as usual. "Jack, you never told us who told you the news about Zera."

Jack grumbles something Filomena can't understand.

"What's that?" Alistair says.

"I *said* it was Sadie. We went by her ranch. She's always been a friend of Zera's. I figured she might be keeping tabs on Zera while she's in Snow Country," Jack answers, his arms crossed.

"Sadie? *The* Sadie?" Alistair asks with eyes wide and eyebrows raised.

"Yes, Alistair, *the* Sadie. Whatever that means."

"Oh, you know what it means!" he says, poking Jack in the arm. "Wow. Sadie's back in the picture, huh?"

"No, she's not back in the picture, if she ever was in the picture. Just drop it, okay?"

"How are her reindeer doing?"

"They're still reindeer."

Gretel frowns. "Am I missing something here?" she asks. "Do we know a Sadie?"

"Jack definitely knows a Sadie, that's for sure," Alistair responds with a grin. "We often detoured to Snow Country during our quests, and it wasn't to visit the giants, I'll tell you that much."

"Knock it off, will you, Alistair?" Jack says tightly.

Filomena's starting to get the picture. She feels another crush-induced sting. But Zera is captured! Jack's crush history is *so* not the thing to focus on here.

Gretel leans in and whispers to Filomena, "Are you following this? Does this Sadie own a reindeer ranch?"

"I guess," Filomena whispers back. "Or at least she works on one."

"Well, I'm going to bed," Jack announces, and then leaves.

"I guess he's not hungry tonight," Alistair says sadly as Beatrice calls them to the table for dinner.

CHAPTER TWENTY-TWO

SWAN RIVER

The next evening they finally finish making the star flower shirts. Rosie leads Filomena, Alistair, and Gretel to the frozen river where she says she meets her brothers most nights.

"I usually bring them leftovers from dinner with the giants," Rosie says, leading them down a snowy path. "But sometimes when I start feeding them, I worry that I'm feeding the wrong swans! It's good that swans don't often travel in groups of seven. Makes my brothers easier to pick out."

Filomena gives a light laugh, but she hasn't been in a very fun mood today. Alistair feels morose for teasing Jack when Jack was obviously terribly upset about what happened to Zera. Jack's barely left his giant bed today. Filomena went to check on him at one point in the afternoon, and if he hadn't looked so sad, she would've laughed at the way the bed seemed to swallow him whole.

She'd asked if he planned to come down anytime soon. Without looking at her, he'd said only that he might as well wait until the famous League of Seven was ready; they couldn't do anything until the League was found, anyway.

Filomena had never heard him be rude like that before. *Whoever Sadie is, she can have him!*

Soon enough they arrive at a beautiful frozen river. Not frozen like still water with a thick layer of flat ice on top. Frozen like waves and swirls of water stopped cold in midair. It is stunning, like someone pressed PAUSE during a particularly spiky wave crash.

They're carrying bowls of leftovers from that night's dinner. Alistair made ramen—with luscious noodles, spicy broth, soy eggs, and bok choy—at Filomena's request. She was craving some hot ramen in this cold weather. Plus it was elaborate enough to cook that she thought doing so might distract Alistair from Jack's bad mood.

The four of them sit down on a log, bowls of ramen in their laps.

"This ramen is actually a great lap warmer," Gretel says.

"And an even better internal warmer once you eat it!" Rosie adds. "Alistair, seriously, it was so good."

The three girls all ooh and ahh over Alistair's cooking skills, hoping to lift the spirits of the evening a bit. It doesn't appear to be working. Alistair just nods in thanks.

They wait and they wait. No swans appear.

"Rosie, are you sure we're at the right river?" Filomena asks.

"Of course. This is odd. We always meet at this time."

The longer they wait, the more Filomena starts to feel panic rise in her chest. What is it about waiting for something important that's so intensely anxiety inducing? It feels like at any moment the swans could appear . . .

But there are no swans . . .

Still no swans . . .

Seriously, still no swans?

"Alistair and I are going to go for a little walk," Gretel says. "Can you call us when the swans come? We'll stay within earshot."

"Sounds good," Rosie says as they walk away.

Still no swans . . .

"You don't think they got . . . ," Filomena starts. Her brain is racing with worst-case scenarios. "Eaten by ogres?" she blurts out, and then immediately regrets it. They are Rosie's brothers, after all!

Thankfully Rosie just laughs. "Don't worry, I don't think swan tastes very good," she says. "I don't know why the ogres would eat them. They're already cursed by Queen Christina; how much worse can it get?"

They fall into silence, once again waiting. Filomena figures she may as well try to get to know Rosie better while they wait. "What do you want to do when you're able to leave the giants' cottage, Rosie?"

"That's almost too hard to think about," Rosie replies. "Too exciting. I've been in that cottage for so long now, it feels like it's all of Never After."

"I know what you mean," Filomena replies. "In the mortal world, I spend a lot of time inside. My parents can be pretty intense about keeping me safe. Plus I honestly didn't have a lot of friends before I met Alistair and Jack."

"I hope they stay friends for your sake," Rosie says. "Do they fight a lot?"

"No, never! Absolutely never. I've never seen them act like this," Filomena says. "And they've been friends for, like, *ever*. For so long. But don't avoid my question!"

Rosie giggles. "Okay, fine. To be quite honest, all the work I've been doing in my laboratory . . . I really love it. I want to be an inventor, I think. I want to make things that are useful for people in Never After. I think, if I could combine my own ideas with a bit of magic, I could make some really interesting things."

"I love that you can add magic to inventions in Never After," Filomena says.

"Oh, that's right. I forgot you guys don't have magic in

the mortal world. How weird!" Rosie laughs. "I mean, no offense."

They laugh together. Filomena's impressed by Rosie's smarts and her creativity. She wants to be an inventor, how cool is that? That would have never even occurred to Filomena!

They both realize at the same time that it's getting pretty dark.

"I'm sorry to say it," Rosie says, "but it doesn't seem like we're going to have much luck tonight. I don't know where my brothers are, but I don't think they're coming."

Just as Rosie says this, Gretel and Alistair walk back over. Alistair looks at the ramen sadly. "They aren't coming tonight, are they?" he asks. "It's probably stone-cold by now, anyway."

The four of them pick up the ramen bowls and the star flower shirts and start walking back to the giants' cottage.

"Rosie, I've been meaning to ask you if I could get a pair of those glasses . . . ," Gretel calls, running up to walk next to Rosie.

Several paces behind them, Alistair and Filomena walk side by side. It's the first time she's seen Alistair alone since the whole thing with Jack.

"Hey, buddy," she says, bumping his shoulder lightly. "How are you holding up?"

He just shrugs.

"Have you and Jack talked at all today?" she asks.

"Nope. Not a peep."

"That was pretty nasty last night. I've never heard him talk to you like that."

"I don't think he's ever talked to me that way before. He usually loves my jokes. But I was being annoying about Sadie, I suppose. Hey, I'm sorry about that, by the way. That was stupid of me to say in front of you," he adds.

Filomena feels nerves flutter in her stomach. "What do you mean? Why would it be stupid in front of me?"

"Oh . . ." Suddenly Alistair looks nervous, like he's let something slip. "Just because . . . ," he hedges. "Well . . . you know, in case you feel weird about it. Sadie, I mean." He's flustered now.

Did Jack say something to him? Or is Filomena so obvious that everyone in Never After can tell she has a crush on Jack? But does she still, after the way he's been acting? It's all too confusing.

"I don't really know what you're talking about, but don't worry about it," she says quickly.

"It was just a little crush, by the way. Nothing *happened*, they never went on a date or anything."

A date? They're only twelve and thirteen! In the mortal world, kids their age go on group dates to the movie theater and then talk in the parking lot for fifteen minutes before their parents pick them up. That's about as much dating as Filomena knows. But maybe Sadie the reindeer rancher knows about other kinds of dates? Like dates where you go on walks and discuss quests?

"Well, I wouldn't care if they did!" Filomena blurts out.

Alistair looks at her, seeming slightly confused. She needs to steer the conversation away from this.

"While I don't like what Jack said, I hope you know that you don't always have to be funny, Alistair," Filomena says, getting back to the initial topic. "I love your jokes, and thank goodness you are the way you are. You do get us through some rough moments. But you should just know that you're allowed to be whatever you want to be in this group."

"Thanks. I'll never stop joking around, but it's nice to know there are other things about me that you like, too." Alistair looks at Filomena, then stops to give her a hug. "Does it count as a group hug if it's only two people?" he asks.

Filomena laughs and thanks the fairies that she gets to be with heroes who have a sense of humor.

CHAPTER TWENTY-THREE

THE BOYS ARE BACK IN TOWN

The next night is like a groundhog day. *Are there ground-hog days in Never After?* Filomena wonders. Or maybe it would be a chippermunk day. The point is, it feels like the same day all over again. Come twilight, Rosie leads Filomena, Alistair, and Gretel to the river with leftovers from dinner. But this time, Rosie insists that everyone come. So Beatrice and Byron, as well as a very reluctant Jack, are along for the walk, too. Each carries a shirt for one brother.

But it's when they arrive at the river that this night starts to be quite unlike the previous.

Seven magnificent swans with wingspans as wide as Byron's swoop down from the sky. They land gracefully in front of Rosie. She gives the one nearest her a pat on the head.

"Where were you delinquents last night?! We waited practically all night for you!" she says.

The swan she just petted only squawks in return.

"They can't even talk? Are you sure these are your brothers, Rosie?" Jack grumbles.

Filomena rolls her eyes. He's still being a jerk today, sulking and hardly speaking to anyone.

Rosie ignores Jack. "It's showtime!" she says. "Fairies, I really hope this works. Winter Witch, please know what you're talking about."

Rosie instructs everyone to pick a swan and stand in front of it. On her count, they each carefully pull a star flower shirt over their swan and then quickly step back.

At first there's nothing. But then something happens that Filomena's never seen before. Feathers are flying around, and human limbs jut out of the swans' bodies. Then all at once—poof. She can hardly believe her eyes. There they are: seven boys. Wait, seven *naked* boys?

"Don't look at us! Don't look at me!" a teenage boy yells out, covering himself.

Huh, now that's something you don't think of when it comes to curses, Filomena thinks to herself, laughing quietly. She guesses that during the process of transforming into a swan, clothes become sort of nonessential.

But apparently the fashion expert of the group *did* think of this.

"Don't worry, boys, I've got clothes for you," Gretel says, opening her bag and tossing garments at the shivering brothers. Rosie gives her a very appreciative look.

"Blimey, it's much colder having human skin than feathers, I'll tell you that right now," one brother says.

As soon as they're dressed, Rosie throws herself into their arms.

"Rosie, you genius girl!" says a brother, hugging her and giving her a noogie.

"Can't believe you figured it out, Rose!" says another.

"Star flower shirts? How in all the worlds did you come up with that one?"

"I don't even want to know," another says. "We're back, boys! We're back!"

The energy has certainly shifted with their transformation. Rosie's brothers are all slapping one another on the backs, doing little jigs, stretching out their arms and fingers, remembering what it feels like to have limbs and opposable thumbs again. And they all keep hugging Rosie over and over. *Having older brothers seems pretty nice,* Filomena thinks.

Swiftly, two of the brothers lift Rosie up onto their shoulders so she's laughing wildly in the air. The more Filomena sees of the brothers—the goofy, cute, wholesome, rambling crew—the more she begins to wonder if Rosie has a point about the League of Seven thing.

"Let's have a party!" one brother shouts, and the rest cheer. A party?

"Rosie, take us back to the cottage," another brother says. "Let's throw a big bash to celebrate! It's been far too long since we've had a good old-fashioned rager!"

It's become very clear to Filomena that Rosie's seven brothers care a lot more about having a good time than they do about saving Never After. As they walk back to the cottage, Filomena's head is spinning. They have so much to do, so much to figure out. This rowdy group of fraternity bros is not how she imagined the League of Seven, the heroes who will save Never After from doom. Plus they have to rescue Zera, find Colette, transform Charlie, retrieve Princess Jeanne's crown . . . Not to mention two of her best friends aren't speaking. It all piles up in Filomena's chest. And now these boys want to throw a party? It would be funny if it wasn't so sad.

At the front of the group, Rosie's brothers still have her hoisted on their shoulders as they walk, cheering and yelling and joking, back to the cottage. Behind them, Filomena, Jack, Gretel, Alistair, Byron, and Beatrice walk silently, a depressing weight hanging over their heads.

When Filomena enters the cottage, it appears the brothers have already invited the giants and their girlfriends over. Seven giants, seven giantesses, seven brothers fill the cottage, dancing, laughing.

"I don't think I've ever seen the cottage this full!" Rosie says. She looks a little overwhelmed.

"Come on, Rosie," one brother says. "We were just swans for goodness' sake, don't we deserve to have a little fun?"

Rosie shrugs and joins in. Though Filomena is happy for Rosie and her brothers, she's having a hard time pretending to enjoy the merriment. Her heart's not in it. It feels like too many people, too crowded. She needs some air.

Filomena steps outside, putting on her Gretel-made outerwear. She dusts some snow off a bench in the garden and sits down, taking a big breath of cold Snow Country air. The sounds of partying are muffled out here. Through the golden glow of the windows she sees Beatrice and Byron dancing, the brothers laughing, the giants standing on the kitchen table and toasting one another. It's one of those moments when she really feels so far away from home. Her heart aches a tiny bit with the loneliness that comes from being in a crowd.

Suddenly someone is sitting next to her: Jack.

"Hey," he says quietly, hands in his pockets.

"Oh, you're talking to us again, are you?" she replies sharply.

"Just to you," he says.

She softens and her pulse quickens. No matter how big of a jerk he's been, when Filomena looks at him, she just sees Jack and his golden heart. Just to her? It feels like the party doesn't exist anymore, like they're in a snow globe, only the two of them. Still, she wishes he hadn't acted so rudely earlier.

They sit in the quiet snowy night for a moment, looking at the stars. Then Filomena can't take it anymore. "What's going on with you, Jack? Why were you so sharp with Alistair? This isn't you."

He sighs. "I know."

"You know? That's it?"

"It's all my fault, Filomena."

She turns her head away from the stars to look at him. His cheeks are damp from crying, she realizes. "What is?"

"Zera. My oldest friend in all of Never After, the closest thing I had to a mother after my mother died. My guardian, my friend. She asked for my help, and I let her down. In her greatest time of need, I let her down."

Filomena says nothing. She can feel how much he's been holding in. He needs to vent.

The floodgates open.

"It's all my fault for getting hurt! I slowed us down." Jack smacks himself on the forehead, and Filomena grabs his hand to stop him doing it again. Then, somehow, they're holding hands. They keep holding hands.

She's holding hands with Jack the Giant Stalker.

"I've always been the one to make all the decisions. Why does it feel like when I make one wrong move, someone I love dies? Why is this my life?"

"I hear you. But it's not your fault that Zera got captured."

"But it *is* my fault, though!" he yells. "She was desperate and sent for help—"

"And so was Princess Jeanne. Everyone needs you," says Filomena.

"And I let them all down," says Jack. He closes his eyes. "Sometimes it's hard to imagine who I even am without all these missions. Saving people and fighting and plotting . . . That's who I am. I'm nothing else."

"That's not true," she says. But he just shakes his head, disbelieving. "I don't know how much I've told you about this, Jack," Filomena continues, "but before I met you and Alistair, I was really lonely. I was bullied at school. My only friend ditched me. The only thing that made my life feel okay was reading about you and your adventures. And then when I met you in real life, you were so much more than just a hero. You're funny. You're kind. You're my favorite person to be around." She blushes slightly, grateful her cheeks are already rosy from the cold.

"Now you're just buttering me up so I'll stop being upset." Jack chuckles lightly.

"A laugh! That's a victory." Filomena bumps his shoulder with hers. She realizes they're still holding hands. Her heart catches in her throat. "But besides all that, a hero is a pretty amazing thing to be, Jack."

"I hate that word. *Hero.* I'm not a hero, I'm just a kid with no other choice but to do this. You heard Sabine when we were in Vineland: 'Blood of my blood has been shed for millennia to keep you safe.' Do you think I want that? I don't want that!"

"I get it. Both my birth parents died for me. I never even got to know them. Sometimes I wish I was still just reading about your adventures instead of living them alongside you. *Being* brave is a lot harder than *thinking* about being brave. How are you so brave all the time? You never seem afraid."

"Of course I'm afraid. I'm afraid all the time. But I can't let anyone see that; I can't show it. This is the destiny given to me by the fairies."

"You know, I was given this destiny, too, Jack. We're both gifts from the fairies to Never After, remember? We have the same destiny. I just joined in a little later." She smiles. "We can help each other," she says. "If you just talk to me for real, tell me what you're feeling, I promise it won't make me afraid. I won't freak out or think something's really wrong. You're allowed to have feelings."

Jack looks at her for a long time, saying nothing.

"I'm really happy you came to Never After, Filomena. Thank you."

They hug. This hug feels different than their past hugs.

There's something deep here, something that feels like two hearts colliding.

When they pull away, smiling, she removes the Seeing Eye from around her neck and tries to give it back to him.

"Keep it," he says.

"Are you sure?"

"Yeah. I gave it to you."

Suddenly they hear a crash come from inside the cottage.

"I'm okay! I'm okay!" they hear Alistair yell. They watch through the window as he stands up off the floor.

Filomena laughs. "Did he just fall off the kitchen table?"

"It's getting rowdy in there." Jack chuckles. "I guess I should apologize to him, huh?"

In an act of real bravery, Filomena touches Jack's cheek. "Yeah, you should. Hate to break it to you, hero, but you've been kind of a jerk."

They both laugh and go back to the party.

CHAPTER TWENTY-FOUR

Zera's Last Dream

The day after the party, a plan is being formulated. After their talk, Jack and Filomena decided together that they can't waste any more time looking for the League of Seven before rescuing Zera. They'll just have to go without the League for now.

And so, that morning the partyers crowd around the breakfast table.

"My head is killing me," Gretel says.

"The giants' bumbleberry punch packs a mean wallop," Rosie says. "Pun intended."

"What time did we even go to sleep last night?" Alistair moans.

On the other hand, Jack and Filomena, who went to sleep immediately after their chat, are bright-eyed and bushy-tailed. Filomena fell asleep dreaming of their hand-holding. She and Jack can't stop smiling at each other. She hopes no one notices.

"Attention, everyone!" she says, bounding over to the breakfast table. "I have an announcement."

She looks at her bleary-eyed friends sipping their morning teas and juices, rubbing their faces, and stretching their arms. This will not do.

"Jack and I have a plan."

That wakes everyone up. First of all, Jack is speaking again? That's good news. Second, they get tingles just hearing the word *plan*.

"I was wondering when you would say that!" Gretel exclaims. "Don't be shy. Tell us!"

Jack joins them at the table and stands next to Filomena. "Today we're rescuing Zera," he says.

Cue expressions of extreme surprise.

"Here's how we're going to do it," Filomena says. She lays a map out on the table and tells them the plan.

Heigh-ho, heigh-ho, it's off to Queen Christina's castle they go. On the walk, Filomena watches Jack and Alistair, who are talking yards ahead. She can't hear them, but she can see the change in their body language and smiles to herself. Jack's apologizing. She sees Alistair stop, then Jack stops as well, and the two share a huge hug. She grins. If this isn't fuel for their rescue, she doesn't know what is.

When they arrive at Queen Christina's castle, they break into two groups. Gretel and Rosie go to the front doors, and Jack, Alistair, and Filomena wait in the bushes at the back of the castle with one of Rosie's brothers. Timothée is his name.

Part of Jack's and Filomena's plan included a brother coming with them to act as a guide. Since the brothers had been held in the dungeon, Filomena figures they know their way around and may be able to lead the rescue mission to Zera. The brothers all agreed that Timothée should go. Apparently he has a photographic memory. Filomena hopes it applies to dungeon passageways and not just studying textbooks.

The rest of the merry crew had lives to return to, wives and girlfriends who were waiting for them. Once Timothée was done helping, he would leave as well to pick up where his old life left off before he was turned into a swan.

They figure that, for once, it might be good *not* to travel in a huge group, so Byron and Beatrice stayed at the cottage. The less obvious this mission can be, the better—and frankly they were due for a break.

In the bushes, Filomena and the three boys hold their breath as Rosie and Gretel use the huge silver knocker on the castle's front doors. They look chipper, as planned. Filomena had racked her brain for the best sort of distraction. Then she thought, *Why pretend when we can use Rosie's and Gretel's strengths?* So they decided that Rosie and Gretel would act as castle-door-to-castle-door sales reps offering custom-made uniforms for Queen Christina's staff. Hopefully they'll get all the servants to collect in one room for fittings. Then Rosie can distract everyone with her inventions while Gretel takes measurements and talks over outfit preferences.

Gretel, in record time, spent the morning quickly crafting samples from whatever garments were lying around the cottage. Bedsheets turned into gorgeous breathable suit jackets. Floral curtains became chic feminine overalls. Rosie especially loves this idea; she can finally get rid of some of the giants' decor choices.

But will the ruse work? What if the castle staff aren't interested? Gretel is confident the staff will be head over heels for the uniforms. Filomena hopes her friend is right and that Rosie and Gretel won't be tossed out head over heels.

From the bushes it appears as though the plan is working. Gretel and Rosie are grinning like two very charming sales reps ready to sell the world. Then Gretel looks over and gives a quick wink. She and Rosie step through the front doors.

Go time.

"All right, Timothée," Filomena says. "Lead the way."

The four start sneaking, quiet as can be, through the gardens behind the castle. Filomena tries not to be distracted by the creepy shapes the bushes are pruned into. A skull? Is that a dagger? Yikes. Queen Christina seems to have a rather gothic aesthetic, too. They should introduce her to Robin Hood.

Timothée leads them to a tiny door hidden under a dark green shrub at the back of the castle. He lifts the door, revealing a ladder that descends far, far belowground.

"Good thing you've been practicing on Rosie's loft ladder, Ali," Filomena whispers.

"I can't go first!" Alistair whisper-screams back.

"Timothée, you go. Then I'll go, then you, Alistair, and then Jack," Filomena decides. The boys all nod, and they begin making their way down, one rung at a time.

The bottom is pitch-black darkness. This they didn't account for. Filomena wishes she had the headlamp her parents bought her. But then she remembers: She has a *built-in* headlamp!

Quietly she says the spell that activates the mark of Carabosse on her forehead, and suddenly the dungeon is illuminated. Timothée looks at her in horror (or awe), but there's no time to explain now. She motions for him to lead the way and he shrugs it off. Filomena guesses that once you've turned into a swan, shock value fades pretty fast.

"I'm guessing Zera is being held in the most highly secured part of the dungeon," Timothée whispers.

The dungeon is like a maze, with small corridors that lead into one another and low ceilings. Alistair is perfectly fine standing upright, but Jack and Timothée have to stoop as they walk. *It would have been impossible to navigate this without a guide,* Filomena thinks. So even though Timothée's not in the League of Seven, she's still glad to have him on their side. The walls are stone and coated with cobwebs and something slimy. At one point, Filomena reaches out to steady herself and has to hold in a scream when her hand touches something that feels otherworldly.

Timothée leads them through a few more tunnels until finally they reach a wall of solid stone. *Lily Licks,* Filomena thinks. *How are we going to get through this?*

But before she can give it much thought, Alistair is already working his magic. "OPEN SESAME!" and the whole wall crumbles into sand.

Jack grins and slaps Alistair on the back. "I can't believe how often that's come in handy, Alistair."

Alistair smiles proudly. Timothée looks to be once again in shock. He must be thinking, *Who are these people?*

"Alistair's sort of a king of the desert," Filomena explains.

"Well, not exactly a *king*," Alistair says, blushing. "More like an emperor, I guess?"

But their good spirits immediately dissipate when the dust settles and they see what lies within the most secure chamber in the dungeon: Zera.

The great fairy Zera, Jack's mentor and dear friend, is chained to a wall. She's slumped over. She looks so weak.

Jack rushes over to her, kneels, touches her face.

Filomena's heart wrenches in her chest. "Zera," Jack says softly. "We've come to rescue you!"

Zera looks up. Her eyes seem to be gazing into a different world. "Hello, my dear Jack. Bravest Jack. Thank you for coming," she says weakly. All color is drained from her face. "There's no need to rescue me now. I'm already gone."

Jack's eyes brim with tears. "No, no, Zera, that can't be true. You're still speaking, you're still here! We'll nurse you back to health."

"My children, you know how my name appears in the prophecies."

Jack and Alistair look at each other, confused. They have no idea what she's talking about. But Filomena does. She's read the words hundreds of times.

"Clever Scheherazade, who spun a thousand and one dreams."

"Yes, dearest Filomena. You are right. I've spun a thousand dreams now. This is my final dream to spin. This last one I must tell you about, and then I will be gone."

Jack wipes his eyes. Part of him must have known this would happen. "Let us at least take you out of here. A great fairy like you can't die chained to a wall in a horrid queen's dungeon. Let us give you a ceremonial burial," he pleads.

Zera touches Jack's face, looks deep into his eyes. "Jack, it doesn't matter where I die. You can't bury a fairy. When we die, we are reabsorbed into the cosmos, where we remain forever. Just honor me in your actions, dear boy, like you always do."

Jack bows his head. "Zera, I'm so sorry I failed you. I should have been here sooner. I should have rescued you."

"I never asked for you to rescue me, Jack. Only for your help. You've given your help, and you continue to give it. There is no way in which you have failed me." She pets Jack's head. "The only way you can fail me now is to be so hard on yourself that you stop living life. Now, chin up. I have one final dream to weave."

She waves for Alistair, Filomena, and Timothée to join them on the floor. They sit around her.

"I know where my sister Colette is. I know you're with her daughter, Rose Red. You must take Rose Red to Colette. She has a message that only she can relay to you. You need to wake her up. Now listen to me carefully: Colette is in a glass coffin in the forest near the giants' cottages. She is under an enchantment. Only true love's kiss can break her spell." Zera lets her breath escape her now, having said what she needed to.

But Filomena promised Rose Red that she'd ask Zera a question. "Zera, if I could ask one last thing of you . . . ," she starts.

"Of course, my child. Anything."

"Rose Red. She's trying to create a talking mirror. She thinks it could be important in the fight with the ogres. She acquired a truth serum from the Winter Witch, but she still can't figure out how to make the talking mirror come to life. Do you know how?"

Zera chuckles until it turns into a cough. "Colette's daughter, Rose Red, is brave to have gone to the Winter Witch. That witch is a true judge of character, for she has no allegiances. Rose Red must be truly pure of heart if the witch gave her a truth serum. The answer to her question is this: Each mirror must be animated by a fairy. But a fairy can animate only one mirror. That is why talking mirrors are so powerful."

Filomena feels the wind leave her sails. "So it's impossible, then? Because each fairy has already animated a mirror?" she asks.

"It's true that each fairy has already animated a mirror and that is why there are the thirteen talking mirrors of Never After. However, I have a feeling—a strong, deep feeling—that a princess who carries the mark of Carabosse might just be powerful enough to animate one, too," Zera explains.

A princess with the mark of Carabosse . . . Where would they find—wait. Wait! Filomena gasps. "Me?"

"I believe you can, Filomena, Eliana. Now go, my heroes. Go find Colette, go conquer them. I have given you my final dream. Do everything you can with it. For Never After."

And with that, the light leaves Zera's face and her body slowly fades, then blinks out, disappearing.

CHAPTER TWENTY-FIVE

TRUE LOVE'S KISS

They're silent for the whole walk back to the giants' cottage. It is a grave day for Never After. Another fairy gone, another bright beam of goodness in the world extinguished by the ogres and their allies. But amid her grief, deep in Filomena's stomach, there is a burning seed of hope. She might be powerful enough to animate a talking mirror. They can find Colette. They will break the curse and have another fairy on their side!

When they reach the cottage, the sacred silence breaks. They congregate inside. Filomena explains to Gretel and

Rose Red what Zera said about Colette. Rose Red's face lights up.

"Mom!" she cries. "I'll get to see my mom."

"Rosie, do you know who your mom's true love is? Zera said that only true love's kiss will break the enchantment."

Rosie looks puzzled. "Well, it's my dad of course, but he's been dead for years."

The seven friends sit at the table, thinking. No one is coming up with any answers.

"What if we just go find her and see what happens?" Alistair asks. "There's no use sitting around here, trying to pull an idea out of thin air."

Everyone is in agreement. Rosie also can't wait to see her mom. So they decide to spread out and search the forest for the glass coffin.

An hour later, having walked up and down the forest pathways, Filomena hears Gretel shout from beyond a nearby hill: "Come quick, everyone!"

Jack and Filomena, who are walking the forest together, run to meet Gretel. Alistair, Rose Red, Byron, and Beatrice come running, too.

There, at the base of the hill, is a glass coffin caught in a beam of sunshine. Flowers around the coffin glimmer and sway in the breeze, untouched by the frigid weather. Somehow, here in this pocket of enchantment, it's warm.

Rosie runs to the coffin, pressing her hands against the glass. "Mom!" she cries.

There is Colette, as beautiful as can be. It's easy to see Rosie's resemblance to her, even though Rosie's hair is red and Colette's is black as night. They both have skin white as snow.

Colette—*Snow White,* Filomena thinks—is lying with her eyes closed. Her expression is one of neutral contentment. She's deep in a sleeping spell. Filomena wonders if she's dreaming.

"What now?" Rosie says, looking at the group. "Do we go back to the village, try to find some old boyfriend of my mom's? The one that got away or something?"

Filomena can tell that Rosie's grasping at straws. But she feels certain there's no prince coming for Snow White.

Gretel takes a deep breath, then gives a light laugh. "I hate to do this, guys," she says. "I don't want to make things awkward or weird. But I have an idea."

They all look at her, waiting.

"I think we all know there's potential for a true love's kiss right here, with us, in this group."

Filomena's heart starts pounding wildly. Surely Gretel means Byron and Beatrice. They are married after all! But does a fairy-tale true love's kiss count if you've already kissed hundreds of times?

"Are you going to say what I think you're going to say?" Alistair gapes, wide eyed, at Gretel. "You're actually going to cross that bridge?"

"I don't think we have a choice!" Gretel replies.

"Can someone fill me in here?" Jack asks.

Gretel sighs. Then she smiles. "Jack, Filomena, I think you two can break the spell."

Jack's jaw drops slightly open in shock. Filomena feels her face flush bright red, and this time it's not hidden by the cold. She and Jack look at each other shyly, flustered. Then they grin. Are they smiling at each other? Are they agreeing to this? What is happening?! A thousand thoughts run through Filomena's mind.

Gretel ushers Alistair, Byron, and Beatrice behind a tree a few paces away to give the tense moment some privacy. Rosie remains, though, leaning over the coffin, looking at her mom.

"Wow," Jack says. "This is intense."

Filomena laughs nervously.

"I feel kind of shaky," Jack says.

"Me too."

"Are you nervous?" he asks.

"Yep."

"Me too. Do you want to do this?"

"I mean," Filomena says shyly, "if it will break the enchantment."

"Right. Just for the enchantment," Jack says, looking at his feet.

Filomena closes her eyes.

But just as Jack leans in to kiss her, Gretel, Alistair, Byron, and Beatrice yelp from behind the trees and run out. Jack and Filomena pull away in surprise, confused. Disoriented, they see the glass coffin is popped open and Rosie is bent over, hugging her mom and kissing her cheeks.

And then Colette, unbelievably, sits up and starts rubbing her eyes.

True love's kiss.

A kiss from Rose Red to Snow White.

Filomena is spinning from how many feelings she's feeling right now. Elated—Jack almost kissed her! Wanted to kiss her? Wants to still? Disappointed—because he didn't kiss her. Relieved and excited—Colette is awake! And still, amid all this excitement, she feels a deep cut of sadness at seeing Rosie and her mom together, hugging and crying tears of joy. Filomena can't help but think of her own mother, who she suddenly wishes she was hugging right now.

After a few minutes of collective disbelief and celebration, they all decide to give Rosie and Colette a moment alone. Jack and Alistair instinctually walk a few paces away to talk, and Gretel grabs Filomena by the arm and yanks her a couple of steps in the other direction.

"Oh. My. God," she says.

"I know!" Filomena squeals.

"You just almost kissed Jack the Giant Stalker!"

"I *know!*"

"But you didn't."

"I *know*."

"Wait, would that have been your first kiss?" Gretel asks. Her eyes are all excited.

Filomena nods sheepishly.

"So let me get this straight. You just almost had your first kiss with your best friend and huge crush to break an enchantment for Snow White? Fairies, will we ever be normal?!"

They grab each other's hands and giggle.

"So what now?" Gretel goes on. "Do you think you guys will kiss later? Now that it's *sooo* obvious you like each other?"

Filomena's suddenly panicked. What *does* this mean? What does this mean for them now?! Do they kiss later? Do they pretend this never happened? They were going to kiss, but it was for the purpose of their quest. Will they actually kiss just because they want to? Will they date? How do you date in Never After? Oh my fairies!

"Oh no, you're panicking, aren't you?" Gretel says, putting her hand on Filomena's shoulder. "Don't worry, everything's going to be totally chill." But she doesn't look sure of that at all.

"What do I do, Gretel? Do I try to kiss him sometime? But when? In between rescuing a fairy and fighting an ogre?!" Filomena's voice is reaching a fever pitch.

"Breathe," Gretel says. "Just breathe. Everything will happen naturally, all right? We'll figure this out. Plus Alistair and I will always be there as buffers."

Filomena nods, and they don't have time to say anything else before Rosie calls them over.

They all gather around Colette, who's still sitting in the glass coffin. She's smiling the warmest, most brilliant smile. She's beautiful.

"Thank you for breaking my curse, lovely heroes."

They all bow to her.

"As you may know," Colette continues, "I was cursed by Queen Christina. She has a horrible sort of magic. The kind that can't perform any real transformation, can't bring anything beautiful into the world. It can only mimic transformation, make things *appear* differently than they are. That's why her curses can always be reversed. She's more of a trickster than anything. But still, she can do damage."

They all nod.

"Queen Christina cursed me because she was afraid of my presence in Snow Country," Colette continues. "Rose Red told me that in your mortal world, Filomena, I was cursed because of my beauty. Isn't that right?"

Filomena nods. Colette (or should they call her Snow White?) laughs.

"The mortal world. So obsessed with beauty. It was because I'm a great warrior that she cursed me, not because she's jealous of how I look! How ridiculous. Anyway, I have something I need to tell you all, so please listen carefully."

The seven gather close around the glass coffin.

"I know you think things look bleak for Never After.

Almost all the fairies have died, many beings have retreated, many others live in fear. It is a dire time. But there is hope. There is still hope."

Filomena nods. "The League of Seven, right?" she asks.

"Yes, exactly," Colette responds.

"But we can't find them, Colette," Filomena continues. "We've been searching for them, and we don't know where they are! Do you know where they are?"

Colette smiles a smile that could melt all the snow in Snow Country. "I do, Filomena. They're here."

Everyone looks around, behind them, on the hill, through the trees. The League of Seven is here?

Colette laughs a bright, sweet laugh. "*You* are the League of Seven. Filomena, Jack, Alistair, Gretel, my Rose Red, Beatrice, and Byron. You seven who stand before me. You're the League of Seven."

Filomena feels like she's been struck by lightning. But in a sort of good way? No one is coming to save them. The people they've been looking for all along are themselves. They are their own heroes. They are the seven.

Alistair busts out laughing. "How did we not realize that we make seven?!"

The seven friends look at one another with new eyes. They can't believe it. It's so shocking, so surprising, so enthralling, this news, they don't even notice Queen Christina come up behind Colette—and stab her.

CHAPTER TWENTY-SIX

CATCHING QUEEN CHRISTINA

There is a scream so loud and bloodcurdling that windows all over Snow Country shatter in their frames. It's Rose Red, who drops to her knees, weeping, clutching the body of her mother, Colette, who is slumped over. Blood wells from Colette's stab wound, soaking her dress.

Jack, Filomena, and Alistair immediately snap to attention. They draw their Dragon's Tooth swords from their sheaths and stand guard. Out from behind the glass coffin appears the queen they've heard so much about over these past few days in Snow Country: Queen Christina.

She is all angles, with long black hair, pointed teeth, and pointed nails. Whereas Colette's black hair is deep and expansive like the night sky, Queen Christina's is matte like charcoal. Her eyes are of the brightest green, like a cat's.

"You," she spits, her eyes squinting into slits. "You seven think you can do anything you want with no consequences! You break my curse on the swans, you break my enchantment on that traitor Snow White!" She paces around the group.

Filomena isn't sure how afraid to be. They have Queen Christina outnumbered seven to one, but Filomena has no idea how powerful she is. Will she curse them right now?

"You think you're so great? Well, how great are you that your precious Zera is DEAD!" she taunts, walking closer. "Is this the famous Jack the Giant Stalker? You're the one Zera pleaded for, aren't you? The one she cried for, saying you'd come save her. But you didn't, did you? You couldn't. You let her die."

Filomena knows that Jack knows none of this is true, but still he's shaking with rage. He swings at the queen with his Dragon's Tooth blade, but she jumps away and cackles.

"You're all doomed!" She laughs. "All your fairies are dying, and the ogres are poised to take the thrones. Never After is practically ours! The ancient clause is invoked, you know, or haven't you seen the news? The summer solstice is just around the corner!"

From the corner of her eye, Filomena sees Rosie look

at her intently, then make a slight motion toward her hip. There's a sparkle of silver flash. Rumpelstiltskin's sister's silver! Rosie brought her invention!

Filomena steps forward to distract the queen. "So how are you going to curse us?" she taunts. "Have you run out of ideas? Personally, if we get to choose, I'd like to be a bear. Then I can hibernate all winter and attack you in the spring." She chatters away.

"Filomena, what are you doing?" Alistair whispers.

The queen looks at Filomena, disoriented by her boldness.

"Yeah, a bear would be good. Or maybe a snow leopard. Do you guys have those in Never After?" She keeps rambling on and on until Rosie has sneaked around behind the queen.

Just as Queen Christina raises her hands to cast a curse, the silver net drops on her and drags her to the ground.

"Run!" Rosie shouts.

Everyone besides Rosie and Filomena is terribly confused, but they follow instructions. Running, running as fast as they can. Queen Christina screams at them from the confines of the silver net. Filomena squeezes Rosie's hand as they run. She lost her mother and saved them, all in the span of five minutes.

As they run for their lives after a near kiss and a murder and the League of Seven reveal, all Filomena can think is: *What ancient clause was Queen Christina talking about?*

Tick Tock, Tick Tock

Magic mirror on the wall,

Will this deadline ruin it all?

The summer solstice around the bend,

A crown to find, a frog to turn back into a prince, and a kingdom to mend.

The League of Seven has been found,

But can they get their feet on solid ground?

Two more fairies gone, so the clause must hold strong,

But if a thief returns, what will he do wrong?

The heroes continue, split up, go forth.

Only their friendship will be their true north.

Magic mirror on the wall,

There is so much to do.

Can the heroes do it all?

Part Three

Wherein . . .

An ancient clause puts our heroes
on a deadline.

A new talking mirror appears
in Never After.

And spells, coronations, and betrayals
abound!

CHAPTER TWENTY-SEVEN

THE PRIME MINISTER'S ANNOUNCEMENT

The prime minister of Eastphalia stands before the Eastphalian talking mirror, readying for his announcement. He looks into the mirror, which is refusing to engage with him and is posing as a normal mirror. This works fine for the moment; the prime minister could use a glance at his reflection before he appears in front of all of Never After.

He adjusts his cravat, smooths the lines in his suit. He thinks to himself that he looks dignified. Like a real ruler.

He takes a breath. This announcement will change everything. Is he really going to lead Never After down this path? There's a pinch in the back of his mind. What's that feeling? That nag? It's what one might call a conscience. But the prime minister learned how to shut that down long ago, and now it makes an effort to rear its head only on rare occasions. He supposes this is one such occasion.

He assures his conscience that it's fine, he's doing the right thing here. When this announcement is out in the world and the takeover is complete, he'll finally have real power. He won't have to worry about silly things like democracy or elections. He'll be able to make a real impact.

He's a fan of order. A man of regulations who prizes ordinance, the unanimous following of rules. Societies and civilizations must be controlled! Never After is far out of order these days, isn't it? Isn't this what the fairies were always on about, this disorganized idea of letting various communities of Never After rule themselves? The fairies encouraged Never After's monarchs to act as guiding figures to their kingdoms—help with decision-making, run frivolous festivals and silly gatherings, deal in connection and morale—rather than rule with the strict discipline the prime minister intends to deliver.

Yes, yes, quite right. He's settled it with his conscience now. See? He's doing the right thing. Yes, most definitely. No doubt in his mind.

He smooths his suit for the umpteenth time and instructs

the talking mirror to project his image to the other twelve talking mirrors of Never After. The mirror rolls its eyes, unbelieving that, after millennia of being respected and revered, it has to put up with this stodgy try-hard's rules. But the mirror has no choice in the matter.

The prime minister takes a breath and commences his announcement.

"Good afternoon, citizens of Never After . . . ," he begins.

CHAPTER TWENTY-EIGHT
MESSAGE RECEIVED

Even though Filomena has had her fair share of adventure since meeting Jack the Giant Stalker on that fateful day in North Pasadena, this feels like a new level of overwhelm. The League of Seven (which, she's still processing, is her and her friends?!) is running for their lives, so there's no time to debrief even if they want to. Filomena isn't sure she does.

The seven finally reach the giants' cottage and rush in the front door. Rose Red quickly locks the door with several dead bolts. Filomena hadn't realized how sound the security of the cottage is, but then it dawns on her. Of course. Rose

Red has been preparing for this day, the day when Queen Christina catches on to her. Those dead bolts are finally getting put to real use.

The League of Seven collapses on the sheepskin rugs. Well, six of them do, heaving and out of breath. Filomena sees that Rose Red is standing with her eyes closed and her back against the front door, breathing hard.

Filomena goes up to her. "Hey," she says. There are no words. Just when Rosie finally found her mother . . . Filomena shudders remembering the scene. She gives Rosie a hug, and Rosie holds on tight. Filomena feels hot tears on her neck.

Then she feels a body behind her, arms around her. A lot of arms. Group hug. She's impressed: For once, Alistair had restraint enough not to yell.

They stay like that until there's suddenly a wild banging on the windows and door. Not just one pair of fists; seven giant pairs of fists pounding. Filomena can't even see from where she's buried in the group hug, but then everyone breaks apart. It appears the giants are locked out of their own cottage.

"What gives?!" yells Crabby through a frosted window.

But they aren't so grumpy—not even Crabby—once they see the look on Rosie's face. She opens the dead bolts on the door and they rush in.

"She's dead. Christina killed her."

Rosie has gone from breaking down to stone cold.

Filomena gets it. Sometimes it's easier to block it all out. Become void of emotion altogether. It's not a good tactic for the long term, but it's one they've all used.

The giants do their own version of a group hug, though they're so huge, they more or less have to hug Rosie one at a time. No one seems to know what to say in the face of this immense tragedy.

Except there are other tragedies to tend as well.

"I know this is horrible timing," Cap says, "but there's going to be an announcement in the town square. I have a feeling we should be there."

"An announcement?" Jack says. "About what? From who? And how?"

All questions Filomena is wondering, too. Ones she doesn't know if she wants answered.

"We'll talk on the way," Cap says, and ushers them all back out into the cold.

And so, with only a few moments to catch their breath, the group is off again—two lots of seven this time—toward the town square. Cap explains that when the giants were at market that afternoon, the town was abuzz with news of an announcement.

"Apparently they're using Snow Country's talking mirror for the broadcast, which everyone is very excited about," Cap says.

"No one's seen a talking mirror in a long time," Joyful elaborates. "Not since the ogres got a hold of them. And even before that, they were used in the public only on very rare occasions."

According to the giants, no one is sure of the content of the announcement. But they're all curious enough to make sure they find out.

That much is obvious when the giants and the League reach the town square. It's absolutely filled with townspeople! This is Filomena's first time seeing more of Snow Country besides the little patch of giants' cottages and Queen Christina's castle. There are boughs of holly everywhere, carts filled with bottles of cider, fur coats, and people riding reindeer.

Immediately Filomena wonders if Jack's ex-crush, Sadie, is in the crowd. She glances at him, and he looks back at her, shrugging, like *will we ever catch a break?* Filomena feels silly for Sadie being top of mind while so much is at stake. But then again, she did just almost have her first kiss! A dreaminess washes over her amid the throng of Snow Country citizens. Too many emotions, too little time!

The fourteen reach a stopping point where the town square abuts Queen Christina's castle. The queen's balcony sits above the crowd.

"Wait a second," Filomena whispers to Gretel, panic creeping up her spine. "What if Queen Christina comes out? Is she going to put a curse on us in front of all these people?

Or, if everyone realizes she's trapped, are we going to get in trouble?"

Gretel shrugs fearfully. Before they can theorize any further, a large mirror is rolled out onto the balcony. It's pushed by two of—Filomena presumes—Queen Christina's minions, dressed in uniforms trimmed with white fur. The mirror is large, oval, and framed with beautifully sharp cut glass snowflakes.

At first the mirror is simply a mirror reflecting the crowd. Then a mist seems to form within the mirror, and an otherworldly face quickly appears. *Is that the face of the magic mirror itself?* Filomena wonders. But before she can get a good look or see any clues, a different face appears. The head and shoulders of a paunchy, graying, austere-looking man in an impeccable suit.

Jack grimaces upon seeing this person.

"Who is it?" Filomena asks him.

"The prime minister of Eastphalia," he says, scrunching his nose in obvious disgust.

The prime minister, or the vision of the prime minister displayed in the magic mirror, clears his throat. Then he begins to speak.

"As many of you are likely aware, it has come to our attention that the heirs to the three major thrones of our kingdoms have been terribly irresponsible.

"Princess Jeanne of Northphalia, who is set to become queen, has misplaced her crown, if you can believe it. As we all know, by Northphalian law, no prince nor princess can become king or queen without their crown.

"Then we have Prince Charlemagne of Eastphalia. No one has seen the lad for over a fortnight. He's freshly married to Princess Hortense, and yet, while she is at Eastphalia's castle, he is nowhere to be found. I paid her a visit recently; she couldn't even tell me where our prince is. What kind of example does that set for the kingdom? A prince missing in action?

"Finally we have Eliana of Westphalia, the daughter of beloved Rosanna. Eliana, who seems to go by Filomena for some reason, has not been seen in Westphalia for several fortnights, and before that not at all. She clearly doesn't know the kingdom, nor does she care to. She's made no effort to spend time there and learn about Westphalian culture or customs, nor to meet her people.

"Many of us are concerned that these heirs are not taking their roles seriously and, as such, are not fit to run the kingdoms they are set to inherit. In order to encourage these young princes and princesses to take on their roles and responsibilities, I am here to declare that the ogre court would like to gallantly invoke the ancient clause of the nature spirits.

"The clause reads as such: 'If the heirs to the thrones of Never After's major kingdoms, Northphalia, Eastphalia, and Westphalia, do not present themselves to be crowned as kings and queens by the summer solstice, then their thrones will be forfeited to those most ready to take them.'

"In this case, those most ready are Queen Olga and her ogre court.

"On behalf of the ogre court, this announcement serves as an official invocation of this clause.

"I'm sure you all understand the difficult position Never After is in. We must have rulers who take the responsibilities of ruling seriously, and thus the ancient clause, as of this announcement, has been invoked.

"All we can do now is wait and see what will transpire by next week, when the summer solstice arrives.

"Good afternoon, Never After, and thank you for your attention."

Filomena's face is the picture of shock. Her jaw is dropped, her eyes are wide. Did he seriously just tell all of Never After that she doesn't care about her role as ruler of Westphalia?

Immediately Filomena can feel hundreds of eyes on her. How does anyone know who she is? That she's Eliana? Oh, right. Filomena thinks back to Princess Jeanne talking all about her, Gretel, Jack, and Alistair appearing in the *Palace Inquirer* and other tabloids du jour. So much for flying under the radar.

Jack seems to notice all the eyes, too. "I think it's time we head home," he says, nodding toward the town square's exit.

Gretel and Alistair, on the other hand, seem to quite enjoy the attention.

"They're all looking at us," Gretel whispers to Ali. "Wait a second, are we famous?"

"Do I look okay? My outfit's okay? What if there are paparazzi here?!" Alistair answers.

Jack rolls his eyes at their antics, but Filomena catches a brief indulgent smile. He grabs her hand to make sure he doesn't lose her in the crowd.

CHAPTER TWENTY-NINE

THE NATURE SPIRITS' CLAUSE

"That no-good, skeevy, two-timing—" Jack is cut off when Alistair shoves a cookie into his mouth. Back at the giants' cottage, Alistair is dealing with the anxiety of their new crisis through comfort baking.

"Your blood sugar is low. We need to nourish, people! Nourish!" Alistair says, waving everyone to the table.

They all sit down, though no one is in the mood to eat.

Jack picks up his tirade right where he left off. "I knew

he was a bad prime minister, but I never thought he'd stoop this low."

They're all shocked, but Filomena isn't sure she totally understands what's happening.

"The way he twisted the facts . . . It was skillful." Byron frowns. "I'd be almost impressed if I weren't so infuriated."

Beatrice is glowering. "I've heard about the prime minister of Eastphalia, you know," she says. "You hear these rumors—that he rigged his election, that he's cutting kingdom funding to outer regions—and you think, *Okay, that's politics. Maybe I just don't understand it.* But this? Inexcusable."

"Exactly." Jack nods. "He's blatantly siding with the ogres! He's encouraging and legitimizing their violent takeover by pretending that it's not even happening, that this is all for the good of Never After!"

"Poor Hori. She must be freaking out right now," Beatrice says. "First Olga turns Charlie into a frog; now they're spinning it like he's off gallivanting somewhere and not taking his responsibilities seriously!"

Alistair licks vanilla icing off a spatula and frowns. "He made it sound like we're all being irresponsible," he says, "like Filomena just doesn't want to do her royal duties, when really she hasn't had a second to even think about them because we've been too busy trying to save everyone from the ogres!" His chef's toque almost flies off, he's so worked up.

"Took the words right out of my mouth, Alistair,"

Filomena says from where she's sadly slumped on the kitchen table.

"That mirror trick was genius," Jack growls. "They were able to control the whole narrative by talking to all of Never After at once. The mirrors are the only way to do that. How else would they reach everyone?"

Filomena can't help but think how different things in Never After are from the mortal world, where everyone can reach anyone all the time. Is that better for telling the truth, or worse? It seems impossible to know for sure.

Then she remembers the second part of the announcement. Not only did the prime minister make it seem like they aren't taking their jobs seriously; he also invoked some clause.

"Can someone fill me in on this whole ancient clause thing, by the way?" she asks.

Everyone looks at Jack, who sighs. "I'd completely forgotten about the nature spirits' clause. It was created centuries ago, during a time of particular prosperity in Never After. Things were going very well, so well, in fact, that the rulers of the kingdoms were getting lazy."

"I remember hearing about this in history classes," Byron says. "It was a period in Never After that was marked by luxury, excess, parties. The rulers were constantly socializing and throwing events."

"Right," Jack continues, "which isn't a bad thing, per say, of course. But the problem is, the rulers stopped paying attention to their duties almost completely. They weren't doing direct harm, but they also weren't taking the right to rule seriously and were neglecting their people. That's where the nature spirits came in."

"The nature spirits?" Filomena asks.

"The most powerful forces in Never After," Alistair explains.

"I thought the fairies are the most powerful force in Never After," Filomena says, her brow furrowing.

"Typically that's true," Jack says. "The nature spirits don't get involved in Never After politics or anything like that, almost never. They're the very essence of Never After, the force of nature itself. As such, they can't take sides the way the fairies can. They are inherent truth. They broke their neutrality only once: to create this clause."

Filomena is awed. Never After always has more to reveal. She doesn't remember anything about nature spirits from the books. She supposes this is another detail she'll have to add to the thirteenth book.

Jack continues, "They created the clause to encourage the leaders of that time to return to their kingdoms, take their responsibility to rule seriously, and do good by their citizens. But the ogres must have found the clause somehow. Now they're using it in completely the wrong way, manipulating the intention. But still the clause stands, so we all have to follow it."

The group around the table is silent for a moment.

"So when is the summer solstice?" Filomena asks.

"Next week," Rose Red responds. It's the first time she's spoken since they got back from the town square.

Filomena takes a deep breath, gathering her strength. She looks to her six friends. They're all here, worn down, tired, heartbroken. And yet they must persevere.

"We know what we have to do," she says. "We have to follow the clause. All the rulers must be crowned within the week."

The weary faces grow wearier still. It seems impossible. Filomena can see they're losing morale.

"Hey," she says, standing up. "We're the League of Seven! Right here, at this table!"

"Oh right," Alistair says. "I kind of forgot about that!"

They all laugh.

"Filomena," Rosie says. "I'm ready. Let's do it."

That gives the rest of the group a jolt. If Rosie can do this right after the death of Colette, then they all can. They must.

Filomena gets an idea. One that will boost their morale and perhaps even give the ogres a scare. Jack said the talking mirrors are the only way to change the narrative. And if all of Never After believes Filomena and her friends to be delinquents who aren't taking their responsibilities seriously . . . Well, then they'll just have to change that narrative. She smiles.

"Everyone, get some rest for the next little while. Rosie, I think we have some work to do."

CHAPTER THIRTY

FILOMENA'S INVENTION

"Are you sure about this?" Rosie says. She's holding an antique handheld mirror, her arms outstretched as far from her body as she can manage.

"Absolutely not at all," Filomena responds, laughing. "But tons of things were invented by accident, right? Penicillin . . . Popsicles . . ."

"Mortal world stuff? I'll take your word for it," Rosie says, laughing, too.

To say it feels good to see Rosie laugh is the understatement of the year. In fact, it feels so good that Filomena temporarily forgets what she's doing and that she's holding a vial of flaming truth serum, which they're attempting to infuse, yet again, into the mirror.

Zera told Filomena that each of the thirteen fairies animated a talking mirror and that's why they are so powerful. Right before she died, she told Filomena that she thought a daughter of the fairies who carries the mark of Carabosse could animate a mirror, too.

But she hadn't gone so far as to actually tell Filomena *how* to do that. Filomena wishes once again that Carabosse or her birth mother were still alive, that she could ask them what to do and turn to them for help. She certainly loves her League of Seven, but there are just a few questions that none of them has answers to.

And so, following Rosie's lead, Filomena is experimenting, which will hopefully lead to an invention.

Rosie had the idea to revolutionize the talking mirror by making it handheld. That way it can be portable! Filomena thinks it'll be a great idea if they're ever actually able to figure out how to animate it.

They've been at it for a few hours now, and so far nothing has worked. They poured truth serum on the mirror. Filomena tried to make up spells (which she's realizing is harder than it seems). They've aimed the light from Filomena's mark of Carabosse and lit the truth serum on fire. Still nothing.

"This is getting a little depressing," Rosie says when another attempt fails.

Gretel's head pops up over the edge of the loft. She's standing on the ladder. "How's it going up here? Any luck?"

"No," they both answer glumly.

"I brought these up for you, Fil." Gretel heaves the thick stack of Filomena's Never After books up into the loft. "I know they sometimes help you think through things."

Filomena shrugs. She's not sure the books can help with something that hasn't happened yet, but she's run out of other ideas.

"Just give them a try, see if they spark any ideas," Gretel says.

"It's worth a shot," she says, then thanks Gretel.

Gretel climbs back down the ladder to the cottage below.

In moments like this, Filomena wishes she could just read the thirteenth book instead of having to write it herself. She flips through her copies of the first twelve Never After books, scanning for anything to do with mirrors.

She stops on a page in book four where Jack is visiting Zera. It makes Filomena almost tear up now. In this part of the book, Zera is telling Jack about talking mirrors.

"The thirteen talking mirrors are special," she says, *"because they have souls. But souls don't form themselves. They come from the truth of those who animate them. Truth begets truth."*

"What do you make of this?" she asks Rosie, showing her the passage.

"Hmm. I mean, scientifically I suppose it makes sense.

Energy cannot be created nor destroyed. It just changes forms, right?"

"Gosh, you really are smart, Rosie. But I'm not sure I'm following."

"Put it like this: As with energy, we can't create a talking mirror out of thin air, right? It has to be created from forces that are already at play in the world. So maybe Zera is saying that the person or fairy who animates the mirror has to give part of themselves to the mirror in order to animate it."

Filomena nods. It's beginning to make sense. *Truth begets truth.* If a talking mirror's soul comes from the truth of the one who animates it, then maybe what's missing is Filomena sharing some part of herself with the mirror. Something true.

"So how do you think I should do that?" Filomena asks.

"Maybe I'll leave you alone up here with the mirror and the serum." Rosie smiles.

"Alone?" Filomena raises her eyebrows.

"I think that's the only way," Rosie says, patting Filomena on the shoulder and descending the ladder.

Alone again. In one hand Filomena holds the antique mirror, and in the other, the truth serum. How can she give part of herself to the mirror? What truth does she have to say?

She closes her eyes. The mark of Carabosse lights up on her forehead, funneling directly into the mirror. The events of the past few weeks, months, flash brilliantly on the backs of her eyelids. An overwhelming sense of fear flows in her body. She feels hot tears begin to pool in the cracks of her shut eyes. It's the thing she hasn't been able to admit to herself. Through all her journeys in Never After, she's always thought she had to be brave, had to be a perfect hero. But now all she feels is fear. Fear of what she can't control. Fear gripping her throat, choking her. Fear that she can't save her mother, that she can't save Never After. Terror at her own fate, that she could die. Terror that she's only twelve and has to rule a kingdom. She's been pretending things are okay, that this is all normal. That she's prepared for this. But the truth is, she's not. She's terrified, and she feels helpless. She's absolutely petrified. She wishes someone could be there to guide her. But there isn't. She's alone, and she's afraid.

"Hello? Hello? This thing on?" says a voice from the direction of her hand.

Filomena opens her eyes. There, in the small surface of the handheld mirror, is a face of mist and color so difficult to describe. It seems made of pure energy, colors Filomena's never seen before.

"Hey, that was quite a wake-up call," the voice says.

Filomena gasps. "Did that really work?"

"I'm here, aren't I? You bet it worked! You got skills, girl!"

"I can't believe this! I'm Filomena, by the way." She bows slightly.

"I know!"

From below, Jack calls, "Filomena, who are you talking to up there?"

Filomena leans over the edge of the loft, waving the mirror around. "It worked! Guys, it worked! We made a talking mirror!"

"Whoa, whoa," the mirror says. "Getting a little motion sickness here!"

"Sorry." Filomena laughs. "I didn't realize you'd feel that."

Downstairs, Jack wakes the rest of the League of Seven from their power naps, and everyone gathers to figure out the next move. Introductions are made to the talking mirror, whose name, they are informed, is Ira Glassman.

"Ira Glassman, I'm Filomena Jefferson-Cho. Pleased to meet you," says Filomena politely.

"Can you, like, see us?" Alistair says, staring into the mirror's face.

"Yeah, of course. What do you think I'm looking at right now?"

"But what about now?" Alistair turns the mirror facedown on the table.

"Alistair!" Filomena turns Ira faceup. "That's so rude."

"Sorry, just trying to figure out the mechanics. We've never had a talking mirror before!"

"I'm not just any talking mirror," Ira says. "I'm a cool talking mirror."

They all laugh.

"Add this to your list of inventions, girl genius," Gretel says, bumping Rosie's shoulder.

"This was all Filomena," Rosie says demurely.

"No way! I'd have never known what Zera was talking about without you. This is a total collaboration."

"So now that we have the mirror, what exactly is the plan, Fil?" Jack asks.

In all the commotion of actually successfully creating a talking mirror, Filomena forgot to tell them about her plan and why they need a talking mirror in the first place.

"Right." Filomena launches into her idea. "So we know that, because of that announcement, all of Never After is now under the impression that we're a bunch of delinquents who don't take anything seriously. But what the prime minister and the ogres aren't anticipating is *us* having a way to communicate with all the other talking mirrors in Never After."

Everyone's nodding along and listening. A conspiratorial smile creeps onto Jack's face.

"I think we need to give an official announcement of our own," Filomena finishes.

Though she fights it for a while, eventually the League of Seven decides it should be Filomena who gives the announcement. After all, she is the one who created the talking mirror and came up with the plan, and she's the only one of them who was directly snubbed in the prime minister's announcement.

Filomena now stands in front of Ira, who Rosie is holding up. Gretel's done Filomena's hair and outfit to look "especially regal." The League of Seven stands behind Rosie, facing Filomena, for support. Alistair is at the ready, holding signs written with the script in case Filomena forgets what she's supposed to say. That was Gretel's idea; she said Filomena would be just like a talk show host. Filomena is the only one who knew what she was talking about.

"You ready, kid?" Ira says. "Just say when and I'll annoy my brethren and show up on the other talking mirrors."

Jack gives her a thumbs-up from over Rosie's shoulder.

Filomena exhales. "I'm ready."

"You got this," Ira says, then gives Filomena a nod and disappears. A singular swirl appears. Filomena realizes her viewpoint must be weaving between those of the other thirteen mirrors. Almost all the mirrors are still in the town squares of their respective kingdoms, looking out onto bustling streets.

"Greetings, Never After!" Filomena begins. "My name is Eliana, princess of Westphalia, but my friends call me Filomena Jefferson-Cho of North Pasadena, California. I'll explain that another time. I want to thank the ogre court and the prime minister for ushering myself, Princess Jeanne, and Prince Charlemagne into the reigns of our kingdoms

Although, contrary to what the prime minister said, I assure you that we *are* taking our roles very seriously; we've just been rather preoccupied with royal matters. However, I'm delighted to announce that the three of us will absolutely, without a doubt, be ready to be crowned the rightful rulers of our respective kingdoms by the summer solstice. I look forward to greeting you all then, as queen of Westphalia. Good night, Never After!"

Ira's face reappears, closing the link between himself and the thirteen other mirrors.

"Talk about a mic drop!" Ira says.

Alistair laughs hysterically. "I wish I could see the ogres' faces right now!"

"I can just imagine it," Rosie joins in. "They're like, *Huh? How'd that girl from the mortal world get access to a talking mirror?*"

Jack chuckles. "They have no idea who they're dealing with."

Everyone's in great spirits, imagining the shock, the confusion, the blood-boiling rage their adversaries must feel. The seven friends sit around the giants' cottage, laughing and laughing, until Alistair suddenly grows quiet.

"You know, there is one thing we didn't really think through about this whole plan," Alistair says. "I know it's important that we change how the people of Never After view us, but we also just sort of gave the ogres a heads-up to our plan."

"Well, did we? I don't think we even have a plan, come to think of it," Beatrice says.

"Good point, Bea." Gretel nods. "What's our next move?"

The group looks to Jack and Filomena.

"Oh, uh, good question." Filomena laughs lightly. She hasn't exactly thought this far yet.

"Well, let's see," Jack chimes in. "We have to get Filomena crowned in Westphalia, we have to turn Charlie back into a prince by breaking Olga's spell, and we have to find Princess Jeanne's crown."

"That's an awful lot to do in one week," Gretel says.

"Especially if we're traveling between kingdoms," Alistair adds.

"I hate to say this"—Filomena sighs—"but I think we're going to have to split up."

No one likes the idea, but it's become obvious. It's the only way. But how do they decide who goes where?

"Gretel, Alistair, I think you should go to Eastphalia and help Hori with the frog situation," Jack decides. "You're both very clever; you can figure out a way to reverse the curse."

Gretel and Alistair nod and smile at each other, happy to be paired.

Jack goes on: "Rosie, Beatrice, and Byron, you guys go back to the North and help Riff stave off King Richard's army and get Princess Jeanne's crown back."

The three nod in agreement.

Wait a second. That means . . .

"Filomena and I will go to Westphalia," Jack says. "If that's okay with you."

Filomena just smiles and nods, a little flustered. More than okay, way more than okay. Does infiltrating a kingdom and taking your place as queen count as a first date around here?

"When will we all see each other again?" Alistair cries.

Filomena gazes at Ira, who's sitting in her lap and nodding at her reassuringly. She feels like someone is watching over her now, in a way. She's bonded to Ira for life. Plus she can see all her friends through her talking mirror!

"If you ever miss me, Alistair, just remember Ira can show me where you are! Isn't that right, Ira?"

"You betcha, kid. I got an all-access pass to Never After, front and center."

The feeling reassures everyone but especially Filomena. No matter where she is, now, because of Ira, she can check in on her friends and talk to them.

"Plus"—Jack smiles—"by the time we all meet up again, we'll have new kings and queens of Never After!"

Filomena cheers with the rest but hopes they're not jinxing anything. They certainly have a long way to go until Jack's words come true.

CHAPTER THIRTY-ONE

GRETEL'S BIG BREAK

"Is it just me or does it feel like we got assigned the farthest-away kingdom?" Alistair says, dragging his feet along the road. "Hey, you know what would be a great invention?" he adds. "If there was some way to tell where swoop holes are. Like, you could just look at a map and go to one!"

"Isn't the whole thing with swoop holes that they always change locations?" Gretel says, kicking stones with her leather boots. Normally she'd never do such a thing, but it's been hours of walking and she's getting so bored, she'll risk scuffing her fabulous boots for at least a semblance of entertainment.

"Exactly," Alistair continues. "That's why it'd be an invention! I should totally tell Rosie about this."

Gretel laughs. At least Alistair always has some far-flung idea to keep them entertained.

"I wish, right now in this moment, that Never After had already invented ride share apps," Gretel says. "Although getting a car from Snow Country to Eastphalia would definitely include a surcharge."

They've been walking for a few hours, and they have only a few more until the sun sets. The road they're following is between kingdoms, meaning there are no villages in which to spend the night. Gretel is starting to panic a little. She still can't forget what happened to them the last time they didn't plan for a place to spend the night: a repeat of her origin story. There's no way she's getting stuck in a gingerbread house again!

Just then she sees something far in the distance and hears the clip-clop of hooves.

"Alistair, I think there's a carriage coming toward us!"

Alistair squints to make it out, it's still so far away.

The solution strikes Gretel. She remembers teenagers talking about hitchhiking in California. Her dad would totally kill her if he knew she was hitchhiking, but what's the alternative? Sleep on the side of the road? That's no safer! This might be the one case in history where hitchhiking is actually the safer choice.

Once she's adequately reasoned with herself, Gretel shares the idea with Alistair. "I think we should try to hitch-hike," she says.

"What does that mean?" he replies.

"Like, we try to get them to give us a ride!"

"But wait, what if this carriage is on the ogres' side? What if it's someone dangerous?"

Gretel considers this. But as the carriage draws closer, she sees it's white gilded with gold and deep purple.

"It's much too glamorous of a carriage to belong to the ogres. But you're right, we can't tell them our allegiances just yet in case they aren't on our side. We have no other choice; we need to get to Eastphalia before nightfall, and we'll never do that on foot!"

Alistair sighs. "One of these days we'll need to start planning our routes ahead of time."

"Why don't we come up with a cover story, just in case the people in there seem fishy?" Gretel tries.

"Hmm . . . I don't really like to lie." Alistair shrugs.

"Consider it acting, not lying. We're playing a part! And if we play the part well, we get a ride to Eastphalia and won't get captured by the ogres overnight. Sometimes you have to weigh the pros and cons, right?"

She can tell that Alistair sees her point. It's not like they would *choose* to lie, but they don't seem to have a choice.

"Okay. Fine. So what's our story?"

"Why don't we say we're tradespeople on our way to

Eastphalia to seek a new life? I'm a seamstress; you're a cook. See? That's barely even a lie."

Alistair nods in agreement. It's decided. Now they just have to get the attention of the carriage. It's barreling toward them. Gretel prays that whoever is inside glances out the window.

"Look as cute and innocent as you can, and wave!" she instructs.

She and Alistair smile sweetly and jump up and down, waving. *Come on! Come on, carriage! Just stop!*

It drives by. *Lily Licks!*

But wait—it's stopping! Gretel and Alistair look at each other in amazement as, several yards ahead, the carriage door opens and a gorgeously decked-out woman sticks her head through. She has a white wig about the size of a bird-cage on her head, and her face is powdered and rosy.

"Children, what are you doing in ze cold on ze side of ze road!" she calls in a thick Eastphalian accent that sounds a lot like the way French people talk in the mortal world.

They run over to her. "We're on our way to Eastphalia," Gretel says, bowing, "but we're hoping we might have the honor of riding with you, if it's not too inconvenient."

"We're tradespeople looking for work in Eastphalia!" Alistair chimes in. "I'm a chef, and Gretel is a wonderful seamstress."

Gretel gives sly dagger eyes at Alistair for saying her real name. This woman might read the *Palace Inquirer*!

The woman surveys the two of them. Alistair is bundled up in his Gretel-made outerwear: a sheepskin-lined suede jacket and matching woolen earmuffs. Gretel is wearing burgundy leather pants and a brown leather trench coat with a thick fur collar. She's been really into seventies mortal fashion lately.

"You are very fashionable for being so young," the woman says with suspicion. She looks at Gretel. "You made zese outfits?"

Gretel grins. "Yes, madam, I absolutely did." An idea strikes her. "I would be happy to make something for you, if you would be so kind as to give us a ride!"

The woman narrows her eyes and pauses. "I am going to my holiday house in Eastphalia anyway. So long as you are very well behaved, it is no problem. Come in."

The inside of the carriage is the most gorgeous thing Gretel has laid eyes on. It's so glamorous! This woman is so glamorous, too. She's wearing a beautiful gown in dark emerald green, and she looks almost like . . .

Wait a minute. This is the famous Eastphalian opera singer Lillet!

"Now, what were you saying about making me somezing?" Lillet says. Her eyes are half-closed and, with her heavy makeup, make her look mysterious and sophisticated.

"Absolutely, I would love to," Gretel replies.

Now that she knows who this woman is, she's even more eager to make her something. Lillet is a famous soprano;

Gretel remembers seeing her all over Never After tabloids. She's a royal performer, going from kingdom to kingdom to perform for the courts. If Gretel makes something for Lillet to wear, it could launch Gretel's fashion career!

"Eastphalia is still a few hours away, *ma chérie*," Lillet says. She smiles. "We have lots of time to go over outfit ideas."

A ride to Eastphalia *and* a networking opportunity? Talk about a big break!

CHAPTER THIRTY-TWO

BEATRICE THE SPY

"So they sent me the backup team, huh?"

Princess Jeanne is standing with her arms crossed in the doorway to her castle. She doesn't look pleased, even though Beatrice has just explained that she, Byron, and Rosie are there to help get her crown back.

The trio arrived in the North to find King Richard's army held back, Riff's fortifications standing (for now), and Princess Jeanne almost feeling smug again. Not quite, but enough to tease the newcomers.

"'The backup team'?" Rosie smirks. "We're definitely the A-team. Have you seen this guy's muscles?" She points to Byron's admittedly bulging biceps.

"I think the A-team is Jack, Filomena, Gretel, and Alistair." Princess Jeanne smirks back. "No offense."

"Offense definitely taken!" Byron says, putting his hand to his heart.

"Look, do you want our help or not?" Beatrice asks.

In answer, Princess Jeanne lets them inside.

As they follow Princess Jeanne through the foyer of the castle, Beatrice can tell Rosie is shocked. Or perhaps impressed. Like Jack said, Princess Jeanne's Northphalian castle is a far cry from the giants' cottage. The ceilings are painted with skies that look like whatever the time of day is outside, depending on how the light hits them. It's quite uncanny.

"Jeez, Jack and Fil weren't lying about this castle. It's huge!"

Princess Jeanne whips around. "What did they say about my castle?" she inquires.

Rosie is suddenly a bit shy. "Oh, only really nice things. They loved your sheets!"

Princess Jeanne smiles, satisfied, and continues walking.

Beatrice tries to remember what Gretel said as they were walking to Snow Country. Princess Jeanne may seem bratty at first, but she's not really. She really does have a good heart. After all, she's standing firm against King Richard. She hasn't given up yet, even though her life is at stake.

Whereas Rosie seems more interested in the castle than in the challenge ahead. "So you live here all alone?" she asks Princess Jeanne. "Like, you have this whole castle?"

"My sister, Little Jeanne, lives here, too, and so do our friends the Merry Men and Women. You'll meet Little Jeanne soon. I'm not sure where she is right now, actually," Princess Jeanne responds, her head swiveling as she looks around.

"Little Jeanne, we have guests!" Princess Jeanne calls out to no response. "Or not guests so much as rescuers, right? So what's the plan?"

"The plan?" Beatrice repeats.

"Don't tell me Filomena and Jack sent you here without a plan!"

"The plan was for us to come up with a plan," Beatrice says, defending herself.

"And did you?" Princess Jeanne responds.

Beatrice looks at Rosie and Byron. To be honest, they'd spent most of the walk getting to know each other. With all the drama and the hubbub in Snow Country, Beatrice had barely even talked to Rosie or learned about her cousin. Can you blame her? They didn't spend a lot of time plotting their next move. Though Beatrice is realizing that might have been a mistake.

"We sort of thought we'd see what the lay of the land is

around here and then figure it out," she says. Not completely untrue.

"Great." Princess Jeanne rolls her eyes.

Beatrice can tell Princess Jeanne thinks that, so far, they're not proving the backup-team theory wrong. "How about you tell us a bit about the crown," she tries out, "and who you think took it, and where it might be?"

Princess Jeanne sighs. "The crown is an ancient Never After artifact. It was made using materials from the Deep and was blessed by the fairies. It was the first crown to be created in Never After, so it holds a lot of importance. There's a legend—and I have no idea if this is true or not—but the legend goes that if the crown thinks the person to be coronated isn't fit to rule the North, it will reject them. That's why it's such an important tradition. Without the crown, Northphalians won't accept me as their queen."

"That's such a beautiful symbol," Byron says, genuinely awed. Beatrice loves how romantic he is. He's so touched by sentimental ideas.

"It is a nice thought, Byron, but it is also very inconvenient, since it's been stolen."

"Where is the crown usually kept?" Rosie asks. "When it's not stolen?"

"There's a special case here at the castle where it's stored between coronations. That's the thing that puzzles me. Robin says he didn't steal the crown. He's a thief, but he's not a liar. Besides, the glass case the crown is stored in wasn't smashed. Whoever broke in must have had a key."

Beatrice wanders the castle halls. She hopes getting her bearings on her surroundings might jog an idea or two. What would Filomena do?

But nothing is helping her think. Not the beautiful sky-like ceiling, not the marble staircase, not the unicorn tapestry hung on the wall. She decides to go back to her bedroom.

She's about to open the door to her room when she hears voices from the other side. She peeks inside and sees Little Jeanne perched on the windowsill. This isn't her room—it's Little Jeanne's! The grandeur of the castle got the better of Beatrice as she was lost in thought; she must have wandered to a different wing of the castle.

But . . . That's odd. Why would Little Jeanne sit in an open window?

Beatrice is about to open the door and say hello, but then the speaking continues. "You ready?" a boy's voice says.

A male voice? In Little Jeanne's room? Something's off. Beatrice tries to position herself so that she can see farther through the crack of the slightly open door without drawing attention. She sneaks another peek.

The boy is none other than Robin Hood!

"You ready?" he asks again.

"Yes. Are you okay? I heard they raided your hideout and got their stuff back. Sorry I couldn't warn you," says Little Jeanne.

"That's all right," says Robin Hood. "Your uncle's waiting. You sure you want to do this?"

"I'm sure," says Little Jeanne.

Robin Hood takes her hand. "You know, I've always liked you better."

"That's not true, but I'll take it," Little Jeanne tells him.

With that, the two of them disappear out the window. Beatrice suddenly understands. Robin Hood is taking Little Jeanne to her uncle Richard, which means Little Jeanne is working against her older sister. And it's clear now who stole Princess Jeanne's crown.

Little Jeanne!

CHAPTER THIRTY-THREE

HEART-TO-HEART

Filomena is dizzy, spinning a little.

"I don't know if I'll ever get used to that feeling," she says, and almost falls over. Jack grabs her by the shoulders to steady her. She tenses and giggles. If she must be thrown about through dimensions, at least she has Jack to keep her grounded.

It's morning now. All night they walked through Snow Country, thinking they'd eventually stop at an inn, but none appeared. And then they found a swoop hole, which led them here, to Westphalia. They were excited to come across one so early in their walk from Snow Country. This is lucky, as Westphalia and Snow Country are pretty far apart. The swoop hole spit them out on a hill overlooking the central village of Westphalia, the settlement closest to the castle.

"Hey, another idea for Rosie!" Jack says. "What about inventing something you can eat that helps you not feel dizzy or nauseated when going through a swoop hole?"

Filomena laughs. Ever since they found out Rosie is a genius inventor, Jack and Alistair have been coming up with ideas for her. The list is already getting long.

"I hate to spoil your and Alistair's fun, but I think part of what Rosie likes about inventing is coming up with ideas on her own."

Jack considers it.

"Nah, I think she'll love our ideas." He smiles that dazzling smile.

Filomena wonders how everyone else is faring getting to their destinations. Then she remembers she can check. Ira Glassman is attached to her belt next to her sheathed sword.

"Hey, want to peek and see where everyone's at?" she asks Jack.

"Let's get our bearings here first," Jack says.

It's a good point. No use checking on friends when they've been apart for only one night and there's so much to do. Surely not much has happened yet.

Filomena is operating on very little sleep but figures, now that they're in Westphalia, they can take a nap somewhere.

Maybe when they get to the castle. Speaking of sleep, Ira Glassman is asleep right now. All the more reason not to check in on her friends. Filomena didn't know mirrors slept, but Ira informed her that talking mirrors require rest to recharge. The mirror is out like a light.

She stretches and rubs her eyes. Looking around, she feels overcome with her surroundings and firmly in the present moment. Westphalia, her kingdom. *Wow. My kingdom?*

The village doesn't look much better than it did during her most recent visit, even though it's been a while since Filomena, Jack, and Alistair broke Queen Olga's enchantment on the kingdom. There's still a lot of work to be done before Westphalia is returned to its former glory. It saddens Filomena that she never got to see what her home kingdom looked like before the ogres demolished parts of it and claimed it as their own.

"Let's start walking, huh?" Jack says.

They begin making their way over hills and through shallow valleys, heading toward the nearby castle. Filomena doesn't say much. Jack must be able to sense her mood, because he bumps her shoulder gently with his.

"Intense, seeing Westphalia again?" he asks.

"It's strange, knowing the whole reason I'm here is to become a queen. But I barely even recognize this place."

"That may be true, but it's in your blood. Even if you don't feel it yet." He smiles reassuringly.

Jack's words do little to reassure her. It's hard to explain, this sickly feeling creeping over her. "I guess I've just always felt out of place, wherever I've been. My family in North Pasadena feels like home, but at school I always felt apart from the group. Of course, I wondered sometimes about being adopted, what my birth parents were like, but my parents make me feel so loved. Even so, I still felt sort of alone. Is that bad to say?"

She knows she's rambling, being contradictory, but there's just too much emotion, too much confusion for her to make total sense right now.

"And then I find out all this stuff about my birth parents," she goes on, "but I never got to meet them. I barely know a thing about them! And now I'm supposed to rule Westphalia and carry on their legacy? How can I rule a kingdom when I don't even live here full time?"

They're silent for a bit. That intense fear she felt when creating Ira Glassman is weaseling its way back into her chest. She tried to suppress it then and, in the hubbub of creating her talking mirror, was able to forget it a little. But now— now that she's actually here, in Westphalia—it's back in full force. She's supposed to rule this kingdom? She doesn't know the first thing about ruling! She doesn't know how to take care of a whole nation of people; she doesn't even know how to take care of herself!

Has she said too much? Is she dumping too much emotion onto Jack? She should never have said all that. She's being too vulnerable. This isn't his problem, and she's being way too open with him. Right? But she can't help herself. *Why isn't he saying anything?*

"If we do succeed in all this," Filomena says, "and I do become queen of Westphalia, what happens then?"

"What do you mean?"

"Like, do I have to choose which world I live in? Do I stay in Never After forever, give up my life in the mortal world, never see my parents again? Do I have to stay in Westphalia permanently? Or do I just visit sometimes? How will it all work? Will I still see you all? Where will you, Gretel, and Alistair be? Will we still see each other?"

Jack is silent for a beat. Then he says, "I think we just need to focus on keeping the ogres out of the castles and on meeting this deadline before we can go that far."

Filomena gets a slight sinking feeling. Does he not want to stick with her after she's crowned? What about Gretel and Alistair? Never After will be just as lonely as the mortal world without her friends.

They start to climb another hill. They're about halfway to the castle from where they started.

Jack's right. Her being crowned is the best-case scenario. Her not meeting that deadline . . . Well, that would mean a reign of terror she can't even imagine. She's barely even had time to think about the deaths of two great fairies, Colette and Scheherazade.

"Jack, I know that no one really brought this up with you, but I'm so sorry about Zera. If I'm torn up about it, I can't even imagine how much pain you must be in."

Jack just nods silently. Filomena can tell it's still too fresh for him to really talk about. But she wanted to say that to him, all the same.

Her fear creeps back in. "Maybe the ogres and the prime minister are right." She sighs.

At this, Jack stops in his tracks. "Whoa, whoa," he says. "Now that can't be true. Right about what?"

"About me ruling over Westphalia. Maybe I'm *not* ready."

Jack is quiet for a moment.

"I'm sorry," he says. "It's just that . . . it's freaking me out a bit, what you're saying."

Oh great. He can't handle her and she's already freaking him out. Guess she can kiss a first kiss goodbye. She looks at her feet as they continue the walk, not making eye contact.

"The thing is, it's freaking me out how much I feel like you're describing me," Jack finally admits. "All that stuff about your parents, about feeling like you're always out of place."

Now that's a surprise. She looks up at him.

"I feel exactly the same, Fil. I've always felt out of place, my whole life. Ever since my village burned down, I've felt alone. I have Alistair, of course, and I have friends in Never After and allies everywhere. But I've been running my whole life. It's always been on to the next adventure, the next quest. Always someone to rescue or something to figure out. It's lonely."

Now Jack's the one staring at his feet as he talks. Filomena's looking right at him, though, silently urging him to go on.

"And what you said about not knowing how to rule Westphalia? I get it. No one taught me how to be Jack the Giant Stalker. Sometimes it feels like it just happened *to* me. Like I had no choice. And maybe that's true."

At this, Filomena can't be quiet anymore. "Aren't you the one who reminded me that we choose our own destiny?"

He smiles at the ground. Then he looks up at her, locking eyes with her own. She feels heat on her cheeks. She almost trips over a rock.

"Sometimes I feel like you're the only one who really understands," he says. "We have a lot in common, even though we also have nothing in common."

They both laugh. They're silent for a few paces. While they're being truthful, Filomena feels the need to say something she's been thinking about ever since they learned of the summer solstice deadline.

But then Jack stops her, touching her shoulder. "Hey," he says.

She turns to face him. They're standing so close now.

"I know at first we were only going to do it to break an enchantment," he says. "But I meant what I said. I don't need a curse to break to know I want to, uh . . ." Suddenly he gets shy. He looks at his feet, takes a breath. "To do this."

He leans in, but before anything else can happen, an all-too-familiar voice calls to them from behind: "Glad to see you lovebirds are going strong!"

Filomena would recognize that voice anywhere. They whip around.

Standing on the hill before them are Robin Hood and Little Jeanne.

CHAPTER THIRTY-FOUR

GIRL, INTERRUPTED

"This is, like, the fluffiest bed I've ever seen," Alistair says, jumping butt-first onto Hortense's princess bed.

"I'm so glad to see you guys," Hortense says, throwing her arms around Gretel for the fourth time since she and Alistair walked in the castle doors a few minutes ago.

Hortense's room at the Eastphalian castle is mega-cool. After the carriage ride with opera singer Lillet and now, being at Eastphalia's castle—whose architecture is highly influenced by the glamorous singer as well—Gretel's starting to get a taste for fashion and decor.

"We are pleased to be at your service, soon-to-be Queen Hortense," Gretel says, doing a little jokey curtsy.

Hortense laughs and swipes at Gretel. "Stop that! You're in no service to me. Though I suppose we do have quite a bit of work to do."

"Yes, thank you both for coming to my rescue," Charlie, in his froggy form, says from his place on Hortense's shoulder.

Alistair just about jumps out of his skin. "Talking frog! Talking frog!" he yells.

"Ali, you know Charlie was turned into a frog," Gretel says. "What are you freaking out for?"

"I know he was turned into a frog," Alistair whispers to Gretel, using one hand blocking his mouth from Charlie's view. "I just didn't think he'd be able to *talk*. It's a bit unnerving, no?"

"Alistair, I can hear as well as speak!" Charlie says. "Just because I'm a frog, it doesn't mean I can't communicate. I'm still my normal self on the inside."

At that moment, Charlie's frog tongue stretches across the room to catch a fly, which he then swallows.

Alistair stares in shock and disgust. "Sure, your 'normal self,' totally," he says.

Gretel turns to Hortense. "So does anyone suspect what's going on? That Charlie's a frog prince?"

"Nope," Hortense responds. "They just think I've become a bit of an eccentric, carrying a frog on my shoulder all the time. The townspeople just believe I'm a little kooky, I guess."

"Quirky girls are very popular in the mortal world right

now," Gretel says. "If it's any consolation. We can totally say it's a trend you picked up from the manic pixie dream girls of the mortal realm."

"There are pixie dream girls in the mortal world?" Alistair is very intrigued. "What are they like?"

"No, no, not actual pixies," Gretel tries to clarify. "Never mind. We'll just say it's a trend."

"Well, hopefully we'll figure out how to turn this frog prince back into a real prince, and then we won't have to make me a manic pixie whatever at all." Hortense laughs.

Gretel is feeling pretty confident in her curse-breaking abilities after the whole Rosie's-swan-brothers thing, plus the Jack-and-Filomena-kissing thing. Wait—hold on a minute! Jack and Filomena are alone on their quest right now! She hadn't even thought of that! Gretel wishes Never After had cell phones so she could get updates from Fil.

Back to more pressing matters.

"Luckily for you, Alistair and I are fresh off a curse-breaking streak. So let's see. How can we break this spell?" Gretel starts pacing the room, circling Hortense and Charlie. "Charlie, do you remember the specific words Olga used when she put the curse on you?"

Charlie scratches his head with an amphibian toe. "It's all a blur, really. I don't remember the words of the spell."

"Okay, so that's not so helpful."

Gretel remembers what Colette told them about being cursed by Queen Christina.

"Hortense, Charlie, both the curses we saw broken were cast by Queen Christina. One of the fairies, Colette—or Snow White—told us that Queen Christina has the sort of magic that can only mimic transformation, or make things appear differently than they are. That is why her curses can always be reversed."

Alistair nods along. "Kind of like the way Charlie's still his 'normal self on the inside' even though he eats flies now."

Gretel ignores this. "So that's good news for us, because I'm willing to bet that ogre queen Olga has the same type of magic, the kind used for evil. That kind of magic is only a thin veil pulled over the truth."

"Okay." Hortense agrees. "I'm following. So what do we do about it?"

"We just have to figure out the right code and crack it. That will reverse the spell!" Gretel says gleefully.

Except that doesn't actually get them any closer. Gretel thinks. She's only ever seen two spells broken in her life, and they both had very specific ways by which to break. May as well try both those methods, right?

"Do you have star flowers on the castle property by any chance?"

An hour later, Gretel and Alistair have realized the answer to that question is no, there are no star flowers. They might be something specific to Snow Country. However, there is an abundance of bleeding heart flowers, which Gretel feels could be a great fit. Bonus: They only need to make one frog-sized shirt rather than seven large swan-sized shirts. They don't even have to dry the flowers!

Alistair and Gretel bring the tiny bleeding heart shirt up to Hortense's room. Hortense has placed Charlie on her bed. She doesn't want him transforming into a human while sitting on her shoulder, after all. They fit the little garment over Charlie's tiny frog body.

Three . . . two . . . one . . .

Nothing. Nothing happens. No transformation, no hint of a breaking curse.

"You're sure this worked last time?" Charlie says. "I'm not feeling anything."

Trying hard not to be deterred, Gretel thinks of the other curse whose breaking they witnessed. "So . . . what about true love's kiss?" she asks.

"We already tried that," Hortense says glumly. "I've kissed those froggy lips so many times, I'm starting to taste flies."

Gretel thinks and thinks. Who else could be a true love's kiss? Maybe it could be between two bystanders. But the only bystanders here are herself and . . .

Alistair?!

Gretel laughs out loud, and everyone looks at her, like *what?*

She has never, never once considered Alistair to be her

true love. Her true *friend* love, sure, but she's not certain that counts. But is it worth a try?

"This might sound crazy," Gretel says to Alistair, "and to be up front, I'm not suggesting I'm romantically into you, dude . . ."

Alistair suddenly starts to sweat.

"But," Gretel continues, "I do love you! As a friend," she clarifies.

"Oh thank goodness! I don't love you either! I mean not in *that* way! Only as a friend," he echoes, wiping his brow.

"But maybe we could still give it a try? For Charlie," Gretel says. "And, again, not romantic!"

Alistair is still incredibly flustered. Gretel's not thrilled with the concept, either. But she can't think of what other solution there might be at the moment. So, okay.

They stand facing each other. Should she close her eyes? No, that's weird. That's too romantic. But isn't keeping them open creepy? She purses her lips a little; so does he. They lean forward and Gretel plants a peck on his cheek.

Nothing.

Charlie's still a frog.

"Oh well," says Alistair, looking relieved it's over. "At least we tried."

Gretel laughs.

"Hello!" a bright voice calls from the doorway. Alistair and Gretel jump away from each other. "Sorry, am I interrupting?" It's a boy their age. He's carrying a tea tray.

"No, come in, John. Come hang out!" Hortense says. "This is John, everyone. He's a page at the castle and also my friend."

"I brought some tea for you all," John says, "and I hope you don't mind, but I overheard a little of your conversation about the curse."

Figures. Gretel can be pretty loud when working out a problem.

"I think I may know how to help," John says. Sitting down on the sofa that faces Hortense's bed, John begins to explain. "What I'm about to tell you is very, very secret information. And I know it might be silly of me to tell the future king and queen of Eastphalia this, but, Hortense, you've been a very kind princess. So I hope I can trust you."

"Of course you can, John! I'd never do anything to put you in harm's way," Hortense says, patting his hand.

"All right, then. I have an aunt who lives in the village. I think she can help you with this . . . situation," he says, nodding to Charlie. He lowers his voice even more. "She's a witch," he whispers.

Hortense's eyebrows shoot up. A witch living in Eastphalia? Everyone knows witches are very rare in Never After and can be very dangerous. Getting involved with one can put a person at great risk.

"I believe she can tell you how to reverse the spell."

Hortense looks troubled by this, but Gretel perks up. "You know, Hori, the way we broke the spell on Rosie's brothers was by carrying out what a witch told Rosie to do. I don't think it's a bad idea."

"I don't know," Hori says nervously.

"If I go with you, she might be more willing to help," John offers. "But you'll have to barter. You should bring her some food."

"Food?" Alistair inserts. "That sounds like a job for me!"

"What do you think, Charlie?" Hori asks.

"I think I'd love to be human again. And I'm willing to visit a witch to figure out how to make that happen," he ribbits.

That seems to settle it. Hori is all business. "John, thank you so much. If you're willing to take us, then I say let's do it!"

"Off to the witch of Eastphalia we go!" Gretel says.

"But first," Alistair pipes in, "to the kitchen! You know what they say: The way to a witch's heart is through her stomach."

CHAPTER THIRTY-FIVE

THE BROKEN MIRROR

It's a lot for a girl to take in all at once. First, Filomena was just about to have her first kiss, she's sure of it. Her first kiss! With Jack! Except it didn't happen because, second, Robin Hood is here, in Westphalia, on the hill before them. And to top it all off, Little Jeanne is standing with him. Which means . . . Filomena was right. There *was* something off about Little Jeanne!

"I'd love to catch up, but we're a bit pinched for time," Robin Hood says, smirking and shrugging. "I'm actually here for something other than seeing if you two finally get together. Finally got some guts there, Stalker!"

Jack glowers in Robin's direction.

Filomena instantly feels fired up. How dare he mock them! That was—that was such a special, sacred moment that's now ruined! She and Jack both pull their Dragon's Tooth swords from their belts and hold them out, readying for an attack.

"What do you want, Robin?" Filomena says, her eyes squinting with suspicion.

"Now this will be so much easier if you just let me do my job. Look, I don't care about the ogres, I have no real moral allegiance to anything. I'm a hand for hire. Can you really fault me for that?"

"Yes," Fil and Jack say in unison.

Robin raises his hands in surrender. "Okay, okay, fair enough. But look"—he places a hand over his heart—"underneath it all, I'm a good guy. I'm a guy in love! You see, let me tell you my story."

Filomena's getting pinpricks of alarm. What does he want? Why is he being so agreeable, trying to be sympathetic?

"Princess Jeanne and I were very close as children. I'm working with the ogres just so I can get her back, all right? And to get paid. It's as simple as that. I have nothing against you folks, really! I like you, even! In my own way."

"You *like* us?" Jack spits, walking toward Robin with his sword poised. "If you like us so much, then how about you stop being so selfish and join the right side? There's a lot more at stake than your childhood friendship, all right? The entire kingdom is at stake here. Do you know how evil the ogres are? Do you know the monstrosities they've caused?"

The two boys are so close now, face-to-face. Jack is seething; every wrongdoing he's seen the ogres commit is flashing before his eyes, Filomena knows. She's watching Robin closely, terrified that Robin Hood will take a swing at Jack when Jack least suspects. She can't bear for Jack to get hurt. But something's tugging on her hip . . . *What's that?*

Suddenly Robin's hand shoots up into the air and catches something. *Ira Glassman!* Little Jeanne grabbed him from Filomena's belt while Robin was distracting them!

"No hard feelings?" Robin taunts. "Just another job that gets me paid, you know. Especially since the last one didn't work out. Ogres say I have to destroy this." And with that he punches Filomena's talking mirror, smashing the surface to bits.

"No!" Filomena screams. All reassurance of her power—that she can do this, can take over a kingdom, can create a talking mirror from thin air—her ability to check in on her friends, her ability to communicate with all of Never After and to tell *her* side of the story . . . All that was wrapped up in her talking mirror.

Having adequately shattered the mirror, Robin drops it onto the ground.

Filomena turns around to see Little Jeanne, who has a scared look on her face. Filomena is filled with rage and lunges with her sword, pinning the young princess to a tree. Little Jeanne screams as if she didn't know Filomena to be capable of this.

"Well, I'll be off! Nice seeing you, then!" Robin shouts, and sprints away.

"You're leaving me?!" Little Jeanne screams after him, but he doesn't turn.

Jack gives chase, but Robin is an expert at sneaky exits and after a few minutes in the hills, Jack loses him. Meanwhile, Filomena keeps Little Jeanne pinned to the tree with her sword.

"He left me!" the princess wails.

"You traitor!" Filomena shouts. "You betrayed your own sister. How could you do this? How could you?!"

"I didn't!" Little Jeanne is sobbing.

But Filomena is sobbing, too. Lowering her sword, she crawls over to pick up Ira Glassman, who's smashed beyond recognition. She loved her talking mirror, she realizes. Ira helped her to feel safe. And now he's broken, completely broken. Robin took away her power, her fairy power. Every fairy can animate only one mirror, and this was hers. She cradles the talking mirror in her arms. There's no smoky face to be found in its smashed surface. Only shards.

Just then, Jack, breathing heavily and cursing, returns from his futile chase after Robin Hood. Little Jeanne is still slumped against the tree, quietly crying. Jack keeps his sword pointed at her so she doesn't move. The three are silent for a few beats as they take in what just happened.

Then Filomena speaks. This time she's not yelling; her voice is measured. "Little Jeanne, how could you?" she whispers.

"It wasn't supposed to be like this," she says. "It wasn't supposed to go this far. I thought if I gave Richard the crown, he would leave my sister alone." She slides down the tree trunk so that she's sitting on the ground, too. She puts her head in her hands.

"Little Jeanne, I think you owe us an explanation," Jack says sternly but not unkindly. His sword is still pointed in her direction.

She looks up, her face covered in tears. "You know Princess Jeanne and Robin Hood were friends when they were kids?" she starts. They nod.

"Well, I was always jealous of them. Jeanne always ditched me for Robin, so I was jealous of him, but I also loved Robin, so I was jealous of her. And how do you think it feels to live in the shadow of a princess for your whole life? And being referred to only as 'Little Jeanne'? I don't even have my own name! I've never been my own person. I've always just been a shadow of her.

"When Robin approached me for help, I didn't really

know what we were doing. I just knew that, finally, it felt like he was choosing me over her, like *I'd* get to be the main Jeanne. I could do something different from her. Then it started to get out of hand. I didn't realize how serious it all was, and then it was too late."

"What was your uncle and Robin Hood's plan?"

"They wanted me to steal the crown. So I did. It was easy. My sister trusts me," Little Jeanne tells them. "But it wouldn't fit Uncle Richard's head. The magic in it rejected him. I know about the legend of the crown so I wasn't surprised but I guess Uncle Richard thought he could fool the crown. But he didn't. So he thought he'd just take the kingdom by force, but the Northphalian people still need to see a ruler wear the ancient crown of the North.

"So they came up with a new plan: They would put the crown on my head, and Uncle Richard would rule as regent. I mean, they already call him king as it is. He figured one Jeanne is as good as another. But the crown didn't fit me, either. It wouldn't accept me. So I was useless. Then I hoped Robin would run away with me, but instead he left me here. I'm so, so stupid."

Jack and Filomena look at each other, unsure of what to do. She feels awful for Little Jeanne and for the crimes she was willing to commit. Filomena looks at the shattered mirror in her lap. The damage is done.

But there are still kingdoms to save.

"Where is your sister's crown now?" she asks.

Little Jeanne slowly reaches into her skirt pocket. "Here." What she reveals is a crown of twigs and leaves—a simple thing, not at all golden or bejeweled. It's a crown from the fairies and the spirits that protect Never After.

"Little Jeanne," Filomena says in a burst of realization. "I remember now—I remember from the books. You have to get that crown on your sister's head. The minute she's crowned, King Richard's army will turn to dust."

Chapter Thirty-Six

Mary, Mary, Quite Contrary

At least the Northphalian kingdom is safe. Princess Jeanne will be crowned queen. After assessing that Little Jeanne was no longer a threat, they let her go. But for now, Filomena and Jack still have a mission to fulfill.

Not only is the castle waiting in Westphalia; a person waits, too. Jack and Filomena walked in silence away from that fateful hill, and now, as they approach, they see a figure—a woman—in the castle's open doorway who stands calm as a still lake.

"Are you finding this unnerving at all?" Jack whispers as they near.

The truth is, the woman isn't unnerving. There's something instantly soothing about her to Filomena. Her shock of white hair, her flowing robes, the warm, welcoming aura of her presence. Filomena's prized possession was just obliterated, and this person feels like a vibe shift.

"I think I like her already," Filomena whispers back.

"Let's withhold any judgments until we know who she is," Jack responds.

Despite her intuition, Filomena knows he's right. Queen Olga's spies are everywhere.

"Hello Princess Eliana and Jack the Giant Stalker," the woman says as they get closer. From far away it was impossible to measure her height; the doorframe to the castle is shockingly large. But at this distance, Filomena sees she is extremely tall.

"I go by Filomena, actually," she says. "At least, that's what my friends call me." She still hasn't worked out how to deal with the whole double name thing. Another complication of living in two worlds.

"Well, Filomena, let us hope that we shall be friends. I will call you by whatever name you like."

"And what should we call you?" Jack inquires, bowing.

"Mary," she says.

Something appears to click in Jack's head when she says this. "Mary Contrary?" he asks.

"Quite," Mary answers. "I was hoping you would be coming by," she says to Filomena. "I have much to discuss with you."

"Pardon me if this is rude to ask," Filomena says, "but who are you?"

"That's an entirely logical question for someone in your position to ask, Filomena. Not rude at all. Logic is never rude."

"Not sure that's true," Jack mutters. Filomena almost laughs. She assumes he must be remembering the time when Rosie told him that, statistically speaking, he's below the average height of a hero.

"Why don't you come to my office and you can ask me all the questions you'd like?" Mary asks.

Filomena glances at Jack, who looks slightly suspicious. He shrugs, and they follow Mary through the castle and up several flights of stairs to her office.

The office itself is unlike any Filomena has been in. Both her parents' offices are quite minimalist—Rosie would love them, come to think of it—with blond wood desks, stacks of papers, and large windows that bathe the room in light and look out onto lemon trees.

But Mary Contrary's office is something else altogether. *Office* doesn't seem like the right word for it exactly. It looks like someplace an alchemist might conduct their work. Large stone arches curve across the ceiling. There are walls of bookshelves with ladders to reach the highest books, right up to the ceiling. And it's so dark! The only window is stained-glass. Everything looks ancient.

"Wow," Filomena says. "Have you read all these?"

"The books?" Mary responds. "Most of them, yes. But I always keep a shelf of unread books, just in case."

Filomena is in awe. She walks around, looking at the spines. Heaven!

"You're welcome to borrow any you like," Mary says.

"Really? That's amazing!"

"You will be living here soon enough, after all," Mary continues.

That stops Filomena a little cold, her excitement dying down a bit. "Right." Brought back to Earth, she recalls the reason they're at the castle. To be crowned, hopefully, and for whatever lies beyond.

"Sit, sit," Mary says, motioning to the red leather couch in front of her desk. Filomena and Jack take seats side by side. Mary Contrary sits facing them, perched on a throne-like chair, which seems to be her desk chair. "Even after the prime minister made that horrid announcement about you not taking your responsibilities seriously, I knew you'd come to claim your place on the throne. And then, when *you* made an announcement? Genius! You've been the talk of the kingdoms ever since. It's caused a real stir. Reignited a lot of hope. I saw some of your mother in you, with that pluck."

Filomena feels flushed hearing this. And proud.

"How did you do it, by the way?" Mary asks. "Did you break into an ogre's lair? Take one of the talking mirrors?"

There's a pause.

"Actually, we sort of DIY'd it," Filomena says.

Mary looks confused.

"She's being modest," Jack chimes in. "Filomena created a talking mirror herself."

Now Mary looks shocked. "You created a talking mirror? I've never heard of such a thing!"

"Zera told me she thought I might be able to, since I—" Filomena cuts herself off. Suddenly she feels uncertain how many details she should share of herself with this person. After all, she doesn't even know who Mary Contrary is. She's filled with sadness, though, thinking of Ira Glassman belted at her waist, smashed to bits.

"Would you mind telling us who you are now?" Filomena asks.

Jack looks relieved that she asked. Filomena gets the sense that he hasn't been totally put at ease yet. His hand's been resting close to his hip, where his Dragon's Tooth sword is sheathed, this whole time.

"Of course, darling. So I'm Mary Contrary, as you know, but, more important, I'm the regent of Westphalia. After your parents died—rest their souls—I was put in charge of the kingdom on a strictly administrative level. You see, I was your parents' adviser during their reign. They found my contrary nature very helpful in the decision-making process. But I was also their close friend."

Filomena sees Jack relax, his hand coming away from his hip.

"You knew my parents?" she asks, surprised.

"Yes, my dear, I knew them very well. Your mother's and father's deaths were the greatest griefs of my life. They were like family to me."

Filomena feels she might cry, hearing this. A swell of relief rises in her chest. Abruptly, and without thinking, she stands and runs to hug Mary. Mary smells very nice, like a garden.

"Oh, oh my," Mary says, flustered. "My dear," she says, stroking Filomena's hair affectionately.

Filomena pulls away and wipes her eyes. Apparently she's started crying. How many times will she cry today? That's not the way to start ruling a kingdom. But then again, she is only twelve.

"Can you tell me what they were like?" Filomena says, sitting back down on the couch next to Jack. She's always been hesitant to ask people about her parents, worried that she'd hear rumors or something untrue. But if there's anyone to ask, it seems like it's this woman. Filomena's distanced herself from the thought of her birth parents almost every time they enter her mind. But being in their castle now, where she was born and where they lived, she's curious. She's ready to hear about them.

"They were the best kind of people. Such full, open hearts. They loved to laugh, to be in each other's presence. They would hold fabulous open dinners at the castle once a fortnight, where any citizen from the kingdom was welcome to drop in. They were beloved, and they loved Westphalia. And they loved you, Filomena, even though they barely got a chance to know you."

Filomena tries not to cry again, but she can't help it. She's leaking. Jack puts his arm around her. Hearing about this set of parents is making her think, too, of her adoptive parents in North Pasadena. How long has she been gone? How is her mother doing now? She wishes she could hug her mom. It all feels like so much pressure, all of this. And now she has to run this kingdom?

"Mary," Filomena says, "I'm scared. Even if I do become queen, I'm so young. How can I run a kingdom?"

"I'm sure this is all very overwhelming for you, Filomena," Mary continues. "I know you grew up in the mortal world and have only recently learned about your involvement in our world. But already you've done such a tremendous amount of good. I've read the papers. People across kingdoms have told me about your bravery, how you've helped them. You have a lion's heart, and that is what the ruler of a kingdom needs. Whatever else you need to know, I'll be happy to guide you through. I'll be here with you. And trust me, I've been helping to run this kingdom for decades—besides during Queen Olga's takeover. I know what I'm doing." She winks.

Filomena feels the tears recede, replaced by something ferocious and daring. Her heart is pumping. She wipes her cheeks.

"Now, I know this is all moving quickly, but I think that it's best to work fast on your coronation," Mary says. "The sooner, the better, as far as the ogres are concerned. To give you a brief update: Since you broke Queen Olga's spell, the reign of terror has ceased, but ogres still patrol the borders of Westphalia, and things have been known to get messy. As soon as they get wind you're here . . . Well, I don't want to know what that will look like. Time is of the essence. We can get some rest this evening, but a ceremony first thing tomorrow might be the ticket. How does that sound?"

Filomena's taking it all in. Ogres on the borders. The kingdom still in danger. Queendom tomorrow. Can she handle this?

She has to. "Good," she tells Mary.

Filomena smiles weakly at Jack, hoping her false confidence is convincing. Ready or not, queendom comes.

But before she can get too comfortable with the idea, a loud crash sounds from the bowels of the castle. Jack sniffs the air. Then a stricken look washes over his face.

"Ogres."

CHAPTER THIRTY-SEVEN

THE WITCH OF EASTPHALIA

Eastphalia's market is a bustling place. Wooden carts drive down narrow walkways filled with rich red carpets, woolen caps, beautiful wicker furniture, and all varieties of fabrics. On each side of the walkways are wooden booths selling everything from marbled cuts of meat to lush vegetables and herbs to the most fragrant flowers Gretel's ever smelled. She's been eyeing one booth in particular: It has a stack of silks she'd love to take a closer look at, but just as she touches the silks to determine if they're real (she has a great sense about these things), Hortense yanks her away.

Now, Gretel, Alistair, Hortense, and Hortense's pet frog—aka her husband, aka cursed Prince Charlie—are all following page boy John down a narrow alleyway.

"Are you sure we're allowed in this area?" Alistair says, tapping John on the shoulder.

John turns around with an impish grin on his face. "Oh, definitely not. We'd get in so much trouble if anyone saw us walking over here. But don't worry, that's why we came at the busiest time of day. No one will even notice, they're too busy hawking their goods!"

The group weaves through alleyways for a few more minutes in silence. Not total silence, since around them is total chaos, but none of them speak, weaving and winding in single file. This is really reminding Gretel of the ancient Greek myth of Daedalus's labyrinth. She really hopes that Hori trusts this John, because if he ditches them, Gretel will have no idea how to get out of here.

Finally they come to a small wooden hut tucked between two rowdy booths serving street food. John motions for everyone to stand back, then knocks on the door with an elaborate sequence of taps and pauses that sounds like an advanced Morse code. They wait.

Then a frail woman opens the door, squinting. "Johnny!" she says, her arms flinging open in a welcoming hug. "What are you doing, my boy? I thought I told you to visit me here only in emergencies."

"I know, *Obasan*, but this *is* an emergency, actually." He motions to the alley's shadows, where Gretel, Alistair, Hori, and Charlie are standing. Except for Charlie, who's actually squatting.

"Oh my, what is going on? These are friends of yours?"

"Yes, they're very kind. This is Hortense, princess of East-phalia."

John's aunt's eyes widen. She motions for them to enter and disappears into the hut.

Once inside, Gretel feels immediate calm. The scents of tea leaves and essential oils are in the air. There are beautiful tapestries on the walls, large rugs on the carpet, and many books and instruments that look meant for cooking or something else. Spells?

John's aunt says nothing, doesn't mention sitting, asks them no questions. She begins to putter around, ignoring them. John looks at Alistair and nods toward his aunt.

"Excuse me, but we've brought you a small offering," Alistair says. He holds out a plate with a pyramid of delicious-looking tiny round treats of various colors, each dusted with soft powder. Green, black, pink. "These mochi are our humble offering to you," Alistair continues, bowing.

John's aunt eyes the mochi for a moment, then plucks a black one from the platter and takes a bite.

"Black sesame." She smiles. "Well done. I'm Eichi. You may sit down."

Gretel is impressed; Ali's cooking skills have come in handy yet again. He whipped those mochi up in no time in Hori's kitchen!

"What do you children seek from me?" Eichi asks.

John lets Hortense take the lead. "Eichi, thank you so much for seeing us. John works with me at the castle, and he graciously led us to you, thinking you may be of help to a very difficult situation I'm in," Hortense says.

"Yes, yes, I know why you're here," Eichi says. "I asked just as a formality, dear. I saw the announcement like everyone else. You're in trouble, are you not?"

"Yes, we are, Eichi. You see this frog on my shoulder? This is my husband, Prince Charlemagne. The ogre queen Olga turned him into a frog, hoping to prevent him from becoming king and me from becoming queen! The prime minister thinks the monarchy should be stopped, but it will be a reign of terror if the ogres take over in our stead. Please, we need to know how to break the curse and transform Charlie back into a human so we can be crowned before the summer solstice."

Eichi eats her mochi in silence for a moment, considering what to say next. Finally, she speaks: "While the prime minister has many faults, he is right in one regard: Monarchy is a complicated way to run a kingdom."

Gretel feels panic bubble in her stomach. Is Eichi against them?

"The right to rule is a serious thing, and it is complicated, monarchy. To be quite honest, we were all uncertain as to what Charlie will be like as a king. But marrying you, Hortense, shows that he has more gumption than we thought."

Hortense seems confused. If Gretel could read frog expressions, she'd say Charlie looks mortified.

Eichi continues: "Hortense, I know you, on behalf of the citizens of Eastphalia, have been battling certain traditions that Charlie's parents uphold. You fight for fairness and for the rights of your citizens even though you don't have to. I can tell you feel accountable to this kingdom."

"I do, Eichi. I really do. And I know Charlie does, too."

"If he doesn't, I expect he will learn from you. And perhaps being a frog will have taught him what it's like to lose control, to have no power over your circumstances." Eichi looks directly at Charlie now. "Maybe you will remember this the next time you make a decision for those less fortunate in the kingdom. Remember what it's like to feel powerless."

Charlie ribbits in agreement. Gretel bets he's too petrified to say anything and is capitalizing off the fact that Eichi doesn't know the curse maintained his ability to speak.

"Now, in terms of breaking the curse . . . Let me take a look," Eichi says. She places her hand on Charlie's head and closes her eyes. "Ah, yes." She chuckles. "This makes perfect sense. This will be a good test, Prince Charlemagne. You will have to see what your citizens are made of and what they are willing to do for you. Only one elixir can reverse this curse. You must consume something your citizens make for you of their own free will."

Gretel glances at Ali. *Something his citizens make for him?* That seems so cryptic. But Eichi doesn't say anymore. She seems to believe that everything they need to reverse the enchantment has been said. She gives a little bow and wishes them the best of luck.

The four kids plus one frog file out of Eichi's hut, bowing to her one by one. Then they're back in the harsh daylight, trying to figure out what exactly she means.

CHAPTER THIRTY-EIGHT
Stone Soup

Gretel, Alistair, Hortense, John, and froggy Charlie walk through the winding Eastphalian marketplace, trying to brainstorm.

"I could make lots of things for Charlie to eat or drink," Alistair says. "Would that count, even though I'm not technically one of his citizens?"

"It sounds like the elixir has to be made by a group of citizens," Gretel says. "I think that's the important part."

"What exactly constitutes an elixir, anyway?" Hortense asks.

"I think it's similar to a potion. So I guess anything liquid?" John answers.

Walking between the market stalls, Gretel tries to jump-start some ideas. Organizing a group of citizens to do anything seems difficult, though organization and event planning are both definitely in Gretel's wheelhouse. They could throw a party? But how can they get the citizens of Eastphalia to create something for Charlie to drink, even at a party? Eichi didn't explicitly say that they can't just tell the citizens to make something, but Gretel knows that curses often have unspoken rules.

They walk by a booth filled with luscious vegetables and Alistair asks to stop. Rolling her eyes, Gretel gives in. As Alistair ogles silky eggplants and tomatoes, vibrant carrots and turnips, and fragrant bunches of herbs, something sparks in Gretel's mind.

It reminds her of a story from the mortal world: a folktale known as "Stone Soup." In the story, in a village not dissimilar to this one, a stranger comes to town and says they're going to make stone soup. The only ingredient they have is a stone, but they encourage the townspeople to contribute ingredients. They end up making a soup for all to enjoy.

The solution dawns on Gretel.

"We're making Charlie stone soup!" she cries.

You wouldn't think it easy to quickly procure a giant cast-iron pot or a roaring outdoor fire, but when you're a princess, many such feats are possible. That's what Gretel's learning. It helps that there's just such a pot left over from the kingdom-wide soup-eating contest Eastphalia held during last year's fall festival.

And so Gretel and Alistair are set up in the town square with a massive soup pot over a toasty fire. Alistair even has a step stool so that he can reach inside the pot to stir. John and Hortense are running through the marketplace and the village, knocking on doors and spreading the news that, in the center of town, a celebratory soup for Prince Charlie is being prepared as a homecoming gift, and anyone who contributes an ingredient can share in the soup and welcome their prince home, a preemptive celebration of his rule to come.

Gretel thinks this is also a good test of Prince Charlie's popularity among his citizens. What Eichi said about monarchy made her think, and she is secretly interested to see if enough citizens care about Prince Charlie's rule to contribute to the soup.

"So far it looks like we have a stone and some boiling water in here," Alistair says, stirring the pot. "Not looking too promising."

"I don't think you need to start stirring until we have some actual food," Gretel adds.

"Good point," he says, getting off the step stool. "So you think this will work? You think enough people will care to come and have soup?"

"I think Hortense doing the rounds will certainly help. People seem to really like her," Gretel responds.

"Yeah, even if they are like, *Why does that girl have a frog on her shoulder?*"

They both start laughing.

"Hey, you know what we haven't talked about yet?" Alistair adds. "We kissed!"

"I only kissed you on the cheek, doofus!"

"I closed my eyes and everything!" Alistair yelps.

They break out in hysterics, this time at the concept of their kissing. Even as friends, it's too funny. Gretel's stomach is actually cramping up with how hard she's laughing. When the laughter dies down and they wipe their eyes, they're shocked to see a whole lineup of Eastphalian folks with baskets of vegetables and meat and bunches of herbs in their hands.

"Is this where we contribute to the soup?" a lady asks kindly.

"Wow!" Alistair jumps up, standing on his stool by the pot. "This might actually work!"

"Yes, come on up," Gretel says. "Please add your contributions! And stick around—Alistair's made peony punch for us all!"

Alistair leans toward the people in line and adds, "My take on peony fizz. It's a bit fruitier, richer. Let me know what you think."

And the people keep coming and keep coming. A little girl carries a bushel of apples. An old lady presents a delicate-looking artichoke. A handsome elderly fellow offers sprigs of sage and thyme.

"These apples are from the orchard by my house," the little girl says.

"This artichoke is from my family's farm," the old lady says.

"These herbs are from my garden," the fellow says.

Gretel starts to worry that these ingredients will create something most foul, but Alistair graciously accepts each item, then quickly measures, chops, and tosses it in. And there's nothing Gretel trusts Alistair with more than creating something delicious. Except maybe having her back. So they're doubly covered, then!

John and Hortense return, having knocked on every door and notified every stall at the market. By the time they arrive, it's a full-fledged party. Everyone's cheering Alistair's peony punch—he tells every single guest his tweaks to the classic Northphalian recipe—and there's dancing, laughter, greetings.

"Princess Hortense!" a girl cries, seeing Hortense join the action. "You're my favorite princess! Is it true that you have a bow and arrows?"

"It is true, lovely girl. I'm a pretty great shot, too," Hortense says, patting the girl on the head.

"*Wooow*," the little girl says, looking up at Hortense in awe.

An older woman approaches Hortense. "Princess, I want

to thank you. I read in the *Never After Post* that you fought to include the outer boroughs of the kingdom in the palace-aid program. I live in an outer borough, and it's helped me so much. It got me through the bad harvest of last fall, kept food on the table for my grandchildren. Thank you for fighting for us," the woman says, patting Hortense's hand.

Gretel almost cries with pride. Her cousin is going to make such a good queen! And the people love her! Eichi, once again, was correct.

Gretel's enjoying this display of community so much that she forgets why they're all there.

"I think it's ready," Alistair says to Gretel. "Who wants soup?!" he asks the crowd.

Hortense, John, and Gretel work to ladle out soup and pass servings down a line to each person who contributed (and to those who didn't). Then, when everyone has a cup of soup, it's time to feed the frog.

Hortense places Charlie on the ground. He can't transform on her shoulder, after all! Gretel's holding her breath. Hortense ladles one spoonful after another into Charlie's froggy mouth until he's eaten almost a whole bowl of the stuff. Then she stands back.

At first—nothing. Gretel's heart drops to her stomach. But then . . . a flicker. And suddenly the frog grows and grows, though he's not looking so green. There, there he is! In human form! Prince Charlie!

Hortense begins to weep and throws herself into her

prince's arms. Gretel thanks the fairies that Queen Olga's spell differs from the curse Queen Christina cast on Rosie's seven brothers: Charlie is not, thank goodness, naked.

A collective gasp goes through the crowd. The faces of the villagers are shocked. Or appalled? They're suddenly very scared. Parents cover their children's eyes. Of course! How did Gretel not think of this? It's terrifying to watch a curse break even when you know what's going on. They need damage control, stat!

But Hortense, already a polished princess, is on it. She stands atop Alistair's stool and faces her people.

"Citizens of Eastphalia! As many of you know, I am Princess Hortense, soon to be Queen Hortense. I know that what you just witnessed is a horrible thing. But it's also the most joyful. Olga, the ogre queen, put a curse on Prince Charlemagne that turned him into a frog, in the hope of preventing him from taking his rightful place as king of Eastphalia. Today you have helped us break that curse. And now Charlie and I are ready to be your king and queen, if you will have us." Hortense bows to the crowd.

There's silence. And then there's cheering. Loud, unabashed cheering! If there were any doubts as to the citizens' opinions of the prince and princess, those doubts can surely be put to rest.

"You are all invited to our coronation! It will happen this evening. Please come celebrate at the castle!" Hortense shouts, her fist pumping in the air.

Gretel exhales, relief washing over her. The rightful king and queen of Eastphalia have returned.

Amid the hubbub, Alistair comes and stands next to her with a cup of soup. "So what do you think?" he asks. "Too much garlic?"

CHAPTER THIRTY-NINE
READY OR NOT, QUEENDOM COMES

It would feel almost comforting if it wasn't so terrifying. Filomena almost thought she'd be able to close the chapter on this adventure without an ogre fight, but that, of course, would be too good to be true.

In Mary's office, Jack smells the stench of ogre, and just after, they can all hear the ogres. A shudder runs down Filomena's spine as she realizes why the ogres are here. They must have gotten word that Filomena is in Westphalia, and now, they're here to kill her in the privacy of her own castle. And then, of course, they'll tell everyone in the kingdom that she ran away from being crowned, deserting her people, and the ogres will step in to salvage the kingdom.

It's chilling, the feeling that you're being cornered.

"How many are there, do you think?" Filomena asks Jack hurriedly. But Jack isn't listening to her; he's looking straight at Mary Contrary.

"Is this a trap?" he says sternly, his voice steely. "Are you on their side?" His eyes are like daggers, his voice like iron. Filomena is glad, for the umpteenth time, that she's on Jack's side.

"Jack, I swear on Westphalia's crown that I am not on the ogres' side. I don't know how they got past the guards! They must have slipped in a secret way."

"They must still have an entryway into the castle," he says to Filomena. "A leftover from their time ruling Westphalia, when it was under their spell."

"The good news, then," Mary says, "is there can't be that many of them."

Jack is still looking at Mary suspiciously, but Filomena needs him to focus. The ogres are getting closer.

"Where should we go?" she says.

"We need to get out of this room. We need a getaway. But, Fil, I think we're going to have to fight them."

"Let me run down first," Mary says. "I'll do my best to distract them, or at least delay them. You two head up to the next floor. Three doors from the top of the staircase, there's a secret passageway. You can use that to escape if you really need to." With that, Mary and her long cape swoosh out the door, and she runs toward the ogres.

"Do you not trust her?" Filomena asks.

"I'm not sure yet. I want to say yes, I really do. Especially because of all that stuff with your parents. But you know how it is, Fil. We can't be too careful. Right now, the only person I trust in this castle is you. So let's fight these ogres, then we'll deal with the rest, okay?"

She nods. They leave the office. Once they reach the floor above, all they can do is wait for the ogres. Running away won't help, not this time, not now.

Filomena tries not to shudder as the footsteps of the ogres, those loud, sloppy footsteps, come closer.

Jack holds her shoulders. "We can do this," he says. His words fill her with a golden courage, a fire. "You can do this. We're so close."

Then, with no curse to break, no dare, no pretense, Jack leans close once more.

Filomena's heart leaps. He brushes a lock of hair out of his eyes and smiles shyly at her. How brave and shy he can be at the same time! Only Jack's face can hold those two qualities at once.

When he leans in to kiss her, she raises herself up to meet him, and when they kiss, it's like she's going through all the swoop holes in Never After at once. Like she's moving through time and space. Like she's floating.

They pull apart and smile at each other.

"That was cool," he says.

She blushes. "Yeah, that was cool."

So much has been said between them, and so much waits on the horizon, but for just a moment, they stand and look at each other and smile.

I just kissed Jack the Giant Stalker. I just kissed Jack! Part of Filomena wants to tell Gretel immediately, but a stronger part is present for the moment to fully enjoy the feeling.

But, of course, nothing can ruin the moment after a perfect first kiss like a bumbling ogre.

"There she is!" one screams, drool pooling out of its maw.

"Olga is gonna be so pleased with us," another snarls, coming up the stairs.

The first ogre has a huge club and swings it right at Jack. Jack ducks and the club goes into a wall. The ogre is mad now and swipes the club backward, and this time it does hit Jack—square in the stomach.

Filomena wants to run to him, but she can't; the second ogre, this one carrying a machete, is taking a swing at her. If the machete hits, it will be deadly. Filomena swipes her Dragon's Tooth sword, slicing the ogre's arm. Wounded and now even angrier, the ogre charges.

Her instinct is to run, but there's only one open door. She runs through, trying to buy herself some time to regroup. She realizes there's a balcony attached to this room and charges out onto it. The ogre follows her, machete swinging.

On the balcony, their weapons clash. The machete is huge, but Filomena's Dragon's Tooth sword is stronger. The machete nearly hits her, but she blocks it with the shield. Back and forth, they swing and land, swing and miss, swords clanging again and again. Then the ogre looks away for one second and she lunges.

The ogre's bent back now, Filomena's sword locked against the machete and held up to the ogre's throat. Now that she has a second to breathe, she realizes a crowd is forming beneath the balcony, which looks directly over the Westphalian town square. Through the haze of battle, Filomena thinks how lovely it is that her castle is so close to her people and not hidden away.

But this is no time for such thoughts! *Focus, Filomena!*

She notices people seem confused. Do they not understand what's going on here?

"People of Westphalia!" she shouts, still holding her sword against the ogre's throat. "I am Eliana, princess of Westphalia, daughter of Rosanna and Vladimir. I have come to disprove the claims of the ogre queen and take my rightful place as your ruler, if you will have me!"

She feels overcome suddenly—not by the weight of responsibility nor fear over whether she will be a good ruler but by a strong, deep desire to protect her people. "All I want is to serve Westphalia well, to bring this kingdom back to its prosperous origins. I know I haven't lived here my whole life, but that was not my choice. That was Queen Olga's doing!

And I'm ready. I'm ready to be connected to my kingdom if you will accept me as your queen."

The crowd, at first awed, begins to cheer.

Filomena removes her sword from the ogre's throat and plunges it into his heart. Her face is splattered with blood. But then the cheers turn to screams. Another ogre is coming up behind her.

"You think, just because of this public stunt in front of these plebs, you'll get to be queen? You don't think we can rework this story?" A huge ogre—one Filomena recognizes as a general in the ogre queen's army—has come out onto the balcony. "We'll kill you and make it look like your fault," he snarls at her. The ogre general paces forward, relishing the moment before the kill. He slowly raises his blade.

But looking past the ogre, Filomena sees a beautiful sight. It's Jack. And he winks at her. There is nothing to fear. Because Jack always has her back.

The ogre cackles and brings down his blade, but before the ogre knows what is happening, vines are wrapped around his weapon, and around his legs.

Jack pulls and the monster falls.

Filomena swings her sword forward and finishes him. Cheers erupt from the crowd again.

Jack waves. He has a black eye and a bleeding arm. But he's standing and he's alive.

Mary appears then, holding the crown in her hand. It's a thin circlet of pure gold, with flared spikes around the perimeter that are meant to symbolize the sun's rays. Filomena gets a jolt when she realizes what's happening.

"Are we allowed to have the coronation without a proper ceremony?" Filomena asks Mary.

"There's no better time for a coronation than in the wake of a battle won. Look, your audience is already here."

And it is. Filomena looks out over the kingdom of Westphalia, at the crowd that has multiplied times ten since she first stepped onto the balcony. *Word sure travels fast around here.*

Mary motions for Filomena to kneel. "Eliana, princess of Westphalia, and rightful heir to the throne: By the power vested in me as regent of this kingdom, I hereby proclaim you queen of Westphalia."

Filomena, panting and with ogre blood covering her face, is crowned at last. She's a queen now. *I'm a queen now?*

"Hey, what did I miss?"

The voice, somehow, comes from her hip. Ira Glassman! Shocked, she grabs the handle and holds the talking mirror up to her face.

"You're still there?" she gasps.

"Here I am, kid. Was just having my nap."

"I thought you were gone when Robin smashed you!"

Ira's misty eyes roll. "That's the thing a kid like Robin, or the ogres, they don't understand. Loyalty. Love. When a talking mirror is smashed, it gives the soul of the mirror— aka *moi*—an opportunity to flee. But I love you, Filomena.

I'm with you for life. I'm not going nowhere." Ira grins and winks.

"I wish I could hug you!" she yells, feeling so relieved.

"How about you just turn me around so I can see the crowd! I need my moment in the sun." Ira chuckles.

She turns the talking mirror around, and together they wave to her citizens. Then she gets an idea. She whispers to Mary. Mary nods. Filomena motions for Jack to come forward and kneel. He does, slightly confused. Standing before Jack, Filomena picks up her Dragon's Tooth sword and touches the flat of the blade to one of his shoulders, then the other.

"By the power vested in me as queen of Westphalia, I hereby knight Jack the Giant Stalker—my first loyal, royal knight of Westphalia!"

The crowd cheers. Filomena realizes then: They all know Jack from the tabloids.

Jack bows his head to her, then stands up. "Congratulations, Queen Filomena," he says.

"Thank you, Loyal Knight of Westphalia. As if you need another title," she teases, pushing his shoulder.

"This might be my favorite one yet." He grins.

Then he kisses her again.

CHAPTER FORTY

QUEEN JEANNE

W ord gets around Never After that the next day is
Princess Jeanne's coronation. Little Jeanne must
have made her way safely back to the North. Now Jack and
Filomena are leaving to attend.

One cool thing about being a queen, though, is that she
and Jack don't have to walk from Westphalia to Northphalia.
Now they get to ride in a carriage.

"Check this out," Jack says, sitting across from her in the
carriage. "They even have complimentary Lily Licks in here!"

He holds up a white-and-yellow, flower-shaped lollipop and starts sucking on it.

"Are you sure your eye is okay?" Filomena asks. Jack's in really high spirits for someone whose eye is surrounded with swollen dark purple skin.

"I've had worse. Don't worry about me," he says.

Eventually, Filomena looks out the little window and sees the Northphalian castle fast approaching. She sighs. "We're almost there."

"They'll all be there, I promise," Jack says. He reaches for her hand and squeezes it.

"But what if they're not?" she asks.

"They will be."

Filomena's coronation was dramatic because of its impromptu nature, but it has nothing on the decorative drama of Princess Jeanne's coronation. There's no sign of King Richard's army nor Riff's barricade.

Everything is peaceful and joyous. As Filomena and Jack ride through the streets of Northphalia, they hear citizens cheer and bang on their carriage door. The Northphalian kingdom's purple flags fly through the streets. In classic Princess Jeanne fashion, this coronation is clearly set to be the event of the decade. But Filomena can't enjoy it yet; she's still holding her breath.

As they arrive at the castle doors, Jack jumps out first and extends a hand to help her step down. Filomena smacks his hand away, laughing, and leaps from the carriage.

"Just because I'm a queen now doesn't mean you can start treating me differently," she says.

"If anyone tells me chivalry is dead, I'll tell them you killed it!" Jack laughs and rolls his eyes. "I am your loyal knight after all." He does a mocking bow.

Filomena pushes his shoulder jokingly, hardly noticing the crew that's assembled in front of them.

"What in all of Never After happened to your eye, dude?" Alistair yells.

Filomena turns, yelps, and bursts into tears.

"Whoa, whoa, girl!" Gretel says, running to her.

"Are we that horrible to look at that she cries at the very sight of us?" Alistair brings a hand to his chest, pretending to be offended.

Through the tears, Filomena breaks into a huge smile and wraps her arms around her friends. The group hugs tighter and harder than ever before. Filomena never feels safer than when in a group hug with Jack, Alistair, and Gretel. They've been through so much, together and apart. But it never feels right when they're separated. Filomena never wants to be parted from them.

"I'm so relieved you're all right!" she says. "Is anyone hurt? Are we all here?"

"Rosie, Byron, and Beatrice are just inside helping Princess Jeanne get ready," Gretel says. "They're totally safe."

"Let's go inside," Alistair says, hugging Jack. "We have a lot of catching up to do!"

They tell Jack and Filomena that the minute Little Jeanne arrived with the crown, they immediately put it on Princess Jeanne's head. And once the crown was settled on her brow, as Filomena predicted, King Richard and his army turned to dust.

But, of course, Princess Jeanne wants a more . . . ahem . . . *public* celebration.

As they wait for the ceremony to begin in the main hall of Northphalia's castle, Jack, Filomena, Gretel, and Alistair sit together in a pew among the lords, the ladies, and the Merry Men and Women of Queen Jeanne's court.

"I can't believe the answer was *soup*." Jack laughs. Then he winces. His black eye makes big facial movements pretty painful.

"It was the most delicious cure to a curse you can imagine," Alistair says proudly.

Filomena feels at ease for the first time in what seems like weeks. The summer solstice is tonight, and she's relieved to see Charlie back in human form—sitting on the bench behind her—and that he and Hortense are officially King and Queen.

Hortense leans forward to talk in Filomena's ear. "So what's with all the fanfare?" she says, motioning to the elaborate decorations, the choir waiting to perform, the stained glass artist currently installing a stained glass panel of Princess Jeanne.

"Northphalia is the most tradition-oriented kingdom of Never After," Jack explains. "They like to take these things really seriously."

"Perfect for Princess Jeanne," Gretel says.

And just like that, Princess Jeanne herself emerges at the front of the hall. She's wearing a beautiful chartreuse silk dress that glints with amethysts.

"That has Gretel written all over it," Filomena whispers to Gretel, who shrugs modestly but smiles.

Once Princess Jeanne sits, Rosie, Beatrice, and Byron sneak over to sit with the others. Filomena gives them each a silent hug as the ceremony starts.

"Seems like Beatrice and Princess Jeanne ended up getting along after all," Gretel says. "Bea said that Princess Jeanne was really mad at her at first when she broke the news about Little Jeanne, but after that, surprisingly, they became super close! Princess Jeanne even wanted Beatrice to help her get ready."

Filomena laughs. "Stranger things have happened in Never After!"

The ceremony begins. The choir starts to sing. Filomena leans back in her seat and watches Princess Jeanne take her rightful place as queen of the North.

Finally—*finally*—all is right in Never After. At least for the moment.

CHAPTER FORTY-ONE

OLGA'S MAGIC POTION

Now that things have calmed down in Never After—the ogres have backed off and returned to their kingdom, and the rightful heirs are crowned—it's time for Filomena to return home. It's hard to know how long Filomena will be saying goodbye to Never After for, but she's leaving Mary Contrary in charge as regent while she goes home. Or goes to one of her homes, at least.

Leaving Never After is never easy, but this time it's particularly hard. After Princess Jeanne's coronation party, Filomena knows it's time. She'll be back, of course, but she can't excuse staying when her mom is sick. She needs to see her, hug her, see how she is, if she's improving. Saying goodbye to Jack, though, feels nearly impossible.

Jack and Filomena kiss one more time, sheepishly and in front of their friends but without caring. Everyone's standing by the portal to send Filomena off. She'll hold on to these moments for a long time. She hopes there will be more—she needs there to be more. Will it always be this way?

That's the thing about being from two worlds, Filomena realizes as she's walking up her street in North Pasadena. You always have to choose between them.

Walking in the front door, Filomena notices things are quiet. This is pretty usual at her house, since both her parents, Carter Cho and Bettina Jefferson, are writers who spend much of their spare time reading. But the air is still in a way that gives Filomena a feeling that things haven't changed much since she was last home. She figures her parents might be at the hospital. They didn't know she was coming home, after all.

"Hello?" she calls.

Filomena's Pomeranian puppy, Adelina Jefferson-Cho, comes running up to greet her. Adelina's little pink tongue gives Filomena's ankles lots of licks. Filomena scoops her up and nuzzles her. It feels like months since she's been home, though she knows that's not true.

"Mum? Dad?" Filomena repeats.

"We're in the bedroom, sweetie," she hears her dad say.

She's so relieved. They're not at the hospital anymore! Things must be better.

"You're home!" he says when she walks through the bedroom door. He gives her a big bear hug. "How are you? How's Never After? What's happening there? Are you safe? Are your friends safe?"

Filomena still can't believe that, after being so protective in the mortal world, they were willing to let her go off on her own to an infinitely more dangerous world. But her parents have always understood the mechanics of narrative, and they seem to understand Filomena's importance in the real-life narrative of Never After.

Before she can answer her dad's questions, though, Filomena looks to her mom, whose eyes are closed. Her mom takes top priority here.

"How is she? Is she asleep? What's going on?"

Carter motions for Filomena to take a seat next to him on the couch that he's set up near her mother's bed. Filomena notices his laptop on the floor, stacks of papers and notebooks piled around the bed, and not to mention a few takeout boxes. It looks like he hasn't left her side in days.

"Sweetie, your mom isn't doing so well," he says. He begins to tear up. Though she's seen her dad cry before—he's not the kind of man who refuses to cry—it still shocks her.

"What do the doctors say?" Filomena asks desperately. "What's going on?"

"They still don't know. But every day, she seems to get

weaker. They told me to keep her at home, to keep her as comfortable as possible. But they don't know what's happening to her."

So there's no news. No news is said to be good news, but this no news is the opposite of good. Things are still as they were the last time she was here. Instead of feeling sadness, right now Filomena feels a deep anger. Why can't they figure out what's wrong with her mother? What's modern medicine good for if not to figure out what's wrong and solve it?

"I think I need to get some water," she says. She has to be alone for a second.

"Of course, sweetie," her dad answers.

"Do you need anything?"

"If you could grab a towel with some cool water on it from the bathroom, I'll put it on her forehead. Helps with the fever."

Filomena gets a glass of water, then walks back upstairs and into her parents' bathroom. She shuts the door and sits on the cool tile floor for a second, curling up into a ball. She puts her head on her arms and starts to cry. She can kill ogres, rule a kingdom as queen, travel across Never After, and break curses—and yet she can't do anything for her mother. Filomena would do anything to save her . . . anything. She wishes she'd never gone to Never After in the first place. This all happened when she left! Maybe if she'd never left, this never would have happened.

Filomena lifts her head, remembering the towel for her mom.

As she's wetting the towel with cool water at the bathroom vanity, she notices some products she's never seen before. Usually her mom swears by all-natural face washes and creams. But these look different. They're completely white with small green type.

Oil of Olga, the bottles read. *For all your skincare needs. Apply Oil of Olga when you wake up and before you go to sleep. Results will be like magic!*

An alarm bell goes off in Filomena's head, but she can't jump to conclusions just yet.

When she gets back to her parents' bedroom, her mom is awake. Filomena places the cool towel on her forehead.

"Hello, sweetie," Bettina says. "How's my darling girl?"

She looks so weak, but Filomena tries not to start crying again. "I'm okay, Mum. I just wish you were, too," she says, crawling into the bed and giving her mom a hug. After a few minutes of the embrace, Filomena decides to ask her: "Mum, what are those bottles in the bathroom? The ones that say 'Oil of Olga'?"

Bettina laughs. "Oh, those. It's a funny story, actually . . . ," she starts, but then she gets too weak to finish. Her energy seems completely drained. She looks to Filomena's dad. "Carter, can you?"

Carter nods and takes over the story.

A few weeks ago, a woman came to the door selling

skincare products. They didn't know people even did that anymore! The woman seemed kind of strange at first, and there was a slight green tinge to her skin. Bettina thought this odd, since the lady claimed to work in cosmetics. But she insisted that Bettina try the products. If she didn't like them, the woman said she could have a total refund. She even gave Bettina a bunch of products for free as thanks for being a first-time client!

Filomena's stomach is sinking. *Green tinge? Olga?* "And you've been using them every day?" she asks.

Her mom nods. "I've been feeling so horrible, it's nice to have a part of my routine feel like I'm taking care of myself."

"Mum, I think you need to stop using those products right away."

"What? Why, honey? Do they test on animals?"

"It's likely, but that's not why. Oil of Olga? I'm almost certain that the woman who came to your door was evil Queen Olga from Never After."

CHAPTER FORTY-TWO

MIRROR'S PROPHECY

You would think knowing the cause of her mother's terminal illness might be a relief, but no part of Filomena is relieved. If anything, she's more freaked out than ever. Just when she thought she'd vanquished Olga for good—the evil queen rises again! Filomena assumed she would be able to spend some time with her parents and let the doctors take care of things. But here she is, being dragged right back to Never After. And now it's time for revenge.

She's also realizing that if she's going back and forth

between the mortal world and Never After, she's going to have to come up with a better system for communicating with her friends. It's been a week in Never After's time, so she has no idea where anyone is! And, of course, when Filomena's faced with a seemingly insurmountable problem, the only place she wants to go (besides to her parents, who unfortunately can't help her with this one) is to her friends. But where in the worlds are they?

Filomena gets spit out of the Northphalian portal and crosses her fingers that her friends are still hanging around Princess Jeanne's castle.

As she approaches the castle, walking the now-familiar path through rolling hills from the portal, she sees something odd. It looks like a girl with bright red hair, except . . . Wait, does she have wings? Is this some Never After creature Filomena has yet to meet? The girl looks like she's about to jump out a window!

"Hey!" Filomena yells. "Hey, stop! What are you doing?!" Even though the girl has wings, Filomena worries she might not yet know how to fly.

"Filomena?" the girl yells back. "Is that you?"

Rosie! Of course. What other brash redhead would jump out a window?

As Filomena gets closer, she sees the wings aren't some magical extension of Rosie's body; they're mechanical wings attached with a harness.

"Rosie, hold up! Wait for me!"

Filomena runs to the castle. Inside, Jack, Gretel, and Alistair are sitting at a table with maps spread in front of them. They all jump in fright at the sight of her.

"What are you doing here?!" Alistair yells. "Didn't you just leave, like, a day ago, for you?"

Jack's confusion is quickly replaced with happiness as he runs to hug her. As he approaches, though, a moment of hesitation appears between them. Their friends are watching. They're no longer just the Filomena and Jack they once were; now they're something else, something that involves *feelings*. Or something. Everything else, all the problems, are wiped from Filomena's mind. But she can't help showing how she really feels about him; she thought it would've been much longer until they saw each other again. She smiles and gives him a big hug. Jack's visibly relieved, closing his eyes and smelling her hair.

"All right, all right, that's enough of the lovefest. My turn!" Gretel yanks Jack off Filomena and gives her a huge hug. In Filomena's ear, she whispers, "Oh my fairies, we have *so* much to discuss about you two!"

Rosie rushes down from upstairs. "Filomena, you interrupted my inaugural flight, you know," she says.

"Not happy to see me, Rosie?" Filomena asks.

"Well, duh," Rosie says, smiling, and gives Filomena a hug.

"Sadly, I'm not so happy to be back," Filomena says. "Not because I don't want to see you all—I do, thank goodness you're here—but because of the circumstance."

Just then, Byron and Beatrice enter the room. They haven't left for Wonderland yet, especially since they're also part of the League of Seven.

"Filomena! Good to have you back!" they tell her.

So Filomena updates them about her mom, how weak she is, how her doctors in the mortal world still can't tell what's wrong, and that she's getting worse every day. And then she tells them the big news. She's practically fuming by the time she gets to this part.

"I think Queen Olga went to the mortal world to poison her. I don't know why, but she gave my mom these cosmetics that I'm sure are making her sick. I had to come back. I feel like if there is a cure or a way to stop this, it's in Never After. I can't believe this! It's one thing to come after me, to have her minion ogres try to stab me to death right before I'm supposed to be crowned, but to go after my *mom*?! In the *mortal world*?! That's a whole other kind of risk. That's too far."

Her friends stand in silence for a minute, soaking in the news. Then they immediately go into solution mode.

"Maybe I can make a reversal potion!" Rosie says. "I can create an antidote, and we can get it to your mom—"

"Olga will pay for this!" Jack threatens.

"No doubt!" rumbles Byron.

"That evil wench!" cries Beatrice.

"Especially in a skincare cream! Truly sadistic!" seethes Gretel.

"What if I make a poisoned cake that gets Olga sick, and then we'll say the only way we'll cure her is if she tells us how to cure your mom?!" Alistair yells.

Filomena is thankful for all their ideas, and for their enthusiasm, but she has no idea in which direction to go.

"Hey, over here!" a voice says. "Come on, pick me up!"

It's her talking mirror. Rosie's been carrying Ira Glassman around with her wherever she goes, but she must have set him facedown on the table by accident. Rosie picks up the mirror so they can all see his cracked face.

"You didn't forget about good ol' Ira here, did you?" Ira says wryly.

"I could never."

"Good, good. Now listen: I may be broken, I may not be able to show you the world through my pretty little looking glass, but I do have quite a bit of ancient knowledge, you know."

Filomena starts to tingle. *Right, mirrors have mirror world knowledge,* she remembers Jack saying.

"I know what you have to do to save your mother," Ira says. Filomena's heart leaps.

"Oh, fantastic, Ira! I could kiss your shiny face right now!"

"Don't get too excited just yet, Fil," Ira adds. "I'm not sure you're going to like this."

Rosie takes Filomena's hand. Jack takes the other. They all stand before the magic mirror, awaiting his next words and holding their breath.

"What you need," Ira tells them, "is the sword of Excalibur. It can heal as well as it can harm."

"Okay, I can do that! That's not so bad," Filomena says. She looks at Jack and Alistair. "Now we know our next adventure!"

Jack the Giant Stalker, Alistair Bartholomew Barnaby, Gretel the Cobbler's daughter, Rose Red, and Beatrice and Byron of Wonderland all look at one another and nod. None of them expected to rest for long. Alongside Filomena, they are the League of Seven, after all.

Filomena feels a wave of excitement and dread well up in her at once. But she looks to her friends. So what if she's had barely a moment's rest? So what if she has to take on another quest? She has her friends by her side, and with them, everything feels possible. More than possible—it feels like an adventure.

But her talking mirror clucks and shakes his head in pity.

"That's not the part that you won't like, my dear," Ira adds. "It's that, this time, you have to go alone."

ACKNOWLEDGMENTS

Book Three in a series is a linchpin book! It all turns here! The hardest but my favorite books to write in a series. I'd like to thank my amazing editors Jennifer Besser, Kate Meltzer, and Emilia Sowersby for making this book the best it could be. Thank you to Brittany Pearlman, Theresa Ferraiolo and everyone at Macmillan for all your efforts to bring this series into kids' hands!

Thank you to all my friends, family, and fans.

Thank you to Richard Abate, my consigliere and confidant. Thank you to Martha Stevens and Hannah Carrende, who do all the heavy lifting. Thank you to the fabulous Ellen Goldsmith-Vein, Jeremy Bell, and DJ Goldberg. Lunch and work with you guys are a blast! Thank you to Brad Krevoy and Amy Hartwick for believing in the TV series!

I would not be able to do what I do without my two: Mike and Mattie Johnston. Everything is for you.